John Sandford is the pseudonym of the Pulitzer prize-winning journalist John Camp. He is the author of eleven Prey novels, and two previous Kidd novels. He lives in Minnesota.

THE EMPRESS FILE

John Sandford

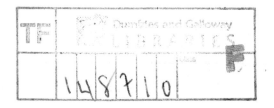

This edition first published in Great Britain 2003 by
SEVERN HOUSE PUBLISHERS LTD of
9–15 High Street, Sutton, Surrey SM1 1DF
by arrangement with Simon & Schuster UK Ltd.
Originally published under the pseudonym *John Camp*.

British Library Cataloguing in Publication Data

Sandford, John, 1944 Feb. 23-
    The empress file
    1.   Kidd (Fictitious character : Camp) - Fiction
    2.   Detective and mystery stories
    I.   Title II. Camp, John, 1944-
    813.5'4 [F]

ISBN 0-7278-5934-X

Printed and bound in Great Britain by
MPG Books Ltd., Bodmin, Cornwall.

For Roswell S. and Anne B.

Prologue

THE HEAT WAS ferocious.

The odor of melting blacktop was thick in the air, like the stink of an oil slick, and the rare night walkers glistened with sweat. A time-and-temperature sign outside the state bank poked scarlet digits down the dark streets: 91, it said, and 11:04. Three doors north of the bank, a janitor at the Paramount Theater vacuumed the lobby in slow motion. The theater was air-conditioned. His home was not.

Across the street from the Paramount, a window dresser at Trent's fussed with an abattoir of dismembered mannequins. He worked only nights, after curfew for children twelve and under. He was setting up the annual bathing suit display, and modern mannequins, the city council observed, had nipples.

In the window lights even the dummies looked hot.

□ □ □

WITH NIGHTFALL an army of insects marched out of the Mississippi river bottoms. Coffee brown beetles, some as long as a man's thumb, scuttled through the gutters. Hard-shelled June bugs ricocheted like stones off the storefront windows. Fuzzy-winged moths fluttered in the headlights of passing cars. They made yellow smears when they hit the windshields; the biggest ones had guts like baby birds, and blood.

The moths and the delicate green lacewings were the tragic stars of the night. By the hundreds of thousands they burned in the eerie violet halos of electronic insect traps. The lucky ones made it past the traps and found heaven in the parking lot lights at the E-Z Way. Under the brilliant floods they danced and died in midnight ecstasy. Their bodies littered the pavement like confetti.

ELVIS COULTIER LIKED the bugs. They made intricate patterns in the boring nightscape, like a living kaleidoscope. In some dumb way they brought him a breath of drama. Once a night, or sometimes twice, a luna moth would appear, huge, green, fragile. He would watch as it circled and climbed, danced, courting the light, and finally burned, fluttering like an autumn maple leaf to the parking lot.

He loved the bugs, but the heat was killing him. He couldn't breathe. His lungs felt as if they were packed with sponges. He had the doors and the big side window open as far as they would go, but never a breeze came in.

Elvis was the night manager at the E-Z Way, a fat young man given to tent-size sweatpants and novelty T-shirts. Tonight's had a tiger-striped cartoon cat, with the caption "I Love a Little Pussy." He'd dripped ketchup on the shirt while eating a hot dog, and five red splotches crossed the Pussy like bloody fingerprints. Elvis mopped his face with a rag he kept in the soda cooler. Reruns of *The Mary Tyler Moore Show* flickered on the portable TV bolted into one corner of the ceiling, but it was so hot that he'd lost the story line. Beige moths the size of penny-candy wrappers battered themselves against Mary's face.

The E-Z Way, the only all-night store in town, squatted beside the A&M Railroad tracks. Both whites from the east side and blacks from the west—anyone looking for milk or beer or cigarettes—patronized the place. "We get 'em all, sooner or later," Elvis liked to say.

AT 11:04 DARRELL CLARK was Elvis's only customer. He stood in the back of the store, peering through the glass of an upright cooler. A dozen varieties of ice cream and sherbet were racked inside: vanilla, Dutch chocolate, strawberry, butter brickle, raspberry surprise, chocolate rocky road. Each name and each color photo evoked a memory of taste. Butter brickle and jamocha were out. Vanilla was good, but too . . . vanilla.

Darrell was dressed in Wal-Mart shorts and a brown short-sleeved polo shirt. The shirt was too small and fit his growing body like a second skin. His hair was close-cropped over his high forehead.

Darrell licked his lower lip every few seconds as he considered the beckoning flavors. After some thought he opened the cooler door, paused to let the cold air wash over him, shivered, selected a two-quart carton of the chocolate rocky road, and carried it to the counter. Elvis counted Darrell's handful of crumpled dollar bills, quarters, and dimes, rang up the sale, and slipped the ice cream into a brown paper bag.

"Now you haul ass, boy," Elvis told him. "That rocky road'll melt faster'n snot on a hot doorknob."

Darrell headed out the door on the run. The brown paper bag dangled from one hand, and his rubber flip-flops slapped on the blacktop as his long fourteen-year-old legs ate up the ground. He crossed the parking lot under the moth-shrouded pole lights and ran down the dirt-and-cinders path that paralleled the A&M tracks.

Two things were going through his head.

The first was the thought of the rocky road, cool and buttery in a blue plastic bowl. A good choice.

Behind that was an algorithm he had been toying with: a way to generate real-time fractal terrain at reasonable speeds on his Macintosh II personal computer. . . .

CLARISSE BARNWRIGHT, whom everybody, including herself, called Old Lady Barnwright, hobbled along Bluebell, a rubber-tipped cane held in one hand, her purse clutched in the other. She lived one block over from the tracks, on the white side of town. She'd spent her entire life in the neighborhood, born in a house not a hundred yards from the house where she expected to die. For thirty-nine years she'd beaten Latin and English into the thick heads of Longstreet's children. White children for the first twenty-seven years, a mix of black and white for the last twelve. Then she gave it up and sank gratefully into retirement.

Her husband's death preceded her retirement by a year. Some people thought that was why she quit. She couldn't face life and work without Albert, they said wisely.

They were wrong.

The fact was, Clarisse wasn't unhappy to see him go. Had, late on hot summer nights in the forties and fifties, lying in the same bed with him, sweaty and suffocating, listening to his burbling snorts and occasional farts, considered helping him along the Path to Glory. Might have done it, if she could have thought of a surefire way of not getting caught. The state had the electric chair, and no particular prejudice against using it on women.

Clarisse sighed as she thought about it. If Albert had lived, he'd have just sat around the house and complained. Complained about paint flaking off the siding, complained about the furnace, complained about the cracking sidewalks, complained about the cotton crop. Never complained about anything interesting.

Never complained about their sex life, for example. She might have been interested if one night he'd looked up and said, "Clare, just what do you know about this here cunny-lingus business?" Old Lady Barnwright cackled to herself. That probably would have finished *her* off.

Clarisse Barnwright lived inside her head. She was so preoccupied with her thoughts that she never heard the soft steps coming up behind.

CLAYTON RAND SAT on his dark porch and watched Old Lady Barnwright coming down the sidewalk. A little late for the old lady, but she still got around good, considering her age. Hell, Clayton was sixty-four, and he'd had her as a teacher in eleventh and twelfth grades. Clayton fanned himself with the sports section of the *Gazette*, watching her hobble down the sidewalk. Wonder what she thinks about? Probably conjugating Latin verbs or something.

When he saw the shadow behind her, Clayton wanted to holler a warning, but his tongue got stuck, and nothing would come out of his mouth. He stood up with his mouth half open as the shadow grabbed the old lady's purse. She went ass over teakettle into the Carters' honeysuckle hedge, yelling her head off, while the shadow went sideways across the street, headed for the tracks. Clarisse Barnwright might have been an old lady, Clayton thought as he pulled open the screen door and reached for the phone, but there was nothing wrong with her lungs.

"Police emergency," Lucy answered in her best bubble gum voice. Lucy had wonderful cone-shaped tits and tended toward pink glitter lipstick and thin cotton sweaters. Clayton felt as if he'd sinned just calling her on the 911 line. "Is this an emergency?"

"Goddamn right it is, honey," Clayton hollered. "This here is Clayton Rand out on Bluebell. Some colored kid just snatched Old Lady Barnwright's purse. Not more than five, ten seconds ago. He's took off lickety-split toward the tracks. . . ."

OFFICERS ROY R. ("TUD") DICK and William L. Teeter had the tac squad that night. That was why the laser-sighted Heckler & Koch MP5, instead of the standard police shotgun, was propped between them. The MP5 was a new weapon. Billy Lee had qualified on it, but Tud had not. He wasn't interested. Tud had little time for guns, and with good reason: The last time a Longstreet cop had fired a weapon in the line of duty, he'd missed six out of six times and got his own ass shot by his brother-in-law. That was back in '71. . . .

The two cops were sitting on a side street, talking about the heat and waiting to see if Annie Carlson would get drunk and take one of her patented summer showers. She never pulled the shade on the back bathroom window, and when she came out of the shower, with the white towel wrapped around her hair, and was framed in the lighted square, Tud thought she looked just like some kind of famous painting. He couldn't tell you which. Billy Lee thought she looked like a potential Playmate of the Month. Which is to say, large.

Tud was sucking on a peach soda when they got the squawk from Lucy down at Dispatch. One second later the black kid ran past the end of the street, lickety-split, just like Lucy said.

"Let's get him," Tud said. He dropped the empty pop can on the floor, hit the lights and the siren at the same time, and they took off, leaving Annie Carlson high and dry. The black kid was running parallel to the tracks and was fast coming to the point where the street went left around a bend and the tracks went straight.

"Shit, Billy Lee, he's gonna get off behind the water tower," Tud said.

"Stop the car. Stop the fuckin' car."

Tud stopped the car, and Billy Lee jumped out with the MP5 and punched up the laser.

"Hold it right there. You hold it right there. . . ." He was screaming as loud as he could.

He put the laser's red dot in the middle of the black kid's back. "You hold it, boy. . . ." A sort of greasy, short-breathed excitement got him by the balls when he realized the black kid wasn't going to stop and Tud said, "Hey, now, Billy Lee . . ." Billy Lee pulled the trigger, and a burst of nine-millimeter slugs went downrange, and the black kid tumbled ass over teakettle into the weeds.

"Ass over teakettle," Billy Lee said aloud in the sudden stunning silence.

Tud called for a backup and an ambulance, and then they walked down toward the body, Billy Lee with the MP5 on his hip and Tud clutching his .38 police special. Lights were coming on in houses on both sides of the tracks, and a guy in a white sleeveless T-shirt was standing on his front lawn, watching them. They found the boy in the cinders and sandbabies next to the tracks, facedown. One bullet punched through his neck; a second took him in the spine between his shoulder blades; a third caught him a little lower and to the left, maybe nicking a lung. Good shooting. The boy must have lived for just a second after he went down, Tud thought, because his mouth was full of dirt and cinders, as if he'd bitten into the earth as he died.

The two officers looked down at him for a minute, and then Tud squatted and dumped the bag the kid had been carrying. Out fell a two-quart carton of chocolate rocky road, steaming in the muggy night air. They both looked at it for a long beat. Then Tud turned his sad hound dog eyes up to his partner.

"Goddamn it, Billy Lee," he said, shaking his head. "You went and shot yourself the wrong nigger."

```
┌─────────────┐
├─────────────┤
│             │
│      1      │
│             │
└─────────────┘
```

THE COMPUTER ALARM went off at four in the morning. When it started buzzing, I'd been asleep for half an hour. The alarm sounds like an off-the-hook telephone, and it took a minute to penetrate.

"Jap phone?" Chaminade Loan made a bump under the sheet across the bed. Her voice grated like old rust.

"Zwat?"

"Jap phone?"

"Yeah." The cat was curled at the foot of the bed and looked up as I rolled out and padded down the hall toward the front room. When I passed the study door, a message was running down the blue screen of the Amiga 3000, and I realized I was hearing the computer alarm, not the phone. A dozen small computers and dumb terminals are scattered around the study, three or four of them plugged in at any one time. Several people knew how to call and dump data to the

Amiga's memory. Only one knew how to tap the alarm.

Bobby Duchamps.

Bobby wouldn't be calling to chat. The alarm sounded as soon as the data came in and repeated one minute out of every five until I turned it off. The message on the screen was straightforward. After the sign-on stuff, it said:

Call Now.

When Bobby said now, he meant *now*. As far as I know, he sits in front of a computer around the clock; Bobby doesn't have a workday and always answered personally when I called his private board.

I yawned, sat down naked at the machine, tapped a key to kill the alarm, switched the modem to SEND and punched in a number for East St. Louis. The number rang eight times, and I pressed the "a" key. It rang twice more and was answered with a twenty-four-hundred-baud carrier tone. A few seconds later a "?" flashed on the upper left corner of my screen. I typed *Hivaoa*, my code name on Bobby's system. It's taken from Gauguin's 1902 painting *The Magician of Hivaoa*, which hangs in the Musée d'Art Moderne in Liège. As a password *Hivaoa* may seem pretentious, but it fills the two main requirements of any computer code word: It's easy to remember, and you don't have to worry that somebody will stumble on it by accident.

Bobby came back instantly:

Friend bad-needs face-to-face ASAP.

When/Where?

Today/Memphis.

Short notice.

Asking favor.

I'll check airlines.

Already booked 4:47 Northwest Airlines Minn-St. Paul-Memphis arrive 7:20.

Booking the plane was presumptuous, but Bobby's a computer freak. Computer freaks are like that. Besides, he was virtually a full-time resident of the Northwest reservation system, so it probably didn't cost him anything.

Bobby and I had met inside a GM design computer back in the old days and had enlarged our friendship on the early pirate boards, the good ones that the teenyboppers never saw. Over the years we'd dealt a lot of data and code to each other. I'd never met him face-to-face, but I'd talked to him on voice lines. A black kid, I thought, still young, early to mid-twenties. A southerner. He had a hint of a speech impediment, and something he said suggested a physical problem. Cerebral palsy, like that. A while back he helped me out of a jam involving the mob, several murders, and a computer attack that wrecked a defense contractor. I still flash on it from time to time, like visitations from an old acid trip. In return for his help, I sent a bundle of cash Bobby's way. So we were friends, but only on the wires. I went back to him:

Where go Memphis?

He meets plane.

OK.

After Bobby signed off, I went back to the bedroom, reset the alarm for eleven o'clock, and crawled into bed. Chaminade smelled of red wine and garlic sauce, a little sweat and a tingle of French scent. She's a large woman, with jet black hair and eyes that are almost powder blue; both her genes and her temper are black Irish. She does electronic engineering, specializing in miniaturization. She was one of the first to crack the new satellite-TV scrambling system and makes a tidy income on pirate receivers.

She was lying on her side, facing away from me. I put my back against hers; the cat turned a couple of circles at my feet. Chaminade said, "Wha?" one time before we all went back to sleep.

□ □ □

I LIVE IN a paid-off condominium apartment in St. Paul's Lowertown, a few hundred feet up the bank from the Mississippi River. The building is a modern conversion of a redbrick turn-of-the-century warehouse.

I have a compact kitchen, a dining area off the front room, a bedroom, a painting studio with north windows, and a study jammed with small computers and a couple of thousand books. I keep a brand-new seventeen-foot Tuffy Esox fishing boat and an older Oldsmobile in a private parking garage up the block. There's another place, quite a bit like it, also paid off, in New Orleans.

When I say the apartments are paid off, I'm not bragging. I'm worried. I screwed up. The run-in with the mob generated quite a bit of cash. I'd never been rich before, and when the money came in, I managed to ignore the annoying buzzing sound in the background. The buzzing sound was my accountant, of course, and she was trying to remind me that I lived in Minnesota, that 40 percent of every dime I earned went for income taxes, either state or federal, plus a couple of more percentages for Social Security and etc. The etc., I suspect, is something I don't want to know about.

Looking back, I shouldn't have paid off the houses. And the trip to Paris and the Côte sometimes seems a tad excessive. I spent a lot of money on food, booze, and women and thoroughly field-tested a faulty baccarat system on the tables at Monte Carlo and what was left, I wasted.

When I got back from France, I was still fairly complacent about the state of my finances. Then the IRS and the Minnesota Department of Revenue showed up. Neither exactly had hat in hand. Tch. I didn't have holes in my socks, but I could use some cash. Soon. Very soon. Like before the fall quarterly estimate was due.

"So what's in Memphis?" Chaminade asked during breakfast, spreading marmalade on her English muffin.

"Beale Street," I suggested.

"Last time I was in Memphis"—she rolled her eyes up and thought about it—"must have been ten or eleven years ago."

"A mere child."

She ignored me. "I went over to Beale Street, you know, because of the blues. I'd been listening to a Memphis Slim tape; it had this great piece called 'He Flew the Coop.' . . . I don't know. Anyway, I went over to Beale, and the whole street was boarded up for urban renewal. I found a big goddamned statue of? Who? Guess."

"W. C. Handy?"

"Nope. Elvis. Right there at the top of Beale. They had a bust of Handy stuck away in a little park. Those Memphis folks got style." She popped the last bite of muffin into her mouth, licked her fingers, split another muffin in half, and popped it into the toaster.

"I don't know the place very well. Seems kind of trashy, in a likable way. The food's good," I said.

I pass through Memphis twice a year, eat a pile of ribs, and move on. From St. Paul to St. Louis is a brutal day's drive. From there you can make it to New Orleans in another day if you don't fool around in Memphis.

When the muffins popped up, Chaminade spread a gob of butter on them, not looking at me. "When you get back . . ."

"Yeah?" But I knew what was coming. I'd been brooding about it for a couple of weeks.

"I'll be out of here." She said it in such a conversational way that we might have been talking about grocery shopping or new wallpaper.

"We were getting along," I said tentatively.

"We were. Wonderfully. Up to a point. Then it stopped. The problem is, I'm something between number four and six on your list of priorities. The way I see it, there's not much prospect of moving up."

"If you could wait until I get back . . ."

"You could go to Memphis some other time. . . ."

"I've got to go today."

She shrugged. "See?"

"Obligations. A friend," I said defensively.

"I'm a friend, too," she said.

"You don't need help."

"See?"

Chaminade looked down the room at the cat, who was daintily picking his way across a radiator to a window. He saw us watching and posed, as cats do, one front foot frozen in midair. Sunlight rippled across his orange coat; there was a potted geranium sitting on a board at the end of the radiator, and the orange fur against the green leaves, all framed by the window, made a nice composition. Beyond the cat, through the window out on the river, a towboat pushed a rust red barge full of coal upstream toward the power plant. Pigeons wheeled overhead, little impressionist smudges against the faultless blue sky. It was quiet and beautiful.

"I'll miss the cat," she said sadly. "And the river."

I CARRY a small wooden box from Poland in my overnight bag. On the flight between St. Paul and Memphis, I got it out. Inside, wrapped in a square of rough silk, were seventy-eight cards, the Waite-Rider tarot deck. I did a couple of spreads. The Empress dominated both of them.

There's nothing supernatural about the tarot. Not the way I use it, as a gaming system. Formal game systems, the kind developed by the military, were intended to force planners out of habitual modes of thinking and to test new theories. The tarot is less structured than the formal systems, but it still forces you outside your preconceptions.

So I had the Empress dominating two separate spreads. In my interpretive system the Empress represents women, new enterprises, new creations, new movements. There's an overtone of politics and a suggestion of sex. That's roughly parallel to the "magic" interpretation, but I don't believe in that superstitious shit.

I sat back and thought about it as the river unwound two thousand feet below. The Empress.

Chaminade? Or someone I hadn't yet met?

MEMPHIS FROM the air looks like any other city from the air, except greener. Just before we landed, the pilot said the ground temperature was ninety-three and the humidity was 87 percent. A Turkish bath.

When I came through the gate carrying an overnight bag and a portable computer, a tall, balding black guy, forty or so, was leaning on the railing that separated the passenger and waiting areas. With his round gold-rimmed glasses, thin face, and high cheekbones, he might have looked like Gandhi. He didn't. He brought to mind a mercenary who had been blinded by a white phosphorus grenade in Biafra, a long time ago and far, far away. This guy wasn't blind, though. He was looking the passengers over, one by one, and finally picked on me.

"You Kidd?" he asked. His voice was tough, abrupt.

"Yeah. Who are you?" He was already walking away, and I trailed behind with my bags.

"John," he said over his shoulder. "You got a suitcase? Besides that stuff?"

"No. John what?"

He thought it over, but not very hard. "Smith."

If he didn't want to talk, I wasn't going to worry about it. He led the way to a two-year-old Chevrolet, one of the bigger models in a nondescript green. We were halfway downtown, sitting at a red light, before Smith said another word.

"I'm not sure we need you." He was staring straight out over the steering wheel.

"I don't know if I want to join up," I said.

"Bobby says you're some kind of complicated computer crook." He still wouldn't face me. "You don't look like a computer crook. You look like a boxer."

"I'm a painter," I said. "I've been hit in the nose a couple of times. The docs never got it quite right."

Now he turned, vertical lines crinkling the space between his eyebrows. "A painter? That's not what Bobby said."

20

"I do computer work to make a living. That's the only way Bobby knows me."

"Huh." The light changed, and we were rolling again. "Can't make a living at painting?"

"Not yet. Maybe in five years."

"You paint ducks?"

"No. I don't paint ducks, barns, sailboats, lighthouses, pheasants, rusty farm machinery, sunsets, jumping fish, birch trees, or any kind of hunting dogs. And I don't put a little pink glow of the setting sun between groups of warm nine-teenth-century farmhouses with hay sticking out of the lofts of the barns in back."

"Eakins painted hunters. Homer painted fish."

"Damn well, too."

"So who do you like? Artists?"

"Rembrandt. Ingres. Degas. Egon Schiele. Like that. Guys who could draw. People who like color. Gauguin. Living guys, maybe Jim Dine. Wolf Kahn. A couple of personal friends. Why?"

"I do some . . . art." He said it reluctantly, almost as a confession.

"Painting?"

"No, no." He slowed for a moment, letting a woman in an old canary yellow Ford Pinto squeeze in front of us. Traffic in Memphis is usually tangled, especially when you get close to the water. The heat didn't help, and the people who weren't sealed in air-conditioned cars were driving with an air of desperation. "I make things. Out of wood and glass and rocks and clay, from down along the river."

"Sell it?"

"Shit," he said in disgust.

"I'd like to see it."

He looked over at me for a moment. "Maybe."

We lapsed back into silence. Ten minutes later we were on a narrow two-lane highway lined with recapped tire joints and motels with signs that said TRUCKERS WELCOME. Memphis was disappearing in the rearview mirror.

"Where're we going?" I asked.

"Downstream," he said. We were running along the river in the gathering evening twilight. "It'll take a while. Town of Longstreet."

"What's in Longstreet?"

He didn't answer. Instead, he braked and turned into a roadside convenience store. When we'd stopped, he said, "I want to get Cokes and ice. I've got a cooler in the trunk."

"Get a six-pack of beer, too," I said. I took a five-dollar bill out of my pocket, passed it to him, and asked again, "What's in Longstreet?"

"A problem. Maybe some trouble. A lot of hate."

"A garden spot," I said.

"It's in the fuckin' Delta," he said, as if that explained everything. "There could be some money in it."

"That sounds interesting," I said.
"Yeah. Bobby thought it might."

WHILE HE WAS in the store, I considered the possibility that Bobby had dipped into my IRS files. I hadn't decided one way or the other when John returned. He stashed the cooler on the backseat, and we each popped a can of Coke. It was a small piece of camaraderie and seemed to loosen him up. He started answering questions.

"Where's Bobby?" I asked, as John barely beat a tractor-trailer onto the highway. "In Longstreet?"

"I don't know. I never met him," John said, sounding a little puzzled. "I thought you'd know."

"No. I've never met him face-to-face."

"Huh. I wonder if *anybody's* ever met him face-to-face."

"*Somebody* must have. He's got to eat. . . . You're a computer jock?"

"No. I work for a legal services company, investigations. The company's got a computer system, with electronic mail. One day I got a piece of mail from Bobby. About a case I was working on—he'd read about it in the papers, developed some information from data bases. He gave me a number to call on the computer gizmo—"

"Modem."

"Yeah. I called, and we've been going back and

forth ever since. Five years. I even got my own computer so I could talk to him . . . privately. He can get anything. Crime reports, credit records, secret research you'd never see. I don't know where he gets it, but it's always right."

"Data bases," I said. "He's a genius with them. But that still doesn't tell me about Longstreet."

THERE'D BEEN a kid named Darrell Clark, John said, fourteen and computer smart. A friend of Bobby's. Knew his math. Knew his logic. At least, that's what Bobby said. Bobby sent him a book called *A Primer for the C Language* along with a pirated copy of a C compiler. Darrell came back three days later with a sophisticated Mac II program. Sent him *Assembly Language for the Mac II*. Talked to him in a month and got back an assembler program of breathtaking complexity.

"The kid was smarter than Bobby. That's what Bobby says."

"You keep saying *was*," I said. "What happened to him?"

"Longstreet cops killed him." John tipped his head for a mouthful of Coke. "They say Darrell came at one of them with a knife and the other one had to shoot. Everybody knows it's bullshit. What really happened was, they thought Darrell was a purse snatcher and they shot him by mistake. In the back. With a machine gun."

"Jesus. A mistake?"

"They had this new toy, this machine gun. The cop had to try it out. Blew the kid all over the railroad tracks."

"So what happened to the cop?"

"Nothing. That's why we're going down there," John said. He glanced over at me. "Darrell Clark won't get justice. His family won't. The town is sewn up tight by an old-time political machine. The cops are near the center of it, and they won't let their man get taken down."

We lapsed into silence again. He seemed to be waiting for a comment, but I had none to offer. The problem with dead people is simple enough. They're dead. There's no point in getting revenge for a dead man because the dead man won't know and can't care.

John was waiting, though, so I eventually gave him a question. "What do you want me to do?"

He was driving easily, one-handed. "We needed somebody who knows about politics, about information, and about security. Bobby says you've done a lot of computer work for politicians, that you're good at planning, and you know about security."

"So you want me to figure out how to get these cops? Why don't you find an NAACP lawyer, get the kid exhumed, and file a federal suit?"

"Because we don't want the cops," John said. "Fuck the cops."

"What do you want?"

"We want the machine. In fact, we want the town," he said, his voice gone low and tight. "That's what we want you to do, Kidd. We want you to take down the whole fuckin' town."

2

WE WERE DRIVING down the river in the long twilight of the summer solstice, a pale witches' moon hung in front of us. Every few minutes we'd go through a raft of river air, cool, damp, smelling of mud and dead carp and decaying vegetation. I watched the moon ghosting through the evening clouds as John laid it out, simply and clearly. They wanted me to destroy the town's political machine, any way I could do it, and leave it in the hands of their friends. Then I asked him another hard question, and he answered that one, too.

When he stopped talking, I cranked back the car seat and closed my eyes, half in contemplation, half in dream.

A long time ago I'd been an idealist of sorts. Somewhere along the line—Vietnam is the conventional answer, but I'm not even sure that's right anymore—the idealism scraped off. After I'd asked him the first hard question, "What do you want me to do?," I'd asked the second: "Why should I do it?" Why should I take any risks for a dead kid I never knew?

"Revenge," John said. He hadn't hesitated. He and Bobby had seen the questions coming and had rehearsed the answers. "Bobby said he was one of you—computer freaks."

"That's not enough," I said. "Good people die all the time."

"Friendship," said John, checking the second item on a mental list. "Bobby's your friend, and he needs your help. He'll do something whether you're there or not. He really doesn't know how. He could fuck himself up."

I shook my head. "I'm sorry. I can't put my ass on the line for something as thin as that. Bobby's a friend, but only on the wires. If he wanted me to do some computer code, illegal code, that'd be one thing—"

"Money," John interrupted. "Lots of it. The town is papered with corruption cash. You could probably figure out a way to grab some of it. And since nobody can talk about where they got it . . . there'd be no comebacks."

"Money," I said, looking out the window, maybe a little bitter. "Everybody's reason."

"To tell you the truth, it bothers me to think you'd do it just for money," he said. "Mercenaries tend to be . . . unreliable." He sounded as if he knew.

"I wouldn't do it just to have *money*, but in this country, today, money is freedom. Anybody who tells you different is bullshitting you," I said, looking over at him. "Freedom's worth chasing."

He nodded. "So you'll do it?"

"Lots of money?"

"Could be," he said.

"I'll talk about it," I said.

THE UNEASY HALF DREAM was shattered when we bounced across a set of railroad tracks. I opened my eyes on a dark town of unpainted shacks, huddled in a grove of dense, overbearing pin oaks. Here and there the ghostly moonlight broke through the canopy of leaves, etching web forms on the shacks, like the work of an enormous spider. We were through the place in less than a minute. If I hadn't later gone through it in daylight—REZIN, POP. 240—I might have remembered the town as a hallucination, a dreamed remembrance of an Edgar Allan Poe story.

"Nightmare place, probably red-eyed incestuous children with crosses carved on their foreheads, creeping through the cotton with choppin' knives," John said, echoing my thoughts. He'd seen me come awake.

"Yeah." I looked back at the town, a dark hole with a ribbon of moonlighted concrete running into it. Then we were around a curve, and it was gone, just another piece of the Delta. I turned to the front and ran my tongue over my teeth. Moss had sprouted during the nap. When I couldn't dislodge it with my tongue, I leaned over the seat for a beer. I'd kill it with alcohol.

"You want one?" I asked.

"Yeah. Another Coke."

I popped the top off a Coke and a beer, handed him the Coke, and said, "So tell me about Longstreet."

Twenty thousand people lived in the town, he said. Nine thousand were white; eleven thousand were black. The city council districts had been drawn to put three whites and one black on the council.

"They fixed the districts so there'd be five thousand people in each one—one man, one vote, just like it's laid down by the law," John said. "One district covers the heart of the black side of town, five thousand people. Hardly a white among them. That district will always elect a black councilman. But when you take out those five thousand black votes, in one bloc, the whites are a majority in all the rest of the districts. There's about two thousand whites in each, and about fifteen hundred blacks."

"That's common enough," I said.

"It's still a son of a bitch," John said.

"These friends in Longstreet . . . are they reliable?"

"I don't know," John said carefully. "I've got solid recommendations, but I've never met them myself. Our main contact is a woman, name of Marvel. She's a Marxist, I hear. That means she's probably got her own agenda."

"I thought Marxism was out of style," I said.

John threw back his head and roared. "In the fuckin' Delta? Listen, even when Marxism was *in style*, you could get lynched for laughing at Groucho and Zeppo, much less believing in Karl."

WE ROLLED into Longstreet after midnight, past a Holiday Inn, a Taco Bell, and a Dairy Queen, a row of white grain elevators, a few dark stores, and a lot of empty streets.

The Mississippi had been a presence all through the trip. We could sense it and sometimes smell it, but with the levee between the highway and the water, we couldn't see it. Longstreet, though, was built on higher ground. As we came to the center of town, to the first traffic light, we climbed above the levee, and the river opened out below. A ramshackle marina, with a few bare white bulbs flickering on an overhead grid, sat at the bottom of the riverbank. A couple of runabouts, a dozen olive drab jon boats, and an aging houseboat swung off the T-shaped pier.

"You know where we're going?" I asked.

"I've got directions," he said, turning at the light. We crossed the business district, passed a well-lit town square with an equestrian statue at its center, and bumped across another set of railroad tracks. On the other side was a convenience store that looked like a collision between a chicken coop and a billboard. A hand-painted sign on the side of the store, red block letters on white, said E-Z WAY. Three tall light poles, the kind used to illuminate tennis courts and Little League baseball fields, lit up the parking lot. Every bug between Helena and Greenville swarmed around them.

"That's where the kid bought the ice cream before he got shot," John said. Through the open doors we could see a fat white man sitting on a dinette chair. He was mopping his face with a rag. John took a left around the E-Z Way and drove another six blocks on a potholed road past a clapboard Baptist church. Then he slowed and peered out the windshield toward the passenger side.

"It's a green house with a porch and some potted flowers hanging from the eaves," he said, half to himself. We rolled another hundred feet down the street. "There it is."

The house was a concrete-block rambler with

an overhanging roof, a small porch, and a picture window. Our headlights picked out a couple of pink metal lawn chairs crouched on the porch. John eased the car into a graveled parking strip. "You wait here. I'll go up and ask," he said.

He climbed out of the car, stretched, walked up to the porch, and knocked. The door opened immediately. John said a few words, nodded, and walked back to the car. I'd cracked the window. "This is it," he said. I climbed out into air that felt as if you could grab a piece, wring it out, and get water. As we walked to the door, John said quietly, "Wait'll you see her."

MARVEL ATKINS WAS Hollywood-beautiful, beautiful like you don't see walking about in the streets. Her black eyes were tilted and large as the moon, her face a perfect oval. She was five-five or five-six and moved like a dancer. She was wearing a thin olive-colored blouse of crumply cotton with epaulets, the kind fashion people think the Israeli Army might wear. She stepped back when she saw me, startled, and turned to John.

"Who is he?"

"Bobby's friend," John said. She kept backing up, looking from John to me and back to John.

"He's white," she said.

"You Commies really got it taped," John said wryly.

"I'm a social democrat," Marvel said, momentarily distracted.

"That's what I said," John answered, showing some teeth.

"Maybe we don't need you," she said. She was in her early thirties and wore round gold-rimmed glasses like John's. You hardly saw the glasses because of the eyes.

"You've been sitting here for a month. There's been nothing but talk and whining and bullshit and more bullshit," John said. "If you think it'll ever be more than that, we'll get back in the car and let you handle it. But I think you need us. You need something. . . ."

Their eyes locked as she considered him, and John watched her with the gravity of a Jesuit. After a few seconds of the deadlock a man eased out of a back room into the living room behind Marvel. He was short, thick, and looked as if he could break bricks with his face. He stepped close behind her and muttered something. She nodded.

"We'll talk," she said. "Then we'll see."

WE TALKED until four in the morning. John stated the proposition as baldly as he'd given it to me: We'd wreck the machine and the town administration. If possible, we'd leave it permanently in the hands of Marvel and her friends.

"A pipe dream," Marvel said flatly.

"That's why Kidd is here. He knows about politics, and he knows about wrecking things. He'll do us a plan," John said.

I tried to look modest.

"I'll believe it when I see it." She deliberately looked me up and down again, not impressed, and John grinned. The thick man, whose name was Harold, watched me impassively.

"He's a technician," John said, letting the grin die. "If you called somebody to fix your telephone, you wouldn't care if the repairman was white as long as he fixed your phone."

"I'd rather he be black, even to fix the phone," Marvel said.

John said, "Right on, sister," and gave her a sarcastic black power salute.

Marvel waved him off. "OK." Then she looked at me and asked, "Why don't you say something?"

" 'Cause you're pissing me off." It came with an edge, and Marvel glanced away, embarrassed. She'd been rude to a guest, a cardinal sin anywhere in the South.

"I try to be civil," she said. "But I can't help wondering what outsiders can do. . . ."

"The town is corrupt," I said. "John says it's in

the hands of a voting minority. If that's right, there may be some way to take it."

"How?"

"I don't know yet. I have to know about the place to figure that out. I have to know about the people who run it. What they're up to."

"We can tell you that, all right," Marvel said. She was looking straight at me with those incredible liquid eyes, and I thought of the Empress card in the tarot. "Anything you want to know. The question is, If you wreck the machine, who runs things afterward?"

I shrugged. "Not me."

"I've got a job and an ... organization ... in Memphis," John said. "I don't have any interest in moving in."

She pursed her lips. "I heard about your organization. Bunch of old lame-ass ex-Panthers, is what I hear."

"Maybe our asses are lame, but they're not getting kicked by a bunch of Delta peckerwoods," John snarled. I was thinking uh-oh. They were knocking sparks off each other, in the angry, confrontational way that tends to lead directly to the bedroom. Harold felt it, too, and was looking back and forth between them.

"How about this?" Marvel suggested, turning to me. "You figure something out. A plan. If we don't like it, we can get out anytime."

John looked at me, and I shook my head. "We

can't have key people bail out at a critical moment. That could kill us."

"How do we handle it?" he asked.

"We lay out a proposal," I said, turning to Marvel. "If you like it, you're in. If you don't, we go home. But you tell us up front."

She thought about it for a moment, then said, "I've got to talk with Harold." She led the thick man into a back room and shut the door.

"THE PROBLEM with Commies is double crosses are built into their system," John said when the door had closed behind them. He was leaning back in his chair, his arms crossed over his chest. "It's all hobby politics. They never have to deal with anything real. They just fuck with each other. We got to think about that."

"Maybe you should hold down the Commie bullshit," I said. "At least until we decide something. And stop talking to her tits, for Christ's sake."

"Was I?"

"Yeah, you were."

Marvel and her friend spent ten minutes in the back. When they came out, she plopped down on a couch, and the thick man moved behind her. They both looked us over. "We're in for now," she said. "What do you want to know?"

I opened the portable and said, "Notes."

◻ ◻ ◻

"IT'S STILL NOT EASY for black folks to get decent city jobs," Marvel said, leaning forward, her elbows on her knees. I'd asked where she got her inside information on the machine. "There are a few black cops and clerks, but most of the blacks who work for the city have menial jobs. Nobody pays any attention to them; it's a hangover from segregation, when a nigger was less than nothing. You wouldn't hide anything from a nigger cleaning lady any more than you'd hide it from her mop. So there are still a lot of invisible people around—cleaning ladies, janitors, garbagemen. Some of them are pretty smart. And we talk. There's not much that gets past us."

There were four men and a woman on the Longstreet City Council. The woman, Chenille Dessusdelit, was mayor and was also the city's chief administrative officer. She had an insatiable hunger for money, Marvel said. And she was intensely superstitious.

"Her mama and her husband died about six weeks apart, and that's when she really got strange," Harold said. "She was always superstitious, but after that it was stars and crystals and talking to the dead. There used to be a Gypsy fortune-teller in town, an astrologer. Chenille'd see her every week. Then the Gypsy died, too.

Come to think of it, a lot of people die around Chenille. . . ."

"What kind of name is that? Chenille whatever it is?" I asked.

"*Deh-soos-da-leet,*" Marvel said, and she spelled it. "It's old French. The French go way back here in the Delta, back even before the English."

"All right."

Of the other four council members, one was black: the Reverend Luther Dodge. Besides presiding over a Baptist church, he ran a city recreation center on the black side of town. He had demanded a special investigation of Darrell Clark's killing but agreed that it should be done by local officers, one black, one white.

"That guaranteed that the cop'd get off," Marvel said. "The local boys wouldn't cut on one of their own." When the final report came out, whitewashing the shooter, Dodge had acquiesced to it.

"If we take down the town, is Dodge a potential front man for whatever's left?" I asked, taking it down on the portable.

"Not for me," Marvel said. "He's as bad as any of them. He's in on the city council deals, and he clips the receipts at the recreation center. We figure he takes a hundred dollars out of the swimming pool receipts on a hot summer day. And we have a lot of hot summer days."

"He has an eye for the girls," Harold said suddenly. It was something of a non sequitur, but he carefully didn't look at Marvel.

"What Harold's saying is, Dodge has been trying to get into my pants since I was twelve," Marvel said.

"So he's human, big deal," John said, not quite under his breath.

Marvel suppressed a grin and started to say something, but I broke in: "We take him, too?"

"Yeah. Take him."

The other three city councilmen were white.

Arnie St. Thomas, Marvel said, was a loan shark—and he used the city's money in his operation. Another, Carl Rebeck, was an insurance agent. He didn't do much, just voted the way he was told, and collected a piece of pie. "He's not smart. I doubt that he even knows that.what he's doing is illegal. To him, it's just business. The councilman does favors for people, and they pay him for it."

"Who's the fifth guy?" I asked, typing.

"Lucius Bell. He's a cutie pie," Marvel said with a genuine smile. "He's a farmer. He's honest, I think, 'cept for one thing."

"What's that?"

"Our bridge fell down a few years back. Got hit by a runaway barge. To make a long story short, it never got replaced. Bell's a farmer, mostly on the other side of the river. He came over here and got himself elected to the council for no other reason than to get the bridge back. Everybody knows it; hell, everybody agrees with him."

"But he's not a big mover with the machine?"

"No. That's the mayor."

The mayor, with the council's advice, oversaw nine city departments. Every one of them was corrupt. Even animal control.

"The dogcatcher is a separate department?" John raised an eyebrow.

"Gotta lot of mean dogs around here," Harold drawled. He said *dawgs*, like a country boy.

"Duane Hill—he's animal control—is the machine's muscle," Marvel said simply.

"Like when?"

"Like we had some young lawyers go through here, from the rural legal services. They looked like they might set up shop. Duane got a bunch of his lowlife friends to hassle them. Every time those boys went out, somebody wanted to fight. The cops were always saying they couldn't do anything, it was just some boys gettin' drunk. That was bullshit. Duane himself beat up one of them. With a pool cue. Hurt him so bad the boy had to go to Memphis to get his teeth fixed. Eventually they all went away, and they never came back."

"Nice guy."

"Duane's the meanest man on the Mississippi

River, I believe," Harold said, with what sounded almost like a note of rueful pride. "He gets a piece of the city council's take, of course, but he also sells dog blood on the side. You know, to veterinary hospitals. He has customers all over the mid-South. The way he gets the blood, he sticks a big needle into the dog's heart and lets it pump out. The more it hurts the dog, the better it is, because the heart beats harder. They say some nights, down at that end of town, you can hear dogs howling for hours."

"Do you have a contact out there?" I asked Marvel.

"I've got somebody I can work on," she said.

"Do it. . . . Now, you mentioned the city attorney a while ago. How does he fit in?"

"He's the fixer . . . and maybe, with Chenille, the brains behind everything," Marvel said. "He drinks too much, and he's a bad man. He doesn't like black people, or anybody else, much. He's got two kids—they're both gone now, up North working—and the word is, he doesn't even like them. I'd say he's right at the heart of the action. . . ."

"Hold that thought," I said. "Who's the center of the machine? That's what we need."

Harold and Marvel looked at each other, and Marvel pursed her lips, then turned back to me. "I'd say the center of the machine is Dessus-delit, the mayor; Archie Ballem, the city attorney; Arnie St. Thomas, the councilman; and Duane Hill, the dogcatcher. Dodge and Rebeck have their own constituencies, but they're mostly along for the ride. They don't make any decisions. And there are a lot of smaller fish. The city clerk helps Dessusdelit run things, and then there are the department heads, individual cops, and so on."

"Does the machine run everything in town? Is there anybody high up we can talk to?"

Marvel was already shaking her head. "Not everybody is on the take, but everybody important is getting something, somewhere. You couldn't make a move here without the machine finding out."

"So it's Dessusdelit and Ballem and St. Thomas and Hill?"

"Yes."

"Power or money? Are they getting rich?"

"Sure," Harold said. "They try not to let it show too often, but every once in a while you see it. With Chenille and Ballem, anyway; Hill, you don't see it so much. But I'd bet every one of them is a multimillionaire, the money they've taken out of this town."

I made a note. I made several notes.

THE DOG BLOOD SALES were only the most bizarre item on a laundry list of corrupt deals and straight-out rip-offs. Crooked public works employees sold tires, gasoline, car parts, even grass seed and fertilizer. The council routinely got kickbacks on city purchases. There was a regular business in false receipts, showing larger-than-actual city purchases of expendables.

The city got suspiciously low rates of interest from the banks where they kept city cash; at the same time it paid suspiciously high interest rates on general obligation bonds issued to build a new sewer system.

As she listed the payoffs, kickbacks, fraud, and outright thefts, Marvel paced the living room, excited. Finally she stopped, turned into the kitchen, and we could hear her banging through the cupboards. A minute later she stuck her head into the living room. "Who wants ice cream?" she asked.

Five minutes later Harold sat behind a bowl of butter brickle ice cream and detailed how you could buy the municipal judge, how the cops took payoffs from the local bars, and how the chief wrote bid specs on new police cars to favor a particular car dealer. The cops stole from the parking meters, took bribes from drunk drivers, and accepted kickbacks from bail bondsmen for steering clients after arrests.

"The fire department?" I prompted.

"Now that's different," said Harold. "They're separate from everything else, not on the take anywhere. Except, like, they handle the dope traffic in town."

"What?"

"Yeah. Ain't that weird? All the cocaine that comes through Longstreet, all the good stuff, comes through fire. They split up the profit right there in the station house."

"Jesus Christ," said John. "I didn't even know they had that shit out here."

"I don't know how it got started," Harold said, "but that's what they do. They're good firemen, though."

"Yeah," said Marvel. "For one thing, they're awake all the time."

"Tell me one really big thing. Something that's going on right now," I said.

Marvel had picked up a pencil, a yellow one, and pressed the eraser against her lips. John was staring at her fixedly, as if he were about to jump on her, and Harold kept glancing at John.

"The sewers," Harold prompted after a moment.

"Yeah . . ." Marvel rubbed her forehead, thinking, trying to get a grip on a complicated subject. "Two years ago the federal government took the city to court for polluting the river. Sometimes our sewage was a little too raw. So we had to get new sewers and a new sewage plant.

"The city got some grants and passed special

obligation bonds, got bids, and hired a New Orleans contractor. The feds were watching it, so the money was all accounted for. Just by accident, we found out that the contractor was buying his sewer pipe from a pipe broker registered in Delaware. Because of the way Delaware registers its corporations, we couldn't find out who really owned the pipe broker. We did find out that the broker was buying the pipe from a regular supplier in Louisville, and the supplier shipped the pipe down here by rail. The broker doesn't seem to do anything except jack up the price between here and Louisville."

"How much?"

"Ten percent. On a contract worth several million bucks. For doing nothing."

"The council?" I asked.

"Sure. We never would have found out, except the cleaning lady at the city attorney's office saw a letter to the contractor from the pipe broker. It was signed by Archie Ballem, the city attorney. We don't know the details, but we know the council is in there; the council's the pipe broker. The council must be taking down a hundred thousand a year, just on the pipe."

I made a note to call Bobby about Delaware and scratched my head.

"What?" asked Marvel.

"These guys are crooks, but they're also running a pretty complicated business. There're dozens of people on the payroll. So they must keep books. They must track what's going where and who gets how much."

"I don't know," Marvel said doubtfully, looking at Harold. He shook his head. "We never considered that possibility."

"Consider it now. Have your people check around."

"OK." We all looked at one another for a moment; then Marvel asked, "Can you do it? Dump them?"

"I don't know," I said after a moment. "We need something spectacular, a crime. A big one. This institutional corruption . . . even if we could get somebody to listen to us, somebody who could do something about it, we'd probably get a slow, long-term, low-priority investigation. It might go on for months or even years. . . ."

"We had one, a few years ago, before Dessus-delit was mayor. It petered out," Harold said.

"That's what I'm talking about," I said. "Politics tangles up everything. We need a Watergate. We need a smoking gun, something dramatic. Something that'll piss people off, that can't be ignored. Once we get that, we can throw all the other stuff in. Then it'll count. But first we need the smoking gun."

Marvel nodded. "Harold and I have been

thinking ever since Bobby called. You don't have to dump the police, or the fire, or public works, or the dogcatcher. You don't have to get rid of all the bad people. Just get us the council. Once we're in, we'll take care of the rest."

WE TALKED for a while longer, but we'd covered the heart of it. I shut down the portable and leaned back in the easy chair.

"It'll take a while to figure this out," I said.

"How long?" asked Marvel.

"A month. I'll need more information. I have to research state law, for one thing. How do you remove a city council? What are the technicalities? What contacts do we have at the state level, who might help? Do we have any influence with the feds? The IRS? I'll be calling you. For anything else—any documents you find, that sort of thing—get them to John. He can be the liaison."

"I can do that." John nodded.

"Can you get to a fax?" I asked.

"Sure. At the legal services—"

"OK. I've got a fax board on one of my PCs. You can pick stuff up from Marvel and ship it to me or to Bobby, depending on what we need—"

"I do have something else to say," Marvel interrupted. We all looked at her. "Whatever you do ... I mean, I know we're dealing with an extreme situation, but there has to be an underlying ethical base to our action. OK? The ends won't justify the means."

We all continued to look at her, and finally John slipped a hand inside his shirt and scratched his chest. "Uh, sure," he said.

"STARS ARE FADING," I said as we pulled away from Marvel's house. "It's getting light. You want me to drive?"

"You see that woman?" John asked, ignoring the offer.

"Marvel?"

"She's something else," John said, and I thought again of the Empress, serving butter brickle ice cream.

"She knows where the bodies are buried," I agreed.

"Ethics." John laughed. "Kiss my ass."

A cop car was parked at the E-Z Way. Two cops were standing over a guy in a T-shirt, who was talking up at them from the blacktop. John pulled in, down at the end, away from the action.

"I'll get it," I said. We needed caffeine for the drive back to Memphis, and the E-Z Way would be the last chance. I hopped out of the car and walked to the door. The cops were fifteen feet farther on, big guys in dark blue uniforms. One of them was dangling a nasty leather-wrapped sap on a key chain. The guy on the ground had brilliant white teeth. He was trying to smile, to placate them, and there was blood on his teeth. He was young, in his late teens or early twenties, with dirty blond hair and a beat-up face. I went inside, got the Coke, and paid the fat counterman. "What happened out there?"

"Danny Oakes, running his mouth again. Boy'll never learn," the fat man said.

"Sounds like a bad town to run your mouth in," I said. I meant it as a wisecrack, but he took it seriously.

"It surely is," he said, nodding solemnly.

At the door I put a quarter in an honor box and took a copy of the Longstreet daily. The headline said something about a hearing on a new bridge for the city. Outside, the cops were putting the blond in the backseat of the squad car.

"What'd he do?" John asked. The cop car's light bar was still bouncing red flashes off the E-Z Way's windows.

"Ran his mouth," I said. John nodded. The Delta.

We rolled along for a while, quietly. I was thinking about the blond kid and white teeth slick with blood and spit when John blurted, "You think she's fuckin' Harold?"

"I don't think so," I said when I caught up.

"They didn't . . . vibrate that way. Maybe a long time ago."

"That's what I think," he said.

"This won't be a problem, will it?" I asked.

John said, "I fear I'm in love." He said it so formally that I didn't laugh.

"Should I . . . chuckle?" I asked.

"I don't think so," he said, and we drove out of town toward Memphis.

3

WHEN JOHN AND I got back to Memphis, the temperature was already climbing into the eighties. Instead of going straight to the airport, he took me through a section of narrow streets of small houses with dusty turnouts in front. The children in the yards were all black.

"Your plane doesn't leave for two hours," John said when I asked where we were going. "I want to show you something."

We stopped at a gray clapboard house with a deep green lawn inside a quadrangle of carefully trimmed hedge. "Come on in," he said, and I followed him through the heat up the sidewalk. He opened the front door with a key and turned on the air-conditioning as we stepped through. The walls were eggshell white, and the floors were blond hardwood. Art prints dotted the walls. I didn't know the artists' names, but all were competent, and some were excellent. The strongest

53

color came from handmade rag rugs spotted through the rooms.

A back bedroom had been converted to a study, with racks of books along the walls. Most of them, judged from their size and color, were histories and political texts. An IBM clone sat on a desk, with a modem and a mouse. Past the bedroom we dropped down a set of stairs into the basement.

"This is my workroom, you know, like a studio," he said as he pulled the strings on a half dozen overhead light bulbs. "I don't bring many people down here."

"You can't work in public," I said. "You get shitty art from committees."

A kiln sat behind the stairs, next to a furnace and water heater. To one side was a workbench made of four-by-four timbers, with a rack of wood and stoneworking tools above it. Welding tanks, along with a torch and mask, were stacked next to the bench. The whole area smelled of hot metal and glass and the pleasantly sharp odor of ceramic glazes.

At the far end of the room a long table was covered with masks. Some were stone; some were baked clay; some were wood. One was glass, apparently made out of melted Coke bottles. You could still see some of the molded-in words. A couple of the objects were in an almost natural state, cut out of dead trees, truncated boles and knots forming lips and eyes. . . .

"Not too good, huh?"

That was patently false modesty. It was better than good; it was exceptional. A pea green ceramic head was fixed on a copper stand made out of some kind of electrical strut. The head might have been Othello's death mask.

"Why this stuff?" I asked, picking up the Othello. "How'd you get started?"

"I saw an exhibit of African masks back in Chicago, in the bad old days. The politicians were afraid the niggers were planning to burn down the city, and they were all running around looking for something to cool us out. Since we were Afro-Americans at the time, they figured we'd get pissed if they handed out sliced watermelon. So they wheeled out the African art exhibit."

I looked sideways at him. "Always a skeptic in the crowd."

He shrugged. "Wasn't no big secret why they did it," he said. Then he grinned. "Funny thing is, with me it worked."

"I get fifteen hundred to two thousand for my good pieces," I said to him.

"Oh, yeah?" he said uncertainly.

"I'll give you a choice of anything I've got on hand, trade you for this mask." I tapped the pea green mask. "I've got a couple of things that'd look great in your living room."

"Bullshit," he said.

"You don't want to?"

"What are you going to do with it? The mask?"

It was my turn to shrug. "Put it on a bookshelf. Look at it. Think about it."

He looked at me for a minute and finally nodded. "Deal," he said.

"I'll get you in touch with a guy in Chicago. A dealer. He's got taste. He ought to come down and look at this."

"So you think it's all right?"

"My friend, if you can't sell this stuff, I'll personally drive you out to Graceland and kiss your bare ass on Elvis's front lawn."

I WRAPPED the mask in newspaper and made the airport with half an hour to spare. John dropped me off and left without a backward glance. While I waited for the plane, I got the tarot deck out of my carry-on bag. The Empress came up in the first spread. Future influences. I put the deck away.

The plane was late, and then I fell asleep on the trip back. A stewardess had to roust me out of my seat in St. Paul. I caught a taxi, growled at the cabdriver, and rode in silence along the riverside road back home. The apartment echoed with emptiness; Chaminade had erased every sign of her short occupation. I made myself busy with unpacking and transferred the notes from the portable computer to my work machine. John's mask went on a shelf in the living room, next to a museum-quality drawing by Egon Schiele. Looking at the mask made me think about buying a kiln, but I wouldn't be any good at it.

Feeling alone, tired, and a little sad, I peeled off my clothes and climbed into bed. After a couple of minutes I got up again, went out to the telephone, and called the Wee Blue Inn, a very bad bar in Duluth. Weenie answered. Weenie is the owner. He's also LuEllen's phone drop.

"This is the guy from St. Paul," I said.

"Uh-huh." Weenie didn't go in for the intellectual discourse.

"I need to talk to your girlfriend."

"Ain't seen her," he said. He said that no matter who called. LuEllen might be sitting across the bar from him.

"If you do, tell her to call me," I said.

"Business or pleasure?"

"Business."

"She got your number?"

"Yeah. She's got my number."

THE NEXT TWO DAYS were beautiful. Blue skies, light, puffy clouds. I spent them on the Mississippi, in the hill country south of Red Wing, working on landscapes and thinking about Longstreet. In the evenings, back in St. Paul, I trained at the Shotokan dojo, then walked up to the center of town to an Irish bar off the main drag. A newspaper friend, who once drank too much, still hangs out in the bars, drinking Perrier lime water at two dollars a bottle. He claims bars are his métier.

"Or maybe they're my forte. Either métier or forte, I get them mixed up when I've had too many lime waters," he said, looking longingly at my bottle of Miller. "You think I ought to change to lemon waters?"

"Don't do anything hasty. You'll wind up in the gutter," I said, dabbing at my fat lip. The pure thing about Shotokan is that when you fuck up, you find out right away.

"Just a lemon water. I could handle it."

"Then it'll be orange waters, and two weeks from now you'll be shooting black tar heroin into your carotid," I said. We talked about the state income tax for a while, and then I asked him about corrupt towns.

"They're all corrupt," he said glumly, scrawling wet rings on the bar with the bottom of his bottle. With his lined and wrinkled face, he looked like an aging English setter. "But they don't think of themselves that way. That's why the politicians get so mad when a reporter goes after them. They convince themselves that the payoffs were really campaign contributions and if they used the money to buy a hat, well, that was just an accounting error. There's nobody more righteous than a guilty Lutheran with a reasonable excuse."

"Have you ever heard of a place down the Mississippi called Longstreet?"

We both looked into the mirror behind the bar. Through the bottles, my hair was looking grayer, and the crow's-feet at the corners of my eyes were cutting deeper. Too much sun probably. Too much time on the river.

"Longstreet," he said, nodding. "Yeah. Don't know much about it. You got something going down there?"

"No, no. I went through there my last time down to New Orleans," I lied. "The place looked kind of . . . funky. Good light, for one thing. Interesting people. I thought I might stop off the next time I go down. Do some painting. But there's an air of violence about the place."

"Hmph." He was looking at me. I don't know how much he knew or suspected about my sidelines, but it may be too much. "There's violence in all the river towns. But the southern ones are the worst. Jim Bowie and the duel of Natchez, shootin' and cuttin' on the levee. Or maybe it was a sandbar." He took another hit on his lime water. "Stay away from the dogcatcher."

"What?"

"The only thing I remember anybody ever told me about Longstreet is, stay away from the dogcatcher. I took his advice. I stayed away from the whole fuckin' town." He raised a finger to the bartender and pointed at his empty lime water bottle.

LATE AT NIGHT, after the days on the river and the evenings in the bars, I sat in front of a computer and went back and forth with Bobby. Bobby's strong on data bases, and there was no shortage of material.

From the federal government he got military and tax records, Small Business Administration loan reports, and criminal rap sheets. All of those are closed, of course, but with the right computer keys, anything is available.

From the state government he got more tax reports and personal driving histories. From the courts he got lawsuits and divorce proceedings. The big credit agencies had records on everybody. So did the insurance companies. He pulled credit card numbers and used them to access billing records. You can learn a lot from bills. Two of the targets, for example, made a couple of trips every year to the gambling parlors in Tahoe. The city clerk showed a whole series of shop-by-mail charges with a supplier of exotic sexual aids.

Got that stuff from Delaware.

Anything good?

60

The council's in up to its chin. Will transmit now.

Go.

As he pulled the information out of the bases, he shipped it to me. Most of it was junk we'd never use. But in this kind of situation you never knew what was relevant, and what was worthless, until afterward. So I printed it out, punched holes in the left-hand side of the printer paper, and bound it in loose-leaf notebooks. I work with computers all the time, but when I browse, I want paper.

IN THE MIDDLE of the third night after I got back from Memphis, I was making clouds in my sleep, nightmare clouds that never came out right. There's a way of making quick, beautiful clouds with watercolor. You lay down a wash of cobalt blue on a good white paper like a 240-pound cold-pressed D'Arches. While the wash is still wet, you bleed in some gray where the shadowed portions of the cloud will be. Then you crumple a paper towel and lightly press it into the wash. When you pick it up, you leave behind a perfect feathery summer cloud. . . .

But in my sleep it wasn't working. I'd pick up the paper towel and find a face. I don't know whose face. A man's. Dead, I think. I struggled with it for a while, then felt myself being pulled up to consciousness. My eyes popped open, and I was awake and sweating.

Something was wrong. The apartment building is old and creaks and groans with temperature changes; those noises were all solidly filed in my subconscious. Something else was going on. I listened, trying to keep my breathing unchanged, and heard nothing but a deep and continuing silence. I turned my head a fraction of an inch to the left, toward the clock. Four in the morning. I'd been in bed an hour.

At the foot of the bed, and off to the right, I could barely make out the lighter rectangle of the open door. As I watched it, a dark shape seemed to slip through. For a second I thought it was my imagination. Then a narrow-beam flashlight sliced through the dark and crossed the bed before it cut out again.

I was trapped under the sheet and a light blanket. If I did a roll, I might make it off the edge of the bed between the bed and the wall, but from there I didn't know where the next move would be.

"Hey, Kidd . . ." The voice was soft, amused, and distinctly feminine.

I sat up, furious, the adrenaline still pumping. "Goddamn it, LuEllen, you scared the shit out of me."

"Aw, poor baby."

I punched the bed light. LuEllen was grinning

at me from the foot of the bed. "What the hell are you doing here?" I asked.

"Well," she said, with a barely audible sniff, "I thought I'd probably find you in bed with that Charade person—"

"Chaminade—"

"Whatever." She made a gesture to indicate that the name was of no importance. "I wouldn't want to disturb you in the midst of a rut, so I tried to be a little discreet."

"Jesus Christ, you almost stopped my fuckin' heart," I growled. "How'd you get in?"

"Professional secret. You got nice locks, by the way." She dropped the miniature steel flashlight into the pocket of her maroon jacket. LuEllen doesn't wear black, because it's noticeable. If you get pinned by a cop's spotlight, a deep red comes off better. And in shadow, where she does her best work, a maroon or burgundy is no more visible than black. "Weenie said you wanted something. Business."

"Yeah. I've got one, but I don't know how much money there'll be." I yawned, dropped my feet on the floor, and rubbed my hair around. "It's mostly a favor for Bobby. Maybe we can work something out on the money."

"Interesting?" She sat on the end of the bed.

"Could be. It's sort of like running a revolution. He wants us to help some people take over a town."

She crossed her legs and stroked a small white scar that dimpled her chin. "I'm so fucking bored I'll take anything."

"How's the coke?" I asked.

"I'm cutting down," she said defensively.

"Right." The skepticism showed in my voice.

"I am. I'm down to less than a gram." She yawned and took a long, deliberate stretch, just to show me that she was staying in shape. "So it's Chemise and who else?" she asked.

"Chaminade took a hike. I don't feel like being teased about it."

"Oops. Sorry," she said cheerfully. "But she was bound to go. You are an impossible mother-fucker to live with."

4

LuElLen SPENT THE night on the sofa. When I wandered through the living room the next morning, she was still asleep. She was wearing one of my old T-shirts for a top and a pair of pink underpants. She had twisted her blanket into a coil and wrapped her arms and legs around it, like a kid climbing a rope. I stepped over to wake her, but at the last minute, with my hand already at her shoulder, I stopped, eased myself into an overstuffed chair, and just looked at her.

She was a burglar. A good one. She stole cash, mostly, because it couldn't be traced. I'd done some work in the same line, though I'd taken something even harder to trace than cash. Trade secrets—ideas, if you will. At first I thought there was a difference; later I wasn't so sure.

When she wasn't working, LuEllen wore hand-stitched ostrich-skin cowboy boots and too-tight jeans. Her shirts had piping on the back and little arrows at the corners of the breast pockets, unless she was wearing one of those little puffy white baby doll numbers that let the black bra show through. . . .

She knew nothing about painting or computers, never made it out of high school. But she was intensely intelligent, a friend, and more than a friend. Sometimes we were in bed together; sometimes not. We tended to develop outside relationships, and we told each other that it was OK.

Maybe I believed it. But in the post-Chaminade *tristesse*, I was glad to have her back. Her legs looked great, not to mention her ass, and I eventually sneaked out of my chair, got a sketch pad, and started to draw. I laid out her body shape in a half dozen lines, blocked in her hair mass with charcoal, laid out the shadow beneath her waist, and stopped. I'd done this before, caught a sleeping woman unawares with a sketch pad. Sure. Maggie Kahn. Lying in the sunlight, on the bed in the Washington apartment, before the world started to come apart.

I was sitting there, staring at nothing, when LuEllen woke up. She woke like a cat, all at once, and spotted me.

"You've been drawing my ass, Kidd."

"I confess," I said. She rolled off the sofa and

walked around my chair to look over my shoulder.

"Pretty good. But what I want to know is, Would you love me without the ass?"

It was a throwaway line. We dealt with each other with a careful sarcasm, with metaphorical pokes and winks. But with Chaminade taking a walk, and the hollow she left behind, with the flashback to Bloody Maggie, I was seized with an instant of what felt like honesty. I looked up and said, "Yeah. I would."

Our eyes hooked up for a moment. Her grin slowly faded, and a tear started down her cheek. "Fucking men," she said. She turned away, banged into the bathroom, and stayed there for half an hour.

When she came back out, we both were struggling to get back to normal.

"So what do you want me to do?" she asked brightly.

"I've got to pound on the computers. Bobby's shipping me more data than I can handle. While I do that, I want you to start looking for a boat. Something we can rent for a month or so."

"A boat?"

"Yeah. You know, one of those white plastic things with a pointed end? They hold out the water when you—"

"OK, OK," she said, waving me off. "What

kind of boat? How big? What are we going to do with it?"

"A houseboat. Good-size. Air-conditioned. Something you'd tend to notice."

"You're going to live on it?" LuEllen has an oval face with dark hair, big, interesting eyes, and a few freckles scattered across the bridge of her nose.

"*We're* going to live on it."

"Down in Longstreet?"

"Yeah. Down in Longstreet."

I SPENT TWO WEEKS compiling Bobby's raw data into economic and psychological profiles of the individual city council members—the same kind of work I often do for politicians. Hill, the dogcatcher-enforcer, was a gambler and probably a loser. Dessusdelit and Ballem, though, were hoarders. I couldn't yet tell how much money they were taking out of Longstreet, but it was substantial. They couldn't invest it legally, because then they'd have to explain where they got it; none of it showed up on their IRS returns. Neither Dessusdelit nor Ballem had a passport, so they weren't personally taking it out of the country. They had to be stashing it.

Marvel talked to a man who worked for Ballem's lawn service and heard a story that Ballem collected stamps and maybe coins. Dessusdelit had been seen by another man in a

Memphis jewelry store, and she'd been looking at unset stones. . . .

"Stamps are great inflation hedges," LuEllen said. "Coins are not so good, but they're OK. Gold sucks, but it gives you some protection. Stones aren't so good either. But all of it stores value, and all of it is easy to move."

She knows what she's talking about.

Besides the research, I put in three hard hours at the Ramsey County Law Library. Every night I talked to John, Bobby, or Marvel.

"How much clout do you have with the black caucus of the state Democratic party down there?" I asked Marvel.

"Me? Not much. But Harold does."

"We may need their help. I'll get back to you. For now I just needed to know if you had any clout with them. Have you made any progress on finding the machine's books?"

"No, but we think you're right; there must be some. We have Xerox copies of letters on the sewer scam, and there's information in them that must be based on other letters, or files, or books. You know what I mean? You can infer the existence of the books from what these letters contain. . . ."

"Gotcha," I said. "When will I get the letters?"

"I gave them to John this morning. He was going back to Memphis, and he said Bobby would scan them in and ship them to you, whatever that means."

"I read an article in the Longstreet paper about the bridge. You mentioned it when I was down there. Tell me again. . . ."

She told me about the bridge. The bridge, she said, was the only reason the town hadn't blown away fifty years earlier. Now that it was gone, the city might go with it.

"Sounds serious."

"For people down here, it's desperate."

LuEllen caught me staring at the ceiling that night, chewing the eraser off a pencil.

"You have something?"

"What?"

"A plan?"

"Yeah. Maybe. An edge of one."

LuEllen found a thirty-six-foot Samson houseboat docked on the St. Croix River and took me down to see it.

"It's a fucking tub." I paced off its length along the dock. A huge tub, a shiny white, plastic behemoth, ugly, ungainly, and slow. Just what we'd need to catch the eye of a small river town. A diminutive American flag hung dispiritedly from a bent stainless steel rod on the peak of the cabin, to one side of a radar antenna. I looked under the stern and found the name *Fanny* inscribed in gold paint.

"Wait till you see the bedroom," LuEllen said.

"The sleeping cabin," I said, correcting her.

"Uh-uh." She shook her head. "I mean the bedroom. The guy who rents it said you don't use nautical terms for a houseboat. It's bedroom and kitchen and bathroom, instead of cabin and galley and head."

"Why's that?"

"Marketing," she said wisely. Everything she knew about marketing you could have written on the back of a postage stamp with a Magic Marker. "They didn't want houseboats to sound like submarines. They don't want the customers to think about sinking."

"Where's the owner?"

"Skiing. In Chile. He won't be back before the first of September."

We went aboard. The forward six feet of the lower deck were open, with a rail to keep drunken passengers from going overboard. Inside, the cabin was divided into halves. The front half was the general living area, with built-in bench seats along the walls, a television cabinet with a stereo, and a general-purpose dining- and worktable. At the very front was a set of boat controls with a pilot's chair, looking out through windows over the bow.

The back half of the cabin was a warren of small rooms and storage cubbyholes. The galley had everything most kitchens have, and it all fitted into a space the size of a closet. There was a minimal bath, with a shower, a fold-down sink, and a head. But the main attraction was the bedroom.

"It looks like a whorehouse," I said when I saw it. I was awestruck; the owner's taste was . . . unique. "That's the only purple-flocked wallpaper I've ever seen—I mean, done in plastic like that."

"How about the smoked mirrors?" LuEllen asked. Mirrors covered two walls and the ceiling. "And notice the electric swivel mount for the video camera. We can make our own movies."

The aft six feet of the deck, like the forward six feet, were open. The engine housing was back there, and the access ladder to the cabin's roof, which served as an upper deck. There was another set of controls on the upper deck, along with mounts for a couple of chairs, a bench seat, and a sunbathing well with removable privacy panels.

"All right, I admit it," I said finally. "It's perfect. Where do we sign?"

The agent was a stocky woman who wore what appeared to be a wrought-iron girdle. She asked a lot of questions, took some bank references, and two days later showed us a contract. She also showed us her husband, a grizzled cigar-smoking river rat named Fred. We spent the next three days pushing the *Fanny* up and down the St. Croix under Fred's watchful eye.

On the third day we nosed out into the Mississippi, took it through Lock and Dam No. 2 at Hastings, and fooled around in the current below St. Paul.

"I guess you can handle her," Fred grudgingly allowed at the end of the day. We were standing on the dock, and he handed me the keys. "When are you leaving?"

"Couple of days."

"Good luck. You take care in that Chain-of-Rocks Canal." He glanced at LuEllen on the upper deck. "And try not to wear out them mirrors."

THE PHONE LINES were burning up. John to Bobby to me to Marvel, out into her network, and back to John. I was piling up detail. Names. Leverage. John called that night. He was in Longstreet.

"We've got the Reverend Mr. Dodge by the balls. And we got him separate from the rest of the council."

"How'd you do it?" We'd decided to keep Dodge on the council while we dumped the rest of it. Since he was tied to the machine, that might not be easy.

"Remember how Marvel said he's been trying to get into her pants since she was a kid? She got to thinking, maybe he's been doing that with other kids. . . . And he has. We got two, so far, young girls. Marvel's gonna have a talk with him."

"Don't push him too hard," I warned. "Don't ask too much. He's a Baptist, and if he thinks he's a sinner, he might decide a public confession is the only way to go. That'd fuck us, along with him."

"She'll handle it," John said confidently.

"All right. I hope you're staying out of sight," I said.

"I'm down here only a couple of hours at a time and only at night," he said. "We never go anyplace in town."

"It's gotta be that way," I said. "Have you got your costume?"

"Yeah. And the motherfuckin' hairpiece looks great, man. I look like Fred Hampton. How about you guys?"

We were getting it together. A crystal for LuEllen, dangling from a gold chain. Her tools, and a small but outrageously expensive Leitz photo enlarger, some basic darkroom gear, and her Nikon F4. She sometimes takes photographs of places and things that she wouldn't want a photo lab to get curious about.

WE'D FALLEN BACK in bed together, though it took a while. After my spasm of honesty on the morning I drew her sleeping, she'd been walking circles around me. I let it go. There was something new in our relationship, but I wasn't sure what it was or if I wanted it.

Three days before we left, LuEllen made a quiet trip down to Longstreet, flying into Memphis, then rolling down the river road in a rented car. She was carrying a fairly expensive piece of electronic equipment from a friend on the West Coast. She got back late that night and checked back onto the couch.

Then, the day before we left, I hauled a carload of personal stuff and computer printouts down to the boat and stowed it. With nothing much left to do, we rented a movie—*Jeremiah Johnson* with Robert Redford—and sat on my couch with a bowl of popcorn between us. About the time the Indians started hunting Jeremiah around the mountains, she picked up the bowl, moved it to the other side, said, "Fuck it," and plopped her ass down beside me.

I couldn't think of anything to say, and she said, "Don't say anything clever."

So I didn't. We sat on the couch, watched the end of the movie, and then fell to necking like kids. Later we moved into the bedroom. LuEllen usually made love the way she wore clothes: like a cowgirl. Lots of enthusiasm, not much finesse. This time she seemed small. Fragile. When we went to sleep, I had my arm around her, and when I woke, eight hours later, we were still like that. She felt too good to move, but the little man in the back of my head was getting nervous: What the fuck is going on here, Kidd?

WE LEFT in the early afternoon, still not talking much. LuEllen took the *Fanny* out, while I got a gin and tonic from the bar, put my feet up, and watched Wisconsin go by. It was a fine day, with sailboats batting around Lake St. Croix, China blue sky with mare's tails trailing across it, and just enough breeze to ruffle the *Fanny*'s dispirited pennant.

THE ST. CROIX enters the Mississippi below St. Paul, at river mile 811.5. From there it was six days to Memphis. One of the days was a hot, unpleasant transit of the Chain-of-Rocks Canal around St. Louis. We were wedged between two river tows, bathed in the fumes of their oversize diesels.

The other five days were as good as days get. The sun was shining from clear pale dawns to rose madder dusks. I painted or tinkered with a little junk shop laser while LuEllen ran the boat, or I ran the boat while LuEllen read or sunbathed. LuEllen would peel off her bathing suit in the most provocative possible manner, warn me to mind my own business, and then roll around nude on the white foam sunbathing pad. Her browning body would relax and open and build a shiny patina of perspiration under the brilliant river sun. I'd keep one eye on the water as we chugged along, another on LuEllen. When I couldn't stand it, I'd drop the anchor and jump in with her. We went along that way until the bad day at Chain-of-Rocks Canal and picked up again on the other side.

Fifty or sixty river miles south of St. Louis, beautiful white sand beaches stretch along the Illinois side of the Mississippi. They are cut off from land access by the marshes along levees and so are virtually untouched by humans. We stopped at a bar on the fifth afternoon, and LuEllen jogged naked along the water's edge, a small woman with a gymnast's body running in a shimmer of heat and sand. She stopped here to look at a piece of driftwood, there to examine the desiccated remnants of a fish or animal that had washed up on the beach.

On her way back to the *Fanny*, a river tow rounded the bend below us. Rather than duck through the screening willows, LuEllen ran gaily along the edge of the water. The boatmen stood transfixed along the edge of their cabin and the points of the barges as the apparition jogged by in all her glory. As they passed, the tow let out a long, appreciative moan on the whistle, and LuEllen threw back her head and laughed.

And we did business.

I had two computers on the boat. One was a big top-of-the-line 486 with enough hard-disk space to store the complete denials of Richard M. Nixon. That machine ran off a portable generator. I also carried a laptop with built-in hard-disk and telephone modem. Every day, at some point, we'd pass a town where we could walk over the levee and call Bobby for another data dump. In the evenings we'd sift through the new stuff scrolling up the screen.

On the sixth day, late in the afternoon, we motored into Memphis and tied up at the docks below the city front. As I paid the slip rental, John Smith walked down the levee wall.

He politely checked out LuEllen—most of her was visible under a ridiculously small two-piece bathing suit—and said, "Ooo."

"How's Marvel?" I asked. He grinned sheepishly, and I introduced LuEllen.

"I got us rooms in a hotel just over the levee," he said. "Marvel called an hour ago and said she and Harold would be here"—he looked at his watch—"just about now."

"Fine," I said. I glanced at LuEllen. "Why don't you get some clothes on? We'll go up and introduce you to the others."

While we waited for her to change, John said, "Byron Lund came down to see me."

I nodded. Lund was my Chicago dealer. "He said he would, but I haven't heard from him. Is he interested?"

"He's talking about a fall show. He took a bunch of stuff with him. . . ." A shyness crept over his face.

"Hey. Congratulations."

"Yeah. You know, I wanted to tell you . . ." He looked as though he were going to dig his toe into the deck. "You know, thanks, motherfucker."

LuELLEN AND I were sitting on the hotel bed, and John was in a side chair, when Marvel and Harold arrived. John let them in.

"Whoa," LuEllen muttered. Marvel was wearing a V neck T-shirt and pleated black slacks. The whole outfit probably cost twenty dollars. On her it looked like a thousand-dollar Rodeo Drive production. She was carrying a white paper bag.

"Isn't she—" I started.

"She sure is," LuEllen said under her breath.

Harold was right behind Marvel, uncomfortable in a brown suit, white shirt, and brown-striped polyester tie. He looked like a magazine salesman assigned to the proletariat.

"Marvel, Harold," John said. "You know Kidd. That's LuEllen on the bed."

"LuEllen what?" Marvel asked, looking her over.

"Uh, just LuEllen," John said.

Marvel nodded. "All right," she said, and turned to me. "Did you figure something out?"

I'd told them bits and pieces on the telephone but saved the overall proposal for the Memphis meeting. If they turned me down, I'd take the *Fanny* to New Orleans with no regrets. Because whether or not they wanted the whole thing, they were going to get at least part of it . . .

"I think we can take them," I said.

Marvel walked over to the countertop that held the sink and dumped the bag. A two-quart carton of strawberry ice cream tumbled out with a box of plastic spoons. She picked up one of the half dozen hotel water glasses that were stacked on the counter, pulled off its cellophane wrapper, and opened the ice cream.

"How we gonna do it?" asked Marvel as she dished the strawberry into the first of the glasses.

"With superstition," I said. "Superstition, an old-time con game, and a little help from the governor."

We talked for two hours. When we were done, Marvel shook her head. "That's the most cynical thing I ever heard," she said. She got up and took a turn around the room. "Do something like that

... how do you square it with any kind of ethical position?"

Harold was smiling in a nasty sort of way. "Fuck ethics," he said. "I like it."

Marvel looked at him in surprise, then took another turn around the room before she finally nodded.

"All right. I guess we're in. When do you start?"

I glanced at LuEllen and told them the first lie.

5

WE'D BE IN Memphis for a couple of days, getting some equipment and taking care of last-minute personal business, I said. Marvel suggested that we eat dinner together that night, but LuEllen vetoed the idea.

"We can't be seen with you," she said. "Even this meeting is risky. We're talking about felonies. If there's ever a trial, I don't want to be tied to you guys by a waitress or a bellhop or a maître d' or anybody else."

"That's kind of pessimistic," Marvel said.

"I'm a pro," LuEllen answered. "I've never been arrested on the job because I try to think of everything in advance. If they ever do get me, I want them to have as little as possible."

The decision to attack the town had been a mood elevator. LuEllen's comments sobered them up, and by six o'clock they were gone. The minute they were out the door, LuEllen made a call.

Five minutes later we were standing on a curb along the riverfront.

"We're running late," I said. "If they don't show soon . . ."

"They will. These guys are good."

"Better be," I said. I was getting cranked and turned away. Below us a string of barges was pushing upriver, driven by a tow called the *Elvis Doherty*. The pilot sat in his glass cage, smoking a pipe, reading what looked like one of those fat beach novels that come out every June. At the tow's stern an American flag, grimy with stains from the diesel smoke, hung limply off a mast between the boat's twin stacks. I was watching the tow, thinking that it would make a very bad Norman Rockwell painting. LuEllen was watching the street.

"Oh, ye of little faith," she muttered. I turned in time to see a blue Continental turning a corner a block away, followed by a coffee brown Chrysler. Neither was a year old. LuEllen held up a hand, as though she were flagging a taxi, and the two cars slid smoothly to the curb.

"Take the Ford," she said. She picked up a black nylon suitcase that she'd carried up from the *Fanny* and headed for the Chrysler. I stepped into the street as the driver got out of the Continental, the car still turning over with a deep, un-Continental-like rumble. The driver, a heavyset, red-faced guy with no neck, a Hawaiian shirt, and zebra-striped shorts, peeled off a pair of leather driving gloves.

"Go easy on the gas till you're used to it," he said laconically. "It's clean inside."

That said, he walked around the back of the car, joined the driver of the Chrysler, and they strolled away down the sidewalk. LuEllen waved and got into the Chrysler. I climbed into the Continental, pulled on my own driving gloves, and spent a minute figuring out where the car's controls were. Then I shifted into drive and touched the gas pedal. The Continental took off like a young Porsche. I never looked under the hood or figured out what LuEllen's friends had done to the suspension, but you could have taken the car to Talladega. On the way to Longstreet I found a stretch of flat, open highway and pushed it a bit, climbed through 120, had plenty of pedal left, and chickened out.

"THAT WAS STUPID," LuEllen snapped. We were in the Wal-Mart shopping center on the edge of Longstreet, with a couple of hundred other cars. It was not quite dark. "A fuckin' speeding ticket would have killed us."

She was in her preentry flow, a weird state of mental focus that excluded everything but the job at hand. She would not be a pleasant woman to be with, not for a while, but she would be frighteningly efficient. "Sorry," I said, and I was.

"Stay with the program, goddamn it." She glanced at her watch. "It's time."

We took the Chrysler, as the less noticeable of the two cars. LuEllen drove downtown, taking the routes she'd scouted in her trip the week before. The city council was meeting, and two dozen cars were parked in the lot sideways across the street from City Hall.

"Chrysler," she said, nodding. The mayor's car was there, identical to the car we were driving. "I don't see Hill's pickup."

"And I don't see the Continental. . . ."

"May be on the street in front."

The Continental would be easy to recognize because it looked exactly like the one we'd left at the Wal-Mart. It belonged to Archie Ballem, the city attorney. We took a left, past the front of the City Hall. No pickup and no Continental.

"Ballem's got to be here for the bond hearing," I said. "Hill, we can't be sure."

"I thought he came to all these things."

"That's what Marvel said."

"I'd hate for her to be wrong this early," LuEllen said. We'd continued down the block past the City Hall. "Let's go around. . . . Wait a minute. There he is. There. Ballem."

A man in a seersucker suit and a white straw hat was walking down the street toward us. He turned to look at our car as we rolled past. "Are you sure?" I asked.

"Ninety-nine percent. I saw him last week, on the street. His office is down this way."

We found the Continental outside Ballem's office, three blocks from the City Hall.

"If we could find Hill . . ."

"If we don't, we'll call it off," she said. "But we've got the other two."

"We go?" I asked.

"Yes."

The phone company was a little redbrick cubicle on a side street, with a lighted blue and white phone booth hung on the side wall. We knew Chenille Dessusdelit, the mayor, was at the meeting. And we knew she was a widow and lived alone. But there might be a guest. . . . We called her home, but there was no answer. With the twentieth ring LuEllen nipped the receiver off the phone with a pair of compact bolt cutters. The phone would still be ringing at Dessusdelit's, and with the receiver gone, it was unlikely that anyone would come along and hang up our public phone.

"Get the portable," LuEllen said. I knelt on the passenger seat, leaned into the back, unzipped her suitcase, took out the cellular phone, sat down again, and plugged it into the cigarette lighter. Dessusdelit's line was still busy.

"Maybe we could get Bobby to kill the call records, so we could just use the cellular and not have to mess with public phones," I suggested after I had hung up.

LuEllen shook her head. "Too complicated. Something could get fucked up and we'd be on paper." She feared paper more than anything: tax records, agreements, leases, checks. Phone bills. Paper left a trail and couldn't be denied.

We cruised Dessusdelit's house just once. A well-kept rambler, it was stuck at the end of a cul-de-sac, in a yard heavy with shrubbery. Trees overhung the streets from both sides, but there were no sidewalks and nobody out for a stroll. Too hot, probably. One light burned in a window at the center of the house, a virtual advertisement that the place was empty. The house on the south side of Dessusdelit's showed a few lights, but the house on the other side was dark. We came out of the cul-de-sac, took a left past the country club, did a U-turn, and headed back. I dialed Dessusdelit's house again, and the phone was still busy. I was looking out the window when I heard LuEllen take the first hit of coke. She carries it in small plastic capsules, one long snort apiece.

"Jesus," I said.

"Don't give me any shit."

The coke was on her in a second, but her driving was rock-steady.

"Zapper," she said.

"LuEllen . . ."

"Get the fuckin' zapper. . . ."

The zapper was a specialized scanning transmitter that looked like a long-nosed hair dryer. It came with its own batteries. I got it out and started hyperventilating. LuEllen likes this part, with the adrenaline. I don't. LuEllen took us into the cul-de-sac and, without hesitating, into Dessusdelit's driveway. When we were still a hundred feet down the street, I pointed the zapper at the garage door and pulled the trigger. After a few seconds the door started up, and LuEllen barely had to slow down before we were inside. I dropped the door behind us, she killed the engine, and we sat in silence.

"Listen," LuEllen said. She was trembling with intensity. I listened and, after a second, picked out the faint ringing of the telephone.

The door to the interior was unlocked. Small towns. Lots of crime but not on the streets. LuEllen led the way in and then quickly through the house, stopping to answer and hang up the phone. There were three bedrooms. One had a queen-size bed, a couple of chests of drawers with jewelry boxes on top, and an antique oval mirror. Neat but lived in. Another was obviously a spare bedroom, with twin beds covered with decorative quilts. The third bedroom had been converted into a small home office with an IBM computer.

The living room was a double-jointed affair with two levels and a big brick fireplace, perfect for political soirees. The kitchen was ample, and there was a small first-floor utility room with a washer and dryer just off the kitchen. A quick tour of the unfinished basement turned up nothing of interest.

LuEllen started with the bedroom while I went back out to the car for my laptop and a stripper program. I was a little surprised that Dessusdelit had a computer at all; women of her age and status don't usually mess with them. Along with the computer were a slow modem, a desperately outmoded printer, and two double-drawer filing cabinets.

I loaded the stripper program into her machine, stripped her floppies and the hard disk, looking for data. I came up empty. There were two application programs, a word processor, and a spreadsheet, but no data.

I dumped the cabinets and again came up empty. Nothing but routine business letters. I carried the laptop back to the car and started working through the kitchen.

There was nothing subtle about what we were doing; we were tearing Dessusdelit's house apart. I dumped the cupboards onto the floor, shook each can and bottle before I tossed it aside, tore the drawers out of the refrigerator, checked the ice cube trays. Halfway through, there was a noisy crash from the bedroom, and I stopped to look. LuEllen had broken the bed apart.

"Loud," I said.

"Go work," she said coldly.

When I finished the kitchen, LuEllen was tearing through the living room. She had cut open the living room furniture and was tearing through a bookcase when I came out. "Where's the circuit probe?" she asked.

"Here." I patted my breast pocket. We'd been in for a while, and I was starting to sweat. LuEllen looked frozen, focused.

"Check the bedrooms, then the bathroom, then the kitchen. I'm going downstairs. . . . I don't know, it should have been in the bedroom." She checked her watch again. "Seven minutes."

We didn't know what we were looking for. We did know that Dessusdelit had taken a lot of money out of the city over the years and that Bobby couldn't find it: couldn't find money, investments, long-distance trips that might point to a foreign money laundry. Nothing. She could have been buying land in some backwoods town under an assumed name, but that didn't feel right. She'd want it where she could see it. She did have a safe-deposit box at the Longstreet State Bank, but Bobby went into the bank records and found that she visited the box only once or twice a year.

Wherever she was putting the money, there should have been some sign of it in the house. There wasn't. The furnishings were good but not great; she hadn't stashed the money in antiques or art. I'd feared the possibility that she'd put it in antiques; we didn't have a moving van.

We hadn't yet found a safe. That's what the probe was for.

A circuit probe is simply a lamp the size of a pencil. There's a plug at one end, a light in the middle, and a screwdriver at the other end. The screwdriver fits the screw in the middle of common everyday home power outlets. Electricians use them to check the outlets to see if they're live.

I checked the outlet next to her bedroom door, one under a window on an outside wall, one next to a closet. I got a light every time. The last outlet, the one behind the bed's headboard, came up dead. I turned the probe over and used the screwdriver to loosen the outlet plate.

Lying on the floor, working, I could feel my heart pounding in my chest; we were getting long on time. I gave the screw a last turn and pried off the plate.

Ah. A wall cache. Inside was a metal box, and I used the screwdriver to pull it out.

"Find something?" LuEllen asked from the doorway.

"Yeah, a cache . . . shit."

"What?"

"Money. Goddamn it." The cash was packed tightly into the metal box, fifties and hundreds. I pulled it out, a folded-over wad some four or five inches thick, and tossed it to LuEllen. In the bottom of the box was a small white envelope. I fished it out with my fingertips, squeezed it, and found three hard bumps like cherry pits.

"Not more than a few thousand here," LuEllen said. "We've got to get going—what's that?"

I tore open the folded envelope and poured a little stream of ice into the palm of my hand.

"Diamonds," I said, holding my hand up to LuEllen.

"Damn, those are nice if they're investment grade," she said. She took the stones and tucked them in a shirt pocket with the cash. "We're running late. . . ."

"Find anything in the basement?" I asked as we headed back toward the car.

"No."

"Goddamn it, we're not doing that good."

"Get the paint."

We had two gallons of paint in the car, red oil-based enamel. We popped open one can and started spreading it around the house.

THIEF, I wrote on one wall, with a newspaper dipped in the paint, STEAL THE CITY BLIND. LuEllen splashed out, YOU DIE PIGGY on another two, and CROOK—CROOK—CROOK. We wrote some more garbage, hitting every wall in the house and most of the ceilings. The last of the paint we poured on the living room carpets.

"Dump the can, and let's go," LuEllen said. We checked the street from the house. Clear. We ran the garage door up and back down and were gone.

"I've never done anything like that," LuEllen said. "It didn't feel that good."

"I know."

We both were private people. Maybe even pathologically so. What we'd just done to Dessus-delit was close to rape. There'd been a point to it, though: We wanted to hurt her financially, beyond stealing her little stash. We wanted her angry, and a little frightened, and disposed to flex her machine muscle. We wanted her scraping for cash when a big opportunity came along. . . .

LuEllen dropped the three stones into a Ziploc bag and put them under the passenger seat as we headed back to the Wal-Mart. "How much?" I asked.

"No way to tell," she said. "Everything depends on quality. If they're a good investment grade, anything between thirty and a hundred thousand."

"Not so good," I said. "There must be more somewhere."

We switched cars at the Wal-Mart, moving to the Continental, the twin to Ballem's car. Next we checked the City Hall. The parking lot was still full, and this time Duane Hill's personal Toyota pickup was in the lot.

"So we got him inside," LuEllen said. "Hope the meeting lasts."

"There's a public hearing. Marvel said it should be a couple of hours at least."

Ballem's car hadn't moved from the spot in front of his office. We stopped at a second public phone on the way to Ballem's house and made the call. When there was no answer, I nipped the phone receiver, and we started toward Ballem's.

"There's going to be hell to pay about those phones," LuEllen said, tongue in cheek. "We're fucking with Ma Bell. . . ."

Two blocks from the phone a cop car turned a corner in front of us, coming in our direction. As we passed, the driver lifted a hand in greeting. The Continental's windows were lightly tinted, so I doubt that he could see much, but I returned the wave.

"He thinks we're Ballem," I said.

"He's supposed to. . . ."

We went on another block when we saw the cop car's taillights come up.

"He's turning into a driveway," LuEllen said.

"Quite the trick. He should be on *The Tonight Show*," I said, the sudden tension forcing out a bad joke. LuEllen paid no attention.

"He's backing out; he may be coming back this way," LuEllen said.

"Do I turn or keep going?" I asked. The cop car was two blocks behind us, then two and a half, and I picked up his headlights.

"Go straight. Let's see what he does. We've got nothing in the car—"

"Except your bag with the wrecking bar and the zapper. And your coke."

"He's got no probable cause. . . ." But she dug into a shirt pocket and took out a half dozen red coke caps. If the cops got too close, they'd go out the window.

"This is the fuckin' Delta, LuEllen. That's probable enough." The lights were still back there but not closing. Then they swerved, off to the side of the road.

"He was looking at something else," she said, the relief warm in her voice. "Let's get out of sight. . . ."

Three minutes later, we were at Ballem's.

"Love those fuckin' automatic garage door openers," LuEllen said as the garage door rolled up. She broke another cap.

"Christ . . ."

"Shut up."

I'm always tense when I work with LuEllen, and the cocaine made it worse. She loved it, the rush of the work and probably, I was afraid, the rush of the coke. She'd have done it all for free. . . .

"Have you ever done a triple-header before?" I asked as we pulled into the garage and waited for the door to roll down.

"Not exactly. One time I went into a players'

locker room during an NBA play-off game and hit every fuckin' locker in the place. That was about a twenty-header . . . if that counts." The door hit with a bump, and we sat, listening, and heard the phone. "Let's go."

BALLEM WAS NOT like Dessusdelit. Dessusdelit kept her wealth hidden, and we didn't know where. Ballem put it on the walls—some of it anyway.

"Jesus," I said when we stepped into the living room. The floors were wood parquet, covered with rich maroon carpets. A floor-to-ceiling bookcase held knickknacks and books and framed a group of black-and-white prints. "Those are real."

LuEllen squinted at the signature on a lithograph of a young girl in a bonnet. "Cassatt?"

"Yeah." I took one off the wall and turned it over. A framer's tag was glued on the back panel, dated 1972. "Ballem would've gotten a great price on them way back then. Now they'd cost you an arm and a leg."

"Take them." She was in motion, headed for the basement. "Women hide stuff in the bedroom and kitchen; men hide it in the basement," she said simply.

I took the etchings. They all were American, by Mary Cassatt, Childe Hassam, John Sloan, George Bellows, Edward Hopper, Grant Wood, and even Stuart Davis and Mauricio Lasansky, which suggested that Ballem had either a catholic taste or an art investment consultant. I don't much care for black-and-white prints, but they all were good, and any one of them would pay for a year at Harvard. I was stashing the last of them in the car when LuEllen came back up. "We got a box," she said. "Come look."

The basement was half finished, with tile floors and painted cement-block walls. The ceilings were open.

"Over here," she said, and led me into a nook behind the furnace.

"It's not exactly a safe," she said, nodding at a foot-square steel door set into the concrete wall. A serious-looking combination dial protruded from the front of the door. "It's more of a fire-proof box."

"Can you open it?"

"I don't know." She glanced at her watch. "We're at two minutes, forty-five." She walked away from the lockbox, looking at the tools hung on Ballem's basement wall, then around the basement in general. A moment later she ran back up the stairs. I followed, but by the time I got to the top, she was already coming back. She was carrying a maul and a wood-splitting wedge. "From the garage. I saw that firewood around to the side."

I followed her back down and said, "What?"

"Stand back." LuEllen lined up with the maul

and gave the box a full-swing whack with the sharp edge. The blade didn't cut through, but it put a dent in it. The impact sounded like the end of the world, like a blacksmith pounding on an anvil.

"Jesus Christ," I whispered. "Somebody'll hear...."

"Not in this neighborhood," she grunted, pivoting for another swing. "Everybody's got air-conditioning, and all the windows are closed."

She took another whack, put another dent in the box. "You do it," she said. "You're a big strong man."

"Fuck, LuEllen . . ." Now I *really* was sweating.

"Hit it," she said.

I hit it. A half dozen blows distorted the door enough to see into it. LuEllen fitted the wedge into the seam of the door just above the lock, handed me the maul, and said, "One more time."

I hit it, and the door popped open. Breathing hard, I looked at LuEllen. She was standing with her arms crossed, waiting, not bored but not nervous either.

Inside the safe we found a leather-bound book of stamps, a freezer bag full of currency, and a metal box filled with American gold coins in sealed packages. The stamp collection wasn't much to look at—a few dozen fading squares of red, blue, and green, each in its own archival envelope. We took it all.

"Upstairs," LuEllen said. She looked at her watch. "Seven minutes, thirty-five seconds."

Ballem had an aging computer setup almost identical to Dessusdelit's. While I checked that, LuEllen tore apart the rest of the house. In the bedroom she found a collection of bondage and discipline magazines, both hetero- and homosexual, a new gun, a Smith & Wesson .357 magnum, fully loaded, and a flat metal box, like a safe-deposit box. Inside were a dozen gold Rolex watches, old but in perfect condition.

"We're killing this guy," LuEllen said enthusiastically.

"Good."

I was bringing the paint in from the garage when headlights swept the windows.

"Car," LuEllen said. She said it loudly, so I'd be sure to hear. I crouched and scuttled back into the house. LuEllen was against the front wall, peering out of a crack.

"It's the cops," she said. "The driver's coming up to the porch."

I heard him outside the door and slid over next to it. If he came in ... I lifted the paint can above my head. I waited, and the doorbell rang.

LuEllen's face was motionless, pale, watching me from her window spot.

The doorbell rang.

LuEllen's face, pale like the moon.

The doorbell rang.

My arms were aching.

And the cop walked away.

"He's going," LuEllen whispered. Then: "He's gone."

"Jesus Christ," I groaned, dropping the paint.

"Fucking cops," LuEllen said. She picked up the wrecking bar, dashed across the living room to the built-in shelves, and smashed them off the wall. She was in a frenzy, moving around the room, breaking everything breakable, knocking holes in the Sheetrock walls.

"The paint," she panted. "Dump the paint."

She went through the house like a dervish, while I threw the paint around. THIEF. CROOK. SUCK ON THIS. WHERE'S THE CITY MONEY?

"Let's go," she said when the paint was gone. "Let's get the fuck out of here." She threw the wrecking bar on the rug, and I followed her back to the garage. At seventeen minutes and a few seconds we were out of the house.

"That's about the longest I've ever been inside a place," she said. Her voice was half an octave lower than usual.

"You sound a little . . . turned on."

She let that sit in the air for a minute, then said, "Yeah. I guess I am."

☐ ☐ ☐

THE LAST PART of our trip took us to the edge of town, to what had once been a farmhouse. It was set back from the blacktop, along a twisting dirt track that ran between overhanging trees. We'd made the phone call and got no answer.

A black form crossed the driveway like a shadow from hell, and the hair stood up on my arms.

"Look at that," LuEllen said. "Jesus, look at . . ."

There were three dogs, black and tan, pointed ears and noses.

"Dobermans," LuEllen said. "All three . . ."

She rolled her window down a couple of inches, and the dogs were there, snapping, nobody to call them down. LuEllen reached over the backseat, got the steaks out, rolled the window down another inch, and pushed them out. The dogs were on them in an instant.

"Eat, motherfuckers," LuEllen said. She broke another cap herself. She wouldn't look at me while she snorted it. "Eat."

Outside, the dogs were starting to wobble. Dobermans, when they're in good condition, look semiskeletal, hard muscle rippled over a frame of bones, the whole thing held together by craziness and tension. When the tension goes, as it will when the load of barbiturates is big enough, the dogs seem to come apart.

"Let's go," LuEllen said.

I stepped gingerly out of the car and around one of the dogs. The dog could apparently pick up the motion because he made a weak attempt to react but couldn't get himself coordinated.

We were parked in the yard, just down the steps from Hill's front door. There was a light in one window, but no movement. From the porch we could hear the phone ringing. LuEllen shoved a pry bar into the door, threw her weight against it, and ripped it open.

"Whoa," LuEllen said. The house stank of spoiled food and cigars, an unwashed human, bad plumbing, neglect. Old wallpaper sagged from the plaster-and-lath walls, and there were water stains on the ceiling.

Hill had no computer. LuEllen went straight into the basement, while I went upstairs and began ripping apart the bedroom. Neither of us found anything, and we met on the first floor.

"Where?" she said, one hand on her hip. She walked slowly through the house, taking it in. There was no question of art; there was nothing on the walls but calendars and a couple of stuffed deer heads. I knocked the deer heads off, but there was nothing inside. I looked in the stove and pulled the drawers out of the kitchen cabinets. Nothing.

"Kidd. C'mere."

"What?"

"Look at this."

When the house had been built a century ago, a bookcase had been built under the first flight of the staircase. Hill had piled the shelves with junk; spark plugs; cans of two-cycle oil; a few paperbacks. LuEllen had dumped one of the shelves and pulled it out.

"They're too shallow," she said. "So I pulled the shelf out, and it looks like it's been cut down."

I looked at it. The shelf had been cut lengthwise with a power saw. Once it had been a foot wide or wider. Now it would barely hold Hill's few paperbacks.

"You check the other side?"

"There's a storage space on the basement side, but it's full of cobwebs, and there's an old wall. No way to get in. I'm thinking the stairs . . ."

The stairs were carpeted with a wool rug that must have been nearly as old as the house. I looked at the bottom of it. There was a loose place, and I grabbed it and pulled. The rug came up with a ripping sound.

"Damn. Velcro," LuEllen said. Velcro tabs had been glued to the rug and floor, to hold it in place. The rug covered the steps, and when we started working on them, three of them came cleanly away.

Tightly wedged into the space beneath the stairs and behind the bookcase's back wall was a pile of ordinary plastic garbage bags. LuEllen pulled one out and dumped it. Cash. She pulled another. More cash.

"Son of a bitch," she whispered. "The mother lode."

We had the bags in the car in five minutes, stepping carefully around the feebly thrashing dogs. They were coming back but not quickly.

"Paint?" LuEllen asked.

"Fuck it," I said. "Anything we did to that place would be an improvement."

"All right."

We saw no more cops. LuEllen dropped me next to the Continental in the Wal-Mart parking lot, and less than an hour after we had pulled into Chenille Dessusdelit's garage, we were gone, out of town, up the highway to Memphis. We dumped the take at the *Fanny* just after midnight. The cars we left in a hotel parking ramp, keys under the front seats. Neither of us had taken off our driving gloves, so they'd be clean.

BACK AT THE BOAT we counted the cash from Hill's safe. Three hundred and seventy thousand dollars, with bills that went back more than ten years. Ballem's coins made the total take much higher. There were sixty-five of them, sealed individually and certified by a numismatic rating service. She called a friend in Las Vegas and got a price: another two hundred thousand, and that might be low.

She was most interested in the stamps.

"Stamps are money if they're not too rare. You don't want a one-of-a-kind, where everybody in the world would notice the sale. But if you get stamps that are worth a few thousand dollars each—investor kind of stamps, like those coins are investor kind of coins—they're just like money. They're money everywhere. Fuckin' Bolivia, Bangkok, Saudi Arabia—there's always somebody who'll buy. Especially these—British issues."

"What if these are one of a kind?" I asked, paging through the book. "What if they're worth too much?"

"Fuck, I don't know," she said. "We throw them away, I guess."

She didn't know any stamp freaks but was hot to peg the values. I called Bobby.

Need number of philatelic data base.

Hold.

Three minutes later he came back. He knew only one that was on-line twenty-four hours. He gave me numbers, code names, and patched me into an anonymous telephone line out of Memphis. The first stamp was worth thirty-five hundred dollars if it was perfect. To me it looked perfect. The second stamp was worth forty-two hundred dollars if it was perfect. It looked perfect, too. They all looked perfect.

"A hundred and forty stamps. Say, thirty-five hundred to four thousand each . . ."

"Another half million," I said.

"All right," she said, satisfied. "And I've got a friend who can handle it all."

"What about the diamonds?"

"Another friend. He can sell them, but it'll take a while. We'll get fifty percent of face."

"I wonder about Dessusdelit. I don't think we touched her."

"Maybe we'll get another chance."

"Maybe."

LuEllen was examining the Cassatt lithograph, a sweet child from another age. "I don't know about the art."

"That's the problem," I said. "There's a worldwide registry of stolen art, out in New York."

"Dump them?"

"I won't do that," I said, shaking my head. "Let me think about it. I'll stick them in a safe-deposit box for now."

She nodded, looked at the loot scattered around us.

"This was a good job. Really good. I mean, it was great." She stepped over next to me, like a cat approaching a sardine. "A little tense maybe."

I got up and took a turn around the cabin,

walking away from her. "So we're rich again," I said.

"I don't give a fuck about the money," she said. "I like the way I feel."

I looked at her for a while, then got down a couple of tall glasses, two bottles of diet tonic water, a jug of Tanqueray, and a lime. "I was afraid it was getting like that," I said as I cut up the lime.

"Why afraid?"

I passed her a drink and tried mine. It was tart. Very tart. " 'Cause addicts always get caught."

6

BEFORE BED LUELLEN made two calls from a public phone, and the next morning we did some running around in a rental car. We dropped the gold coins at a dumpy motel near the airport, the diamonds at a bar downtown. She wouldn't let me come inside at either place.

"No need for you to show your face," she said.

She came back from the motel with an expensive black leather briefcase. I opened it and found cash.

"A hundred and twenty-seven thousand," she said. "On the low side, I think, but it was take it or leave it."

We did better than expected with the diamonds. Just after noon we left about a half million dollars in a safe-deposit box in downtown Memphis. The stamps, with Ballem's prints, went in another box at another bank.

"Satisfied?" I asked.

"Mmm," she said. "Tell you the truth, it's the best I did, for money. But the rest of it . . ."

"We owe people now," I said. "We'll do it and get out. Lay low for a while. Mexico. The Caribbean. There won't be any taxes on this money. . . ."

"I'll teach you about offshore banks," she promised.

We left that evening for Longstreet, running the *Fanny* down the river.

To WRECK the Longstreet machine, we had to wipe out a majority of the council—three people—at one stroke.

By state law a city council could replace members who died or resigned. If we got only one or two of the machine's councilmen, the rest of the council could legally appoint replacements. They'd simply appoint other members of the machine. But if we could take out three, the council could no longer legally act; it needed at least three members for a quorum.

If it couldn't get a quorum, the replacements would be appointed by the governor.

The governor, as it happened, had already served two terms in the statehouse and was barred from succeeding himself. Not ready to retire, he was looking at a race for a U.S. Senate seat. He had a shot at it, too, as long as the black wing of the Democratic party didn't raise too much hell. The black caucus had been complaining that it wasn't getting enough goodies in return for the votes it delivered, and there were noises that sounded like the beginnings of a revolt. If the blacks bolted and the party fractured, the governor would be retired whether he liked it or not. . . .

And right there was the crux of a deal.

Marvel and Harold would talk to the leaders of the black caucus. They, in turn, would talk with the governor's hatchet man. If the governor agreed to act on Marvel's request to clean up Longstreet, the black caucus would back off. . . .

When I outlined the idea to Marvel at the hotel meeting, she first thought it over and shook her head.

"It's an idea," she said, taking a lick of the ice cream. "But no matter how much he wanted to help us—help himself—the governor couldn't appoint a black majority to the council. That'd kill him for sure. The black caucus has got some clout, but there's a country boy caucus, too. They've got more clout than the black caucus, and they wouldn't stand for that shit."

"The governor doesn't have to appoint a black majority," I said. "Suppose we take out three white council members, leaving the Reverend Dodge and this Lucius Bell, the guy you say might be honest. OK?"

"OK," she said, nodding.

"So the governor appoints the replacements: one of our people and two more machine members. They can be the worst rednecks in the state, we don't care. But they have to be from our list, the list of people we can control—"

"That we got dirt on," Marvel chipped in.

"That's right. When the council is legally functioning again, we take out those two. We either sic the state cops on them, or the IRS, or just go right straight to them, show them the evidence, force them out—"

"Blackmail," said Harold.

"Right. Push those two off the council. That still leaves three: our appointee, the reverend, and Bell. Three council members is a quorum. Three members *can* appoint replacements. You've got the reverend by the balls, for diddling these little girls, plus our new guy. . . ."

"And those three appoint the two new members. That gives us four to one," Marvel said, sitting up straight, the ice cream forgotten.

"With four to one, we've got the votes to redraw the election districts," I said. "We gerrymander it just like the machine did, but in our favor."

Marvel stared at Harold. "It could work," she blurted.

IT COULD WORK, but everything had to go right.

Longstreet was six hours down the river. We

did two hours that night and anchored behind the point of a sandbar. I hadn't shaved since we left St. Paul, and the beard was coming on.

"There're too many white whiskers in it," LuEllen said. "Writers have white beards; painters are supposed to have black. I've never seen a movie where the painter had a white beard."

"I look like Hemingway," I suggested. "Except taller and better-looking, of course."

The next morning I added to the effect with my artist outfit: tan baggy-assed shorts, Portuguese rope sandals, a New York Knicks T-shirt, and a broad-brimmed canvas hat. LuEllen admired the outfit extravagantly. During the final run down the river she fell into periodic bursts of the giggles. I put it down to stress. We arrived at Longstreet at eleven o'clock and eased into the ramshackle marina I'd seen on my first trip down.

The marina operator wore a cap that said "Port Captain." He had an easy, sun-lined face that hadn't seen much of anywhere and didn't much care.

"How y' doin'?" he asked cheerfully. He took a quick look at me and a longer one at LuEllen. LuEllen was wearing a beige sundress that had a pattern of small rectangular holes across the bodice. There was no indication that she was burdened by a brassiere.

"Pretty good," I admitted. "You got hook-ups?"

"Sure do," he said. "Y'all planning to stay awhile?"

I hopped up on the dock. "Maybe a week, maybe two, it depends," I said. Up in the town I could see the tops of Victorian-era clapboard houses lapping around the edges of the business district. "I'm a painter. Last time I came through here, I saw some nice landscape."

As soon as I said the word *painter*, his eyes shifted, and I figured we'd be paying in advance.

"I'm sure there is," he said.

"How about if I give you a week in advance? If it works out, we'll give you another week."

My stock went back up. He hadn't had to ask for the money, and we had avoided an awkwardness. "That'd be fine," he said. "It's fifty cents a foot, up to twenty dollars a day, with another dollar for every person over four?"

There was a question in his voice, and LuEllen said, "There are only the two of us."

"So that's twenty dollars a day for seven days; that'd be a hundred and forty dollars," I said. I took out a pad of traveler's checks. "Do you take American Express?"

AT THE MEMPHIS MEETING, we'd talked about how we'd bring ourselves to the attention of the mayor in the most natural way. Harold suggested that we catch her during lunch.

"She eats a political lunch every day, with the city attorney or the city clerk and maybe one or two other people," Harold said. "You could bump into her there at the restaurant."

We paid the marina operator, and he moved us to a permanent slip. While the two of us did the phone, power, and sewage hookups, LuEllen went back into the houseboat to make a quick addition to her wardrobe. When we walked up the levee into town, she was wearing a slender, glistening quartz crystal the size of my little finger, wrapped in gold wire and strung around her neck on an antique gold chain. The crystal rested between the swell of her breasts, the swell provided by her new uplift bra. You'd have to be blind to miss it. The crystal, not the bra.

Most of the Mississippi River valley below Memphis had been wiped out by the great flood of 1927. In rebuilding, a lot of towns turned their backs on the river, fortifying themselves behind the levees. Some of them simply picked up and moved away from the water altogether.

Longstreet hadn't been hurt as badly as other places. The residential heart of Longstreet was on naturally high ground. When the flood came, it took out the first couple of blocks of the business and warehouse districts along the river, but most of the town stayed dry. As a result, the rebuilt business district was a collection of redbrick thirties and forties architecture, backed up by a residential area that was much older.

The town square, Chickamauga Park, was on the first major terrace up from the river, at the center of the business district. Two blocks beyond that, the business buildings started shading into the white residential neighborhoods. The white neighborhoods went on up the rising ground, across the crest to the railroad tracks. The black neighborhoods were on the far side of the tracks.

We didn't get that far. We took our time strolling up the ridge, getting acquainted with the town. It was hot but not yet unpleasant. The mix of river odors and flower perfume was as rich and interesting, in its own way, as new-mown hay.

"Uh, by the way, what's your name today? Your last name?" I asked.

Across the street, a heavyset woman in a sunbonnet was tilling a garden with an ancient Case lawn tractor.

"Case," LuEllen said, watching the woman in her beans. "LuEllen Case, okay?"

"Sure," I said. "And thank Christ she wasn't driving an International Harvester."

The restaurant where the mayor ate lunch

was a ferns-and-antique-bricks place called Humdinger's, down the block from the City Hall. Most of the local movers and shakers would be there between eleven-thirty and one o'clock. I knew the mayor's face from political advertisements Marvel had sent us, and LuEllen had seen her on the street during her scouting trip. Her face fixed on us as we crossed the street toward the restaurant.

"There she is, like Harold said," LuEllen murmured.

"I see her. Ballem's with her," I said. I took LuEllen's elbow in my hand as we crossed the street. "There's an open booth just before theirs. That's the one we'll take. You sit closest to the door, so you're facing her. Let her get a look at that crystal."

"I'm cool," she said. I glanced at her, and her face looked dewy from the heat and humidity, but otherwise serene.

"You didn't put any of that shit up your nose, did you?"

A flash of irritation crossed her face. "That's only for hard targets," she said.

"Just checking."

"You're not my father."

"No, but—"

"But what?"

"Nothing."

Humdinger's had creaky wooden floors and

rough brick walls and framed reproductions of English sporting prints, a place that strained for sophistication without quite making it. The general lunch hour buzz dimmed noticeably when we stepped inside, heads turning in our direction. There was a sign near the cash register, PLEASE WAIT TO BE SEATED. The waitress who came to seat us took a good look at LuEllen, a shorter one at me, decided LuEllen was in charge, and said to her, "This way please."

We were headed toward the windows, but just to make sure, LuEllen touched the woman on the arm and said, "I wonder if we could have that window booth."

"That's where I was taking you, honey," the waitress said.

I sat in the booth with my back to Dessus-delit, so she could see LuEllen. Even without the sundress, the uplift bra, and the breast exposure, the crystal would have been hard to miss. The light flickering off it made it seem alive.

"She sees it," LuEllen said in a low voice, around the menu.

LuEllen ordered a chicken breast salad, and I had an open-face hot beef sandwich, which arrived swimming in brown gravy. We talked about painting locations in town, LuEllen worried about the cholesterol in my lunch, and we both tried unsuccessfully to eavesdrop on the booth behind me. I was just finishing the sandwich when I felt the mayor and Ballem slide out of their booth. LuEllen winked.

"I don't mean to interrupt," the mayor said, pausing by our table. She was looking at LuEllen. Ballem walked on a few steps before he stopped and turned. "That is a beautiful crystal."

"Why, thank you," LuEllen said sweetly. "It's a Herkimer diamond. My great-great-grandmother found it near her farm in upstate New York. . . . It's sort of our family channel—"

"Oh, you're *interested*," Dessusdelit said with enthusiasm. She had a narrow, sallow face framed by a short, dark, thoroughly lacquered hairdo. The bags under her pale eyes seemed fairly new, as though she hadn't slept for a couple of nights. A chain of braided gold, like LuEllen's but thinner, hung around her neck. She fished it out. "I have one of my own. . . ."

Her crystal was bigger than LuEllen's but not quite as clear. And while LuEllen's was double-ended, the mayor's had a rough cleavage at the bottom, where the crystal had been broken off its base.

"From Mount Ida," she said.

"Oh, sure," LuEllen said knowledgeably. "They're famous. Did you collect it yourself, or—"

"Yes, yes, I bothered Ralph, that's my late hus-

119

band, I said to Ralph, 'Ralph, I swear, if you don't take me, I just don't know what I'll do.' One day he said, 'Let's go, girl. Then maybe you'll leave me alone.' I looked at crystals until I thought my eyes would fall out. This one just sort of *spoke* to me, you know?"

"I know exactly, I know," LuEllen gushed. "Sometimes I wake up in the middle of the night just having to hold it. I can actually *feel* the spheres intersecting through my diamond. . . . Have you ever tried using a ball?"

"Well, once, when this lady was coming through town, but I didn't see much. I mean, for a minute—"

Ballem was looking bored and impatient, but LuEllen ignored him. "Did you have a chance to warm it with your touch, or did you just look into it?"

"Well, I touched it, but mostly I just looked. . . ."

The conversation was getting serious now.

"You should try a ball again. You'll find it's different from the crystal, but sometimes it's . . . a lot better. Next time roll it in your hands for a while. You have to establish a resonance with the ball . . . and it has to be real. The more a ball's used, the more open it gets. . . ."

"I don't know if I could find, just offhand . . . they're expensive, the good ones."

"Well . . ." LuEllen looked at me, as though

for permission, "I have an antique ball down in our river yacht. You'd be welcome to come down and try ... I mean, if you're really an enthusiast ..."

Dessusdelit looked from LuEllen to me, and her voice took on just an edge of wariness. We were moving too fast for the Old South. "Are you ... staying in town?"

"We're down at the marina. You can see the big white river yacht down there. My name is LuEllen Case. Mr. Kidd's a painter, and he's here scouting landscapes. I'm just along ... for the ride."

"So you're not from around here?" But her voice had warmed a notch. We had a large boat.

"No, no. Mr. Kidd has homes in St. Paul and New Orleans. We travel back and forth so he can work on his painting."

"Well, that sounds very nice." Dessusdelit had definitely warmed back up, though the wariness lingered. We were Yankees, after all, and apparently living in sin. Of course, I *did* have two houses and a yacht. . . . "I'm Chenille Dessusdelit, and this is Archibald Ballem. I'm the mayor here, and Archie is the city attorney."

Ballem made a little scrape and bow. From a distance you might think he was sixty. Up close you realized he was probably ten years younger than that, but his face had a dissolute crepe-paper texture, and his nose had the swollen, big-pored quality of a heavy drinker. His eyes, small, sharp, and mean, dispelled any illusion that he was a dumb hick lawyer.

It was time I got into the discussion.

"If it's all right to change the subject for a minute, maybe you can help me," I said. "I'm looking for views . . . you know, overlooks of the town, where I can see some of those beautiful Victorian mansions and still have some sweep of the land. . . ."

Dessusdelit looked toward Ballem, and Ballem's eyes narrowed even further. "Up by the Trent place, you know where that big old oak tree is right on the edge of the hill."

"That would be wonderful," Dessusdelit said, turning to me. "There are several places up there. Excuse me, could I sit for just a moment?"

LuEllen moved over, and Dessusdelit perched on the end of the bench seat and took a silver pen and small pad of paper from her purse. "Now this is Front Street," she said. "If you walk south on Front to Longstreet Boulevard and then turn left . . ."

She gave us directions out to the Trent place, which was perhaps ten blocks from the center of town. I asked about the possibility of renting a car for a couple of weeks.

"Well, Mary Wells's brother—she's our city

clerk—has the Chevrolet dealership here. I believe he rents used cars off the lot—"

"He does," said Ballem.

They gave us directions to the Chevrolet dealer, and Dessusdelit and LuEllen agreed the mayor would visit the next morning to look at the crystal ball. Dessusdelit was just getting up to leave when we had one of those odd encounters that happen from time to time. The door opened, and a man stepped in. Dark-haired, dark-complected, he was wearing a white straw hat, a light cotton sports jacket over a T-shirt, faded blue jeans, and loafers. He started down the aisle headed toward the back, said, "Hello, Archibald," to Ballem, and then saw Dessusdelit sitting next to us.

" 'Lo, Chenille," he said. His eyes moved on to LuEllen, paused, and then to me. He started slowly past, but Dessusdelit stopped him. "You'll be there, Lucius? We're votin' on the pool improvements."

"Of course."

"It's important. You may be the tiebreaker."

"I realize that, ma'am, and I shall be there, as always."

Dessusdelit remembered her manners. "Lucius, this is Miz Case and Mr. Kidd. Mr. Kidd is a painter, and they are going through to New Orleans, on the river. Mr. Kidd plans to stop and work here for a few days . . . and this is a member of our city council, Lucius Bell."

"Pleased to make your acquaintance," Bell said. He had been politely trying to stare down LuEllen's sundress until Dessusdelit mentioned our names, and then his eyes fixed on me. "Are you the fellow represented by the Cale Gallery in New Orleans?"

"Uh, yeah, as a matter of fact." I was startled by the question.

"I believe I have one of your paintings hanging on my dining room wall," Bell said.

My mouth was hanging open. I'd never before blindly bumped into someone who owned one of my paintings.

"Are you serious?" I said.

"*Sunrise, Josie Harry Bar Light 719.5,*" he said.

"Jeez, that's a good one," I said. "How's it holding up? I mean, to look at?"

"I still like it," he said with a thin grin. "You're welcome to come over and have a look. . . ."

"I'd like to do that," I said. I turned to LuEllen. "It's a good one."

"They're like children," she explained to Dessusdelit, whose head had been swiveling between Bell and me. "He hates to let them go."

"Give me a call when you want to come. I'm home most weekday evenings, except council nights," Bell said. He borrowed Dessusdelit's pen and wrote his phone number on the paper next to the map. "And you'd be most welcome, too, Ms. Case. Anytime."

LuEllen clapped her hands, and I thought she looked a little like Alice in Wonderland. "What a good town," she said. "And we've been here only a couple of hours."

7

BALLEM HAD A good eye. The Trent place was a white clapboard Victorian castle with turrets and stunning bay windows. Brick-colored pots of scarlet geraniums were spotted along the railing of a wide front porch. A natural-wood swing hung from chains at the closed end of the porch, and a healthy old bridal wreath hedge grew up from the foundation below. Peonies were spotted around the yard, among the carefully placed oaks, and in back, a grape trellis was already loaded with wide, shiny leaves. The whole thing was surrounded by an antique wrought-iron fence. From the boulevard you could look diagonally across the street and take in the house, the yard, and the sweep of the river below.

I'd rented a three-year-old station wagon from the Chevy dealer and hauled my painting gear up the hill to start working on my reputation. I hadn't expected much; I'd figured on a mildly picturesque view of the city. What I got was more

127

subtle and more difficult, reminiscent of several Winslow Homer paintings of the Caribbean, with the splashes of red geraniums against the white clapboard and the green river valley below.

When I found the right spot, I unloaded a French easel, set it up on the boulevard, and put out my water buckets. Then I sat down in the grass with a sketch pad and began blocking out possibilities. I'd been working for a half hour when an elderly lady in a sweatsuit and Nike running shoes strode out through the porch door, through the gate in the wrought-iron fence, and across the street.

"Painter, huh?" she asked cheerfully.

"Yeah. I suppose you get a few of them," I said. "It's a heck of a view."

"We get a few. Local amateurs," she said. She shaded her eyes and peered down at the sketch pad. I'd made notes on a dozen or so pages, figuring out the moves I'd make when I got the painting going. At the beginning, on a big picture, which I'd decided this might be, I intellectualize the process. After I've figured everything out with a pencil, I go to the paint. Then it usually takes three or four tries before I get it. "Chenille Dessusdelit called and said I might see you. She said you were OK."

"That was nice of her."

"Well, you like to know who's on your street," she said.

"Sure . . . Look, my name is Kidd, and after I get done with this—it'll take me a few days—I might knock on your door and ask if I can set up someplace in your yard. I'd like to get a better shot at that bridal wreath with the geraniums."

"That'd be fine. I'm Gloriana Trent. I'm home most mornings. If I'm not, go ahead and set up," she said. Then, just as abruptly as she arrived, she said her good-byes and left, striding away with the determined stretch of a speed walker. Too much of the time, when I'm working outdoors, people linger, curious about the painting process. It can drive you crazy, trying to work with somebody looking over your shoulder.

When I was satisfied with my sketches, I got my water jugs out of the car, filled the buckets, and started with the paint. I was so deep into it that I didn't hear the van behind me until the driver warped it against the curb.

"What's this?" the driver asked, climbing out. It was a plain white van. When he slammed the door, I saw the ANIMAL CONTROL sign on the door. This was Hill, the dogcatcher. And he looked like his house: ugly and mean. He was maybe forty, an inch under six feet, deep through the body with a short, thick neck. His face was permanently tightened in a frown, making knobs of his cheeks and chin and nose. He wore his hair in a Korean War crew cut, and his forehead had that flattened, shiny look that you see on bar brawlers. Like Dessusdelit, he wore a stressed-out face, compounded of anger and weariness. We'd taken well over three hundred thousand out of his house. . . .

"Painting," I said. I was sitting on a canvas stool, and he moved in close, looming over me. He stuck out one thick finger and tapped the French easel, making it shiver.

"I can see that," he said. "You got a permit?"

"I didn't know I needed one," I said. "The mayor didn't mention it."

His eyes tightened. "The mayor? You got permission?"

"She sent me up here," I said. "She and Mr. Ballem."

"Huh." He looked skeptical but backed off a step. He was about to say something else when the screen door on the Trent house slammed and Gloriana Trent came striding across the yard.

"Old bitch," the dogcatcher muttered under his breath.

"Duane Hill, you get out of here and leave Mr. Kidd alone," she said. Her voice was pitched up a notch. Under her flinty exterior she was afraid of the man.

"Just goin'," Hill muttered. He looked at me, his lips moving silently, as though he were memorizing my face, glanced resentfully back at Gloriana, got in the van and slowly pulled away. Gloriana watched him go.

"Bluff sort of fellow," I said.

"He's a chrome-plated asshole," Gloriana snapped. She looked back at me. "The people downtown say he has his uses. Sometimes I wonder."

"He's not one of your friends," I said. It wasn't a question.

"No. When he was in third or fourth grade, he used to steal from my husband's store; we own the department and sporting goods stores in town, the family does. I caught him once and sent him on his way. The second time I took him by the ear and dragged him down the street to his parents' house, for all the good that did. The Hills were always . . . trashy, I suppose. The third time I caught him, I took him down to the police station, and he went to juvenile court. He's not forgotten those trips with his ear stretched out like a rubber band." She smiled. "I like to think his head is lopsided, but I suppose it's wishful thinking."

She had me laughing. "I hope this won't cause you any trouble," I said.

"Oh, no. Duane knows where the lines are drawn. He came to look at you because the way things work here, he's sort of the town—" She groped for a word.

"Dogcatcher," I said.

She looked at me, no longer smiling. "Exactly," she said. "I hear from the rumor mill that he's had some trouble lately. Someone broke into his home."

"Crime is everywhere these days," I said distractedly, in my flattest voice.

"Yes, it is." She looked at the painting on the easel, and the smile came back. "Very nice."

"Not so good," I said. "I'm just getting a feel for it. It's a complicated subject. I'm not really painting the house, you know. I'm painting the light."

"I understand from Chenille that Lucius Bell owns one of your works, bought it in N'Orleans."

"That's what he says."

"He's a nice boy, Lucius," she said. "Grew up poor, put together a very nice farming business. Educated himself."

"Poor but not trashy?"

"Definitely not trashy. Poor and trashy don't have much to do with each other, do they?" she said.

"Not much," I conceded. "Listen, Mrs. Trent, you want a Dos Equis? I got a couple of bottles in a cooler."

"Well . . ." She looked around, as if spotting neighbors peering from behind curtains. "Well, yes, as a matter of fact, that would be nice on a hot day. But why don't we sit on my porch?"

WE HAD a nice talk, and then she went back to her air-conditioning, and I spent the rest of the afternoon working on the painting. LuEllen was in town, ostensibly shopping but also checking out the City Hall and the city attorney's personal office. About four o'clock the dogcatcher's van crossed the street a block down, slowly, and I could see Hill's face in the driver's side window, looking my way.

There's a myth that bullies can't handle a real fight, that if they get into a real fight, they fold. My experience is just the opposite: Bullies like to fight. They go far out of their way to fight. They are men who look for slights—imagined ones will do nicely—as an excuse. Hill, I thought, was probably one of them. He had that look, the narrow, scarred, righteous eyes of a sociopathic brawler. I hadn't seen the last of him.

A little after five, when the light started to go red, I dumped the water, closed up the easel, and put the painting gear in the Chevy. On the way back to the marina I stopped downtown. Just a look, I thought.

The Longstreet City Hall was kitty-corner from Chickamauga Park, the town square. The square was a busy place; there was a children's play area, with swings, a slide, monkey bars, and a huge sandbox. Metal benches lined the walks, and one or two old men were perched on each of them. The equestrian statue, of old Jim Longstreet himself, was at the center of the square, a major attraction for passing pigeons.

The City Hall looked like most of the other business buildings in town: squat, brick, undistinguished, vaguely *moderne*. The streets on the front and one side were not particularly busy and were fronted mostly by service stores selling hardware, office equipment, auto parts, and so on. An alley ran down the back of the building, to a small blacktopped parking lot and an entryway with a lighted glass sign that said POLICE. On the fourth side, the side with no street, was a hardware store. The store was separated from the City Hall by a ten-foot-wide strip of grass.

I walked through the square, stopped to look at Longstreet on his big fat horse, then waited for two traffic lights, crossed to the City Hall, and went up the steps. Inside, it was cool and slightly damp, the kind of feel you get with old-fashioned air-conditioning. Following the hand-painted signs, I climbed a flight of stairs to the city clerk's office and asked the woman behind the counter if she had a city or county map. She had both and was happy to give them to me, free. There was a built-in safe at the back of the office, with a black-painted door and gold scrollwork. The combination dial was big as a saucer and right out on front, just as Marvel said it was.

THAT NIGHT LuEllen and I drove the station wagon out to the Holiday Inn, which had the trendiest bar and best dining room in town. It was also the most expensive. Crossing the parking lot, I noticed a white BMW parked at the corner of the inn, nudged LuEllen with my elbow, and nodded toward it.

"I like the boat better," she said.

Inside the restaurant a dozen couples were scattered around at other booths and tables, peering at each other in the half-light of little red candle bowls. We raised a few eyebrows when we came in, especially since I was carrying a leather shoulder bag. Men's shoulder bags are not a big fashion along the river. But we needed a place where we could meet with John Smith, Marvel, and Harold, and we also needed a reason to go there. Like drinking.

I finished most of a bottle of wine during dinner and could have gotten thoroughly pissed in the bar afterward if I hadn't been dumping most of the drinks into a planter. We were still building the image: If the rented Chevy was often seen in the parking lot, it was just the drunk painter in the bar, or, if not in the bar, then the dining room. If not either, then probably in the can. . . .

I stopped at a phone on the way out, carrying my shoulder bag.

"On the way," I said.

John had a room on the ground floor. We walked out of the bar toward the parking lot, took a left instead of a right, down an empty hallway, and knocked once on a door that opened instantly. John shut it behind us. Marvel was on the bed, cool as always.

"Whoa," I said when I turned around.

"Sharp-dressed man," John said a little awkwardly. He plucked at the seams of his trousers. "How do I look?"

"Like a thirties nigger from Harlem," said Marvel.

"Supposed to look a little like that," John said. He was wearing a dark blue double-breasted suit with pinstripes, a white shirt, a wine-colored power tie, and slightly pointed black wing tips. The jacket's padded shoulders were a hair too wide, the waist a bit too narrow. The *pièce de résistance*, a toupee with long straight hair, sat on top of his head. It fitted him well and had been combed through with an oily dressing until it shone. He looked sharp, like a subtle parody of a banker. Like a gangster.

"Think you can do it?" I asked.

"Yeah. I been in street politics long enough, and Marvel's backed me up with some people who'll say they know my name. People down in the capital."

"OK. How about—"

Marvel interrupted. "Did you rob Dessusdelit and Ballem and Hill?"

I was ready for it. I glanced at LuEllen, my forehead wrinkling, then back to Marvel. "What?"

"Did you hit the mayor and Ballem and Duane Hill's house?" She was watching me closely, but I can tell a lie.

"No. What the hell are you talking about?" Behind me LuEllen was shaking her head.

"Somebody hit their houses, really fucked them up," John said. "Two nights ago. We thought—"

"Not us," I said. "This could complicate things. If the cops are tearing up the town, looking at new people . . ."

"No, no, they're not," Marvel said. "Matter of fact, we've mostly heard rumors. . . . There hasn't been any official police report. A couple of white boys been picked up and squeezed, but that's about it."

"I don't know," I said. "We'll have to watch it. Can you have your people—"

"Sure. We'll stay in touch," Marvel said. She was still suspicious.

I turned back to John. "How about the rest of it?"

"I called this Brown guy, the landowner. He didn't make any bones about the land being for sale. He sounded pretty anxious; he was also curious about why anybody would want it."

"That's an element in a good con job," I said. "Somebody suddenly sees value where nobody else could see it. It makes them wonder what's going on."

"I hope," John said. He had been taking in my

137

costume and now cracked a smile. "You look like you're in a movie, like an *artiste*. You oughta dab some paint on your shirt."

"We all look like we're in a movie," I said. "We've gotta be careful not to overdo it."

"You see the Beemer out in the parking lot?"

"Yeah . . ."

"Love that car. It turns the head of every god-damned good-looking woman in Memphis—"

"A small exaggeration," Marvel said.

"I didn't know the power of cars on women," John said, a light in his eye. "I really didn't."

"Just drive carefully," LuEllen said. "That thing is costing us a fortune."

"Did you check Ballem's office?" Marvel asked LuEllen.

"Yeah. Going into the building could be tough. The door is right out in the open. People in small towns keep an eye on strangers. Especially at night."

"This help?" Marvel asked. She tossed a key ring with two keys on it to LuEllen. "The brass one's for the building door, and the other one's for the outer office door. Couldn't get one for Ballem's personal office without asking somebody we were afraid to ask."

"This is great," LuEllen said. "Once I'm inside, I can handle his office."

"When are you going to do it?"

I shrugged. LuEllen hated to give away any

kind of security. "Sometime this week probably," I said. I picked up my shoulder bag, opened it on the bed, and took out LuEllen's Nikon F4, along with an instruction book.

"The camera's all set up," she said to John as I handed it over with the book. "The film is loaded, and it's on silent mode. You'll have to focus it when you get there and lock in the exposure." She dipped into my bag and took out another piece of gear. "This is the radio control. . . ."

John peeled his coat off, and Marvel moved forward on the bed to peer at the camera. "Show me how to do this, exactly," he said. "I don't want to fuck up."

8

SMALL-TOWN PEOPLE tell a story on themselves, an illustration of their closeness to their neighbors. Folks in small towns don't use the turn signals on their cars, they say, because whoever is behind them *knows* where they're going to turn.

Longstreet wasn't that small. It was a city, with better than twenty thousand good citizens and a few hundred rummies, bums, and lowlifes. It was not quite big enough to have a real slum, but it did have Oak Hill, which wasn't so much a hill as the back end of the white cemetery. The city also had a lot of middling and a couple of good neighborhoods in both the black and white areas and one upper-middle-class subdivision spread around the Longstreet Golf and Country Club. During our stay a half dozen people mentioned that two black families lived out by the club: a doctor and a veterinarian.

One thing Longstreet didn't have was apartment buildings. Most of the town's apartments were in the business district, above stores. That was a problem.

When we left the Holiday Inn, we went straight back to the boat and changed. Gym shoes and jeans. LuEllen wore a deep red long-sleeved blouse, and I put on a long-sleeved navy blue polo shirt with a crushable white tennis hat. When we got close to the target, I'd pull off the hat and stick it in my pocket.

We'd put the computers out of sight, but now I needed them and got down the portable IBM clone and a piece of gear called a Laplink. With the Laplink, I could dump the contents of one computer's hard disk to the hard disk in the portable. The whole works fitted in a black nylon bag that looked like a briefcase.

"Ready?" LuEllen asked. She was carrying the leather shoulder bag I'd had the camera in. It looked better on her than it did on me.

"Let's go."

"Don't try to hide when we get to the door," she said. "Don't look around; don't get up next to the wall; don't touch me; don't stand too close to me. Try to slump a little bit. Look tired."

"All right."

The night was hot, and the flying insects were fluttering up from the weeds around the marina into town. The streets were well lit; we walked from one pool of orange sodium-vapor light to the next. We passed one man, a black man, who nodded and disappeared around a corner.

We strolled. Ambled. There were lights above the stores, and I saw a woman's shadow on a beige curtain and, below the window, walked through the strong, acrid smell of home permanent. Metallica pounded from a radio down an alley.

"The problem with nights like these, where you've got apartments above the stores, is that people without air-conditioning sit in the windows, in the dark," LuEllen said. "If somebody sees us go in, I hope they don't notice that no lights come on inside. . . ."

It was just after ten o'clock. The time and temperature sign on the Longstreet State Bank said eighty-three degrees.

"There it is," LuEllen said. "The one with the brick."

The door was set at a shallow angle into the wall, surrounded by yellow brick. A brass plate was screwed onto the brick.

"Easy," LuEllen said. "Not too close to me. Look tired and impatient."

She walked up to the door, tugged at it, and used the key. The whole entry took five seconds. We pulled the door shut behind us and stopped to listen. We could hear the buzz of the lights from outside. The sound of an air conditioner in the building. Nothing else.

"When did Marvel say the janitor left?"

"Never misses a Cardinals game. He'd have been home an hour ago," LuEllen said. The hallway was lit by a single dim light. LuEllen led the way past a bank of elevators and into a stairwell, picked out the steps with a miniature flashlight, and led the way up one floor. At the landing she opened the door a crack, watching, waiting. Nothing. Then a sound. A voice. Muffled.

"Shit," she whispered. "There's somebody up here."

We listened some more.

"Two people. Man and a woman. They're . . . fooling around," she said.

"Where's Ballem's office?"

"Down to the right."

The sounds were coming from the left.

"So what do we do?" I asked.

"Let's go." She led the way into the hall, holding the door. When I was through, she eased it shut, and we walked carefully down to Ballem's office. The unseen woman laughed. LuEllen paused at Ballem's office door, her ear to the glass panel, waited five seconds, then unlocked it. Inside, she stopped me with a hand and disappeared into the dark. A moment later her light flicked on, and she said in a low voice, "All clear."

Ballem's personal office was at the end of a short hallway. LuEllen tried the door, found it locked, knelt on one knee to look at the lock, and grunted.

"Hold the light," she said. I took the flash, and she dug into her bag, coming up with a cloth roll tied with a string. Lockpicks. She unrolled the cloth, laid it on the floor, and, after a few seconds' study, selected a pick and a tensioner.

One miserable winter afternoon in St. Paul, with sleet beating against my north windows, we lounged in bed and LuEllen tried to teach me how to pick locks. I failed—I'm not patient enough—but I learned some of the technique and the names of the picks: the half-round and round feelers, the rakes and diamonds and double diamonds, the readers, extractors, mailboxes, flat levers and tensioners, circulars and points.

The lock on Ballem's door was a pin tumbler, in which a lock cylinder rotates to throw the bolt. The cylinder is prevented from rotating by five spring-loaded pins. The ragged edge of a key moves the pins up to a sheer line; when all the pins are moved up exactly the right distance past the sheer line, the cylinder can rotate.

LuEllen was locating each of the lock's five pins and gently moving them, one at a time, up to the sheer line. At the same time she kept pressure on the cylinder with a spring steel tensioning tool. It took time. I was sweating when she said, "Ah," then, "Wait." She made some more delicate movements; then, with a quick twist of her wrist, the door was open.

"Got too enthusiastic with that last pin, got it up too high," she said. She was panting from the stress; when you're picking a lock, you tend to hold your breath.

Ballem's office smelled of pipe tobacco and paper, with an undertone of bourbon. Most of the furniture was turn-of-the-century oak, practical, sturdy.

"Watch the light," LuEllen said quietly. A flashlight beam on a venetian blind will bring the cops faster than an alarm. We didn't really need it anyway; the windows were at the same level as the streetlights, and enough illumination came through the shades that we could easily move around the office.

Two walls of the office were given to lawbooks, another to a series of English court prints taken from *Punch*. A narrow worktable ran along the fourth wall, with a row of file cabinets at one end. A half dozen plaques and framed certificates, testifying to service and study, hung on the wall above the table. The computer was on a walnut side table next to the desk. An IBM-AT, Marvel had said, and it was, with a low-tech printer on a stand behind it and a small three-hundred-baud modem. I breathed a sigh of relief. If it had been a Macintosh or an Amiga, I'd have had to dump the high-capacity internal hard disk to smaller floppy disks, and that might have taken a while. As it was, I should be able to do the job in a few minutes.

I hooked up the Laplink, then handed the light to LuEllen, brought the machine up, stuck in a disk, and loaded a utility program of my own. A minute later I was looking through the hard disk, sending to my machine any text or financial files.

While I did that, LuEllen looked around the office, checking drawers. The file cabinets were locked, but she opened each in a matter of seconds and began going through the files.

"Not much here," she said. "It's all routine legal stuff. Real estate transfers, car accidents, workers' compensation forms. There's some city work, but it all looks like insurance and ordinances and printed budgets. Public stuff, nothing secret."

"Check the desk."

The desk was locked. She opened it, glanced through a few files, and shook her head.

"Nothing financial," she said. "No taxes, no books. Couple of *Playboys*. Toothpicks. Floss. Bottle of mouthwash."

"I'll be done in a couple of more minutes," I said. "I'm almost there."

She walked down the length of the bookshelves, pushing her hand over the tops of the books, feeling behind them. Then she got on her hands and knees and crawled around the perimeter of the room, pulling at the carpet. There was an expensive *National Geographic* globe in one corner, on its own rolling stand, and when she pushed it out of the way and pulled on the carpet, the corner came up.

"Got something," she said. She folded back the carpet and lifted the board underneath. I stepped over and squatted beside her. There was an old green metal cashbox set in the floor. She popped the lid. Inside were a stack of cash, a chrome-plated .38-caliber revolver, and what looked like legal papers.

LuEllen lifted out the cash and the papers.

"Two thousand," she said, thumbing the cash. She put it back in the box, in exactly the position that it had been. I went back to the computer while she examined the papers. "There're copies of a will and some kind of inventory and divorce papers. You want me to copy them? There's a Xerox out in the hall."

"Do it."

I finished pulling the files from Ballem's computer, shut it down, unplugged the Laplink cables, and started stuffing them back in the black satchel with the portable. I was zipping the satchel when LuEllen came into the room, moving fast, said, "Ssst," and eased the door shut.

"Somebody's outside," she whispered. She scrambled over to her satchel, took out two pairs of black panty hose, and threw one at me. I could hear the outer office door opening as I pulled it over my head. LuEllen, with the panty hose on her head but not yet pulled over her face, was digging in her satchel. She came up with a potato and a gym sock, put the potato in the sock, and stationed herself behind the door. I hid behind the desk.

On other jobs we'd decided that the only answer to detection was flight or surrender. We wouldn't hurt anyone for money. But in Longstreet surrender would not likely result in a trial. We wouldn't be talking to lawyers. And we decided after the episode with the cop at Ballem's, when I was prepared to hit him with a paint bucket, that we'd better come up with a new answer.

The potato in the sock made an excellent sap, and neither the potato nor the sock was illegal. And the potato, LuEllen had heard, was soft enough to be non-lethal.

We waited, LuEllen dangling the sock. The late visitor did not turn on the office lights but came straight down the hall, moving in the dark. From the light footsteps I decided that the visitor was female. The steps passed Ballem's door, went on for a few feet, then stopped. There was a moment of silence, then a distracted humming. A woman's voice, and a saccharine tune from the fifties called

"Tammy"; I remembered it from my piano lessons.

We waited, stressing out, huddled in the dark, and the Xerox machine started. And went on. And on. For more than half an hour, without stopping, the copy light flashing under the door like distant lightning. Then, just as suddenly as she'd shown up, she left, whoever it was. The Xerox machine stopped, the footsteps retreated down the hall, and the outer door clicked shut.

"Jesus Christ, she must have been copying her fucking novel," LuEllen said. I stood up, pulled the panty hose off my head, and handed them to her. She stuffed them in her satchel, returned Ballem's will and the other papers to the hidden box, folded down the carpet, and wheeled the globe back into place.

After a final, meticulous check of the office, to make sure that everything was back in place, we were out. In the hallway we heard the unseen woman laugh again.

"Her boyfriend must be a sex machine," LuEllen muttered as we went down the stairs.

"This is no time for jealousy."

I talk a good burglary, but on the street I was gasping for air. "I'm glad you didn't have to slug anybody," I said after a while.

"So am I," she said. "I'd do it, but I think . . ."

"What?"

"Whacking people on the head . . . I don't know. The theory sounds OK, with the soft potato and all, but I've got a feeling that some of them might die."

AN ENTRY FLOODS your system with adrenaline. Riding the high, with sleep an impossibility, I spent most of the night reviewing the files from Ballem's computers. And found nothing but two cryptic, and nonincriminating, letters about the sewer pipe company.

"Nothing at all?" LuEllen asked.

"Nothing," I said. But the letters about the sewer pipe bothered me. "You're sure there was nothing in his desk or the files about the sewer pipe company?"

"I'm sure. That's one of the things I was looking for."

"Well, shit. The thing is . . ." I called up one of the files. "Look at the numbers in this thing. He was using some kind of reference . . . you don't just remember those kinds of pricing and engineering details; you don't pull them out of thin air. Marvel noticed the same things about those letters her people found: too many details without references."

"Maybe he dumped whatever reference he was using."

"Yeah, maybe. But none of Marvel's friends knows about any books, and they know everything else. . . . And Ballem had that modem hooked into his computer terminal. I assumed he used it for the on-line legal data bases, but I wonder if they might not have the books on-line somewhere. If they're plugged into a data base somewhere, anybody who knew the sign-on codes could call it up and work . . ."

She shrugged. "How do we find out?"

"Bobby," I said.

I was still mulling it over when she asked me if I'd looked at the papers she'd copied.

"I'd forgotten," I said.

The papers were a find.

Ballem's will listed bank accounts in Grand Bahama and Luxembourg. The inventory listed household goods, noting the value of specific items: paintings, Oriental carpets, coins, and stamps. The stamp collection "should be assessed by a certified philatelic appraiser." The divorce papers indicated that he'd paid his ex-wife an aftertax half million dollars over three years.

"We got a good chunk of him, but most of it is out of town," LuEllen said. Her voice reflected a mixture of satisfaction and disappointment.

"We did just right," I said. I walked over to the computer and punched it up. "I'll ship this to Bobby. If we can nail down these accounts, we might have the leverage we need against him."

"How's that?"

"I doubt that he bothered the IRS with the details of his income," I said. "So when the time comes, we tell him, 'Get out of town, or deal with the feds.' And we send along the numbers on these very pretty accounts. . . ."

9

LuEllen roused me out of bed at ten o'clock. She doesn't like getting up early any more than I do and was grumpy about it.

"Visitor coming," she said shortly. She was staring at a bowl of Honey Nut Cheerios like Somoza reviewing the Sandinistas. "Get your ass in gear."

I try to stay away from breakfast as much as possible. Instead of eating, I brought up the computer, called Bobby, and told him that we'd failed to find the books. I gave him the names of the banks Ballem had listed in his will and suggested a wide-gauge search of credit company files for more background. And I mentioned the modem hooked into Ballem's computer.

Possible Ballem on-line w/books somewhere.

Will check.

How?

Phone analysis.

Fast?

Don't know. Toggle auto-answer 2nite, I'll message progress.

OK.

Before Bobby got into data bases, he was a major phone phreak. Still is, I guess; he's made the combination of the two into an art form. I wasn't sure what he was planning—not the details, anyway—but I suspected he'd look at the pattern of Ballem's office phone calls and try to spot possible on-line hookups. Then, in the evening, he would check those numbers for a computer carrier tone.

When I got off-line, I locked the big computer, unplugged it, and toted it back to the bedroom. The portable I tucked away in a cupboard. Computers were not part of our image.

While LuEllen set up the main cabin for Dessusdelit's visit, I cleaned up and got back into the shorts and Knicks T-shirt.

"Are you ready?" I asked LuEllen when I got out of the bathroom.

"Yeah, just about. You better get up above."

I climbed on top of the cabin with a bucket of water and a sketch pad and did a few quick studies of the waterfront. I don't get too much in-

volved with detail, going instead for the pattern
and emotional impact of the color. The waterfront had some nice effects. The river water
formed a long olive band across the bottom of a
composition, with the longer darker band of the
levee above that, then suddenly the vibration of
sunlight on orange brick— Never mind.

Dessusdelit showed up a few minutes before
noon, stepping carefully down the levee steps. She
was wearing a snappy black-and-white striped
dress that looked both summery and businesslike
at the same time and low heels.

"Mr. Kidd," Dessusdelit said as she came out
on the dock.

" 'Lo," I called. "Come aboard." I stamped
twice on the deck, and LuEllen popped out a moment later, saw Dessusdelit, and waved. LuEllen
was wearing a bleached-out Mexican peasant top
with an oatmeal-colored skirt and leather sandals,
with Indian turquoise-and-silver earrings. Sartori-
ally it was a standoff.

"I've made a light lunch, a salad, and some
white wine," she said. "You come on, too, Kidd.
You've been up there for hours. You'll burn your
brain out."

Dessusdelit disappeared into the cabin, and I
took a last look at the sketches, washed my
brushes, and followed her down.

"Need a shower," I said. I grabbed the bottle of

white wine as I went by the table. "Back in a minute."

I shut myself in the head, poured a couple of swallows of wine down the sink, sloshed some more around in my mouth, and took the shower, spending some time with it. When I got back, LuEllen and Dessusdelit were halfway through their salad.

"LuEllen has been telling me that you're an expert on the tarot, Mr. Kidd," Dessusdelit chirped brightly. She reminded me of a sparrow with fangs.

"I use the tarot, but I don't believe in any mystical or magical interpretations," I said. "I use it in a purely scientific way."

LuEllen snorted. "He says that because whenever he does one of his scientific spreads, he can't figure it out. When he does what he calls a magic spread, it usually reads right."

"That's interesting," Dessusdelit said, peering at me. "I didn't think such things as the tarot would work if the person wasn't sincere in using them."

"Oh, Kidd's sincere about using them," LuEllen said before I could answer. "He's being insincere when he says he doesn't believe. He had this scientific training in college, and the implications of belief . . . frighten him."

"Is that so, Mr. Kidd?"

"I leave the pop psychology to LuEllen, Miz

Dessusdelit." I poured myself another white wine. "This is my idea of a great lunch," I said jokingly, saluting her with the glass.

A vague look of disapproval crossed Dessusdelit's face, but she was southern, and in the South, where men drink, nothing is said.

AFTER THE LUNCH LuEllen cleared the table and sat Dessusdelit with her back to the bow windows. I retreated to an easy chair at the rear of the cabin while LuEllen brought out her crystal ball. It was real crystal, antique and six inches in diameter, bought at a store in Minneapolis. One day after we'd been out on the river, learning about the houseboat, she left it on the table while she went to shower. When she came back, I was juggling the ball, a broken Ambassadeur 5600 bait-casting reel, and a conch shell. She'd gone visibly pale and snatched the ball out of the air, causing me to drop the reel.

"You know how much this fuckin' thing cost me?" she hollered. I hadn't messed with the ball since.

"It's very old," she said now, in a dark, hushed voice, unwrapping the ball's velvet sleeve and passing it to Dessusdelit. "There are rumors of Gypsy blood in my family, way back, and this ball supposedly came from them."

"It's so heavy," Dessusdelit said, marveling at the size and weight. The ball was a perfect sphere, but the interior was a complicated geological dance of inclusions and tiny fractures. A rainbow of colors flickered inside, depending on how the light hit it.

"Just sit and hold it," LuEllen said.

"Lots of colors in there," Dessusdelit said, peering into it.

"Let your mind go, but try to track the color," LuEllen said. "Look for greens for opportunity, red for danger or conflict. Those were my grandma's interpretations. . . ."

"OK," said Dessusdelit, fascinated.

"I think yellow might have something to do with prosperity, blue with peace; black, I think, is death. . . . Orange is warm; I think that may mean excitement in the good sense or pleasure. I saw a lot of orange in the ball before we started down the river. This whole trip is kind of new for me, kind of exciting. . . ."

"Wonderful," Dessusdelit said. She was rolling the ball in her hands. "I don't see too much just now. Maybe if I were closer to the window and the light . . ."

"No, no, stay where you are," LuEllen said. "I put the good chair there for a purpose. You should be comfortable. Don't worry, if you have the ability to see things, the colors will come."

That's when she gave the laser a goose with a foot pedal we'd wedged under the rug. The laser, a little two-hundred-watt deal with an output that was no bigger in diameter than a filament of spider web, was mounted in the bedroom. I'd fixed it to do a skittering scan across the area of the chair, a tiny dot of light moving so fast it was virtually invisible. Except when it hit the ball. When it hit the ball, the crystal fluoresced, and the veil lit up with some of the pulsing reaction of the northern lights. I knew when the laser hit because Dessusdelit suddenly caught her breath.

"It . . . did something," she said.

"I thought it might," LuEllen said. "I thought you had the power when I saw you in the restaurant. Were you able to pick out any particular colors?"

"Well . . ." Dessusdelit was rolling the ball in her hands. "There was green."

"Opportunity, that's wonderful. Maybe it means the opportunity to explore your psychic self," LuEllen gushed.

"Is that what it usually means?" Dessusdelit asked, looking up. She was hooked.

"It can mean any kind of opportunity—often money, frankly—but in this case . . . unless you're expecting some money?"

"No, no, nothing special. In fact, there have been some problems in town. . . ."

"Then it may simply be the opportunity to explore yourself," LuEllen said, brushing away the hint at the burglaries. She touched the laser again.

"There it is," Dessusdelit said, brought back to

the ball. "There's a lot of red, and my God . . . I can feel the power. And I thought I saw . . ."

"Yes?" LuEllen prompted.

"My mother's face. She's been gone now for ten years. . . . Is this possible?"

"Anything's possible if you have the power and the right crystal," LuEllen said.

I broke in. "This is not my style, I'm afraid. I'll leave you alone. I'll be on top."

"I think that would be best," LuEllen said, her voice now dreamier than ever. "I think Chenille and I have some work to do. . . . Red, you say? Red sometimes means danger. . . ."

THEY WERE at it for an hour. I was deep into the painting again, sucking on a Dos Equis and cursing the asshole who invented Hooker's green, when the door popped open. LuEllen stuck her head out and called, "Chenille's got a favor to ask. She wonders if you could do a quick spread."

"Oh, boy," I said. I didn't want to read for her without notice. I wanted the deck ready, so it'd read *my* way. "That would be . . . my head's just not right for it."

"That's all right," Dessusdelit said from inside the cabin, but I could hear the disappointment in her voice.

"How about if we cut the deck just for a taste?" I asked.

"Would that work?"

"Sure, just for a taste," I said.

I dropped down into the cabin, got the Polish box, took the silk wrapping off the deck, and shuffled. Seven times. Nothing mystic in that; the good gray *New York Times* Tuesday science pages carried an article that said a good seven shuffle gives you the best approximation of a random distribution. When the shuffling was dead, I spread the deck across the table and looked at Dessusdelit.

"Do you know about the tarot?" I asked before she picked a card.

"Just a bit," she said diffidently.

"I like to warn people that the Death card doesn't mean death. It means change, often for the good. I don't want somebody to pull the Death card out of the deck, misinterpret it, and drop over dead of a heart attack. . . ."

"I know about Death," she said. She drew a card, held it for a moment, facedown, then flipped it over.

The Empress. I sat back, a little startled. "Have you actually done tarot readings before?" I asked.

"Yes, a few times."

"What card did you choose to represent yourself? Was it the Empress?"

"No, no. Usually the Queen of Cups."

"Which is a minor arcana analog of the Empress," I said. I tapped the Empress with my index finger. "Perhaps you underrate yourself. In any case, the Empress would suggest success, fulfillment in an enterprise you're involved with. Something you rule or manage. But that's just a taste."

"Just a taste," she said.

"Sure. I have to warn you, I really don't believe in this stuff," I said. And if I did, I wouldn't have picked her for the Empress or even the Queen of Cups. I pushed the cards together and rewrapped them in the silk.

"Well, I thank you," Dessusdelit said. She found her purse, and we went back out into the sunshine, with LuEllen trailing behind.

"If you're really interested . . ." I said.

"I am," she said promptly.

"I read best in the morning. Frankly, I like to . . . have my beer, you know, and alcohol seems to interfere with the necessary connections. . . ."

"I thought you didn't believe in the magical interpretations," she said in amusement.

"Well." I shrugged. "You got me, I guess."

"Come down tomorrow," LuEllen said. "About ten o'clock. Kidd can do a reading, and we can do the ball again. And then maybe you can tell me where the best shopping is. . . ."

"I'll be happy to," Dessusdelit said. She looked at me again. "The Empress . . ."

"Just a taste," I said.

LuEllen and I watched her step off the end of

the dock and start up the levee. "How'd you do that?" LuEllen asked, shading her eyes as she watched Dessusdelit disappear over the top of the wall. "Produce the Empress card?"

"I didn't," I said.

LATER, while I put the computer back up, LuEllen went out to a grocery store and ran into Lucius Bell in the fresh produce department. He was the councilman who owned my painting.

"He wants us to come over tonight," LuEllen said as she unloaded her bags into the refrigerator. "After dinner. For bourbon and branch, whatever that is. . . ."

"Water," I said.

"Whatever." She closed the refrigerator door and stretched like a cat, as she tends to do when she's feeling sexy. "That boy could develop a serious case of the hots for me."

"And would it be reciprocated?"

"Could be," she said, grinning. "He has the nicest eyes, good shoulders . . ."

"Probably wears nylons and lipstick when there's nobody around. Does strange things with carp."

"Not my Lucius," she said in a southern simper.

"Why, God?" I asked, appealing to the ceiling. "Why women? Wasn't the fuckin' bubonic plague enough? Wasn't the H-bomb—"

We were kidding. On the way over to Bell's, though, I noticed she was wearing her Obsession.

I'D DONE *Sunrise, Josie Harry Bar Light 719.5* five years before, in about twenty minutes, sitting awkwardly on a sandbar a few feet from a rented pontoon boat. I've done a lot of traveling on the river over the years, though never before in the style of the *Fanny*. It had always been in little fourteen-foot bass boats and rented pontoons and even canoes.

Josie Harry was one of the good ones. I spotted it, hung on a white wall between two built-in book cabinets, as soon as I walked into Bell's dining room.

"Wonderful," I said. "Who did the framing for you? The gallery?"

"No, I had it done here in town," he said.

"You found a good framer," I said. "It looks fine."

I went over it inch by inch. After a minute or two LuEllen and Bell wandered back to the sitting room, chatting. They liked each other, all right, but I didn't expect any trouble. LuEllen had a penchant for variety but only when her security wasn't at stake. She would never let sex step on that.

"Satisfied? That I haven't done anything embarrassing to it?" Bell asked when I finally joined them. He did have an engaging way about him, not diminished by the fact that he owned one of my paintings and was taking good care of it.

"I'm more than satisfied; I'm delighted," I said, looking back at the painting. "It's got a good spot, good light, protection. That's what it's made for."

"I had an offer for it. An old lawyer guy here in town. Five hundred over what I paid."

"Tell him to get his own," I said.

He nodded. "I did, and he said he would. Don't know if he has, but he gets down to N'Orleans often enough."

So we sat and talked, passing pleasantries about the river until I mentioned the bridge. He suddenly got serious.

"Those peckerwoods—pardon the language, LuEllen, but I get mad thinking about it—up in the legislatures, they won't help us. See, the people across the river say, 'Hell, if we build a bridge into Longstreet, the people on our side will just go over there to spend their paychecks.' The people on this side say, 'Why should we pay the whole cost of a bridge?' So they dicker back and forth, and nothing gets done. It's killing me, is what it's doing."

"How's that?" LuEllen asked. She was picking up some of the southern rhythm of his speech.

"I'm a farmer. Most of my land is over there on the other side. Before the bridge got knocked down, I'd haul my beans to the elevators over here and ship it downriver. When the bridge went, we had to haul the beans out by road, and it's forty miles down to the nearest elevator on the other side. That's an eighty-mile round trip for my trucks, what used to be a five-mile round trip. The cost of gas, the wear and tear . . . That's why I got myself elected to the city council. They weren't getting anywhere with the bridge—crooked sons of guns probably looking for a cut somewhere. So I got myself elected, thinking I could push it harder. But shoot, I'm not getting anywhere either," he said. He finished his bourbon in a single gulp and got up to pour himself another.

"So what happens if you don't get a bridge? I mean, to you personally?" LuEllen asked.

He shrugged. "It used to be that in a good year I made a lot of money. In an average year I'd make a little, and in a bad year I'd find some way to break even. Now, in a good year I make a little, and in an average year I maybe break even, and maybe not. In a bad year I lose my shirt. I can't go on farming like that. Not for long. I've had a run of good years here, and they've had some drought problems up North, and that's helped the markets. But a bad year is always just around the corner, and they tend to come in groups." ·

"You couldn't build a barge landing on the other side?" I asked.

"Naw, not for miles, not the way the levees run. Nothin' but swamp behind them, no roads. Be more expensive than truckin' it out. . . ."

He was still brooding about it when we left.

"Nice guy," LuEllen said. "With major problems."

"But it's a help," I said. "We maybe couldn't pull this off without the bridge problem."

"Doesn't make me feel any better about it," she said as she got in the car.

After a moment of silence I said, "Well, you like him."

"Yeah." And after another moment of silence she asked, "Does that bother you?"

"A little bit."

"It never bothered you before," she said.

"That was before."

More silence, then: "Kidd, you're making me nervous. I mean, like really nervous."

10

THE COMPUTER ALARM was beeping when we got home, and I phoned Bobby.

Found on-line.

Where?

Animal control.

Dogcatcher?

Number is right; old 300-baud carrier.

Thanx; will check. Could you monitor line, look for access code?

Yes. Will call.

I dialed Marvel's house and got John.
"You ready?" I asked.
"All set. I'll go in as soon as the place opens and wait. Mary Wells parks her car in that lot sideways across the street. If you can get a window seat in that Coffee Klatch Café, 'round

171

about eight-fifty you'll see her go in the lot. Red
Ford. She usually gets there between nine-oh-five
and nine-fifteen. You can meet her in the street
and walk up with her. I'll be ready."

"Marvel says the map books cost twelve dollars?"

"Yeah. Have a twenty ready; maybe a fifty
would be better," John said. "I think she'd open
the box anyway, but with a fifty it'd be a sure
thing."

"All right. And you've got the focus figured out
and all that. . . ."

"I've been working with it, and I'll check it
again before I go in to make sure it's turned on,
that it's on silent mode, that the radio's at-
tached. . . . It'll be peeking out of the briefcase."

"The briefcase handles . . ."

"Yeah, we thought of that. They'll be out of the
way. We've got them taped. And I'll go out to talk
to this Brown dude as soon as we're out of the
place."

"OK. I'll see you tomorrow morning. Let me
talk to Marvel."

She must have been standing next to him because she was on the line a second later.

"Everything OK?" she asked.

"Bobby says there's a computer out at the animal control building. Ballem calls it with his
computer and apparently does some work with
it. You got anybody out there?"

"There's a girl I could talk to . . . but I don't know. She's not the most trustworthy."

"I'll try to raid it from here, but if I can't, we might have to go into the place. We could use another key."

"Oh, man, I don't know," she said doubtfully. "My friend's pretty shaky."

"Is she a secretary? What?"

"She's fuckin' Duane, is what she's doing."

"Ah, shit . . ."

"It's no big love affair; she thinks she needs the money."

"Well, talk to her. But don't give her any hint of what's happening."

"I'll think of something," she said. "A story."

"Be careful, for Christ's sakes. Hill's goofy. If there's any question, back off. We'll try to go in without her help."

LuEllen didn't like it. The worst thing, she said, was that too many people knew that we'd be hitting a particular place.

"Our security," she said, "is fucked. You know what the state women's prison is like here? I don't need some two-hundred-pound baby-killer sitting on my face for three to five."

"If it looks bad, we won't do it," I said. "Let's check it out tomorrow. Right after our session with Dessusdelit."

"It's kind of remote. We'll be noticed if we hang around."

"Nah. I looked at the map, and the place is right on the river. We'll chug down the river, look it over with the glasses, chug back, and look it over some more."

We were off the boat early the next morning, walking through town to the Coffee Klatch Café. The morning was warm and humid: pleasant but with the thick, hazy feel that foretold an insufferably hot day. It'd be good to be on the river. We got the window seat we needed at the Coffee Klatch and lingered over coffee and cheese Danishes.

"John," LuEllen said, and I turned my head to the street. John was climbing the City Hall steps, carrying the briefcase. He was wearing the dark pin-striped suit we'd seen in the motel. He looked hot.

Ten minutes later LuEllen said, "There she is. Let's go."

We slid out of the booth, left a dollar tip, paid the rest of the bill at the counter, and hurried outside. We'd been in the café only fifteen minutes, but you could feel that the day had gotten hotter and closer. Across the street Mary Wells was climbing out of her car. We walked down to the corner, waited for a car to pass, and strolled across the street toward the City Hall.

"Radio on?"

"Just looked," LuEllen said. The hand-size transmitter was in her shoulder bag. We were ten feet behind Wells as she climbed the steps into the City Hall. We paused for a moment at the directory inside, then followed her up the second flight to the clerk's office.

"It's going to be a scorcher today . . ." Wells was saying as we walked in. She was talking to a woman behind the service counter. John was standing at a table to one side, poring over a book of plat maps. Wells's eyebrow went up as she looked from John to the assistant; the assistant caught it and shrugged. John's briefcase, its mouth opened toward the safe on the back wall, was sitting on a flat-file cabinet.

"Could I help you folks?" the assistant asked, looking past Wells.

"Yes, I was told you sell Corps of Engineers navigation maps for the Mississippi."

"The map book? Sure . . ."

Wells walked through a wooden gate on the public counter to a glass-enclosed private office at the back. The clerk dug in a drawer, found a map book, and said, "That'll be twelve dollars. There's no sales tax on government publications. . . ."

I dug out my billfold and handed her a fifty. "I'm afraid I don't have anything smaller."

"That's OK. I'll just be a minute."

She walked back to Wells's office and said something. Wells nodded, stood up, came out, and walked to the safe. LuEllen put her hand in her purse. Mary Wells turned the combination dial on the safe, pausing briefly to align each combination number, and took out a cashbox. We got the change for the fifty, and two minutes later we were back on the street.

"OK?" I asked.

LuEllen shrugged. "Seemed to be. I'll have to look at the film. She turned the dial slowly enough, though. If the camera worked, we should be clear."

We were back aboard the *Fanny* before ten. John called a few minutes later.

"It worked. If the camera was aimed right, we got it because the film advanced four frames."

"Good," I said. "We've got to talk to Dessusdelit, and then we're going out on the river. I'll see you tonight at the Holiday Inn."

WHEN DESSUSDELIT came over the levee wall, I turned to LuEllen and said, "We're on," and fled toward the head.

"OK. So after she cuts the deck, as soon as you pick it up, I say, 'What'd you do to this ball?' " LuEllen said, following me.

"Yeah. *Right* after I pick it up. And you've got to put something extra in your voice—like awe. Like gee whiz. Don't overdo it, but I'm not good at this, so you've got to turn her around. Just glancing your way won't be enough. . . . Maybe you could hold the ball in that light beam," I said, nodding at a shaft of sunlight coming in the bow windows.

"OK . . . here she is."

I went on back to the head, stripped off my tennis shirt, and turned on the water, while LuEllen went to the door.

"Come on in," I heard LuEllen say cheerfully. Dessusdelit twittered a few words, and LuEllen led her to the same chair she'd sat in the day before.

While I splashed water on my face and neck, LuEllen got down the crystal ball and passed it to Dessusdelit, "just to warm it up." I wandered out of the head a minute later and posed in the galley, rubbing my wet face with a towel, yawning. Dessusdelit was wearing a bright print summer dress and beige low-heeled shoes. Even with the color, she still looked like a venomous sparrow, spooky, nervously glancing this way and that, as though a predator were about to jump out of a bush. She had the crystal ball cupped in her hands, rolling it, staring into it.

"You in a mood for a reading?" LuEllen asked me.

"Sure, I guess," I said lazily.

Dessusdelit knew something about tarot, so we couldn't fool her with a fake spread. LuEllen kept her working with the crystal ball while I got my deck from the cupboard. It was a common deck, the Waite-Rider. There are hundreds of tarots in circulation, but you can buy a Waite-Rider any-place that handles occult stuff. It's a standard, which is a good thing, because when I needed the second identical deck, I had no trouble finding one. The second deck was in a little cardboard box we'd taped under the edge of the table.

"It's amazing," LuEllen said as I sat down across from Dessusdelit. My knee touched the box under the table. "We must have caught Miz Dessusdelit at a critical juncture. When she handles the ball, it lights up like a Christmas tree: money and adventure. . . ."

She paused, artlessly, and let a wrinkle crease her forehead, as if a new thought had just occurred to her. "And romance?" LuEllen looked down at Dessusdelit. "Do you think that peculiar flux and intensity could have something to do with romance?"

Dessusdelit blushed. "Well, I wouldn't be . . . there isn't anything—"

"Could be something wicked this way comes," LuEllen said. I jumped; LuEllen surprises me sometimes. She'd just quoted a piece of Macbeth, which later became a Ray Bradbury title. Dessus-delit obviously recognized at least the sound of it, and I wondered if it were the Shakespeare or the Bradbury.

While Dessusdelit was mumbling over LuEllen's suggestion, I thumbed through the deck and put the Queen of Cups on the table, faceup.

"Significator," I said. I glanced at LuEllen. "Would you pull the blinds just a little and kill the lights? I'd like it a little dimmer to help focus the concentration. . . ."

LuEllen started pulling blinds, and I put the deck, less the single card, in front of the mayor. "I want you to shuffle. At least seven times, and after that, as long as you want," I told her. She took the deck and began riffling the cards. When she was done, she placed it squarely in front of me.

"Do you want to cut it?" I asked.

"Should I?"

"That's purely up to you. Look inside yourself, and make a decision."

Dessusdelit closed her eyes, and after a moment her hand came out, groped for the deck, and cut it.

"Good," I said, picking up the deck.

"What'd you do to this ball?" LuEllen blurted suddenly. She'd been juicing it with the laser. When Dessusdelit turned her head to look, the crystal was fluorescing like a piece of cold fire.

"My God," Dessusdelit said.

"It just never stopped," LuEllen said.

As Dessusdelit turned, I switched the decks. The new deck was identical to the first but thoroughly stacked.

"You know what it is?" Dessusdelit volunteered. She turned back to me, her voice dropping to a whisper. "It's the tarot, focusing the energy in the room."

We all looked at the deck in my hand. "This is getting scary," LuEllen said. I agreed. Dessusdelit's voice had such a deadly intensity that the hair stood up on my arm.

I shook it off and did a spread. The Empress came up immediately, overlying the significator, the card that represented Dessusdelit. She grunted, and I realized that she knew more about the tarot than she'd let on. I rolled out the rest of the spread, and she grunted several more times, little underbreath ummph noises. For the possible future, she got the Wheel of Fortune, upright, which generally means good luck; for the environment card, the Queen of Pentacles, which stands for success in business and the accumulation of property; and as the final outcome, the Ten of Pentacles, upright. The wealth card.

"Something's going on here," I said. "I've never seen a reading so consistent across the board."

I began the interpretation, and she nodded and then reached out to the spread. "But this . . ." she said, tapping the future card. Death riding a white horse.

"I told you about the Death card," I said. "It doesn't mean Death; it means change. Usually welcome change."

"Yes, but it's a frightening image."

"Does the image strike you as particularly

strong this morning? Did the image catch your eye, rather than the philosophical position behind the card?"

"Well . . ."

"There are times when you must look at the image. You know, the tarot speaks on a lot of different levels. Sometimes it's on a mystical level that seems far beyond anything I can interpret," I babbled. She was listening intently. "On other occasions it's as simple as the picture printed on the card."

"It did seem sort of special. . . ."

Of course it did, with my implicit prompting.

"I don't know what it might mean, though," I said, putting new doubt into my voice. "A dark knight, a black knight, arriving on a white horse. That hardly seems to fit modern times—especially coupled with the wealth cards we see everywhere else. I don't know."

Jesus, I thought, am I overdoing it? Behind Dessusdelit, LuEllen was biting her lip.

I picked up the Death card and placed it in front of Dessusdelit. The room had grown tense, and Dessusdelit sat frozen for a moment, studying Death. Then, with a sudden release of breath, she pushed her chair back and stood up. Her eyes were wide and distant, as though she were stoned.

"Let's get some light in here," LuEllen said suddenly. She pulled a shade, and daylight cut through the gloom. "Boy, I've never seen anything like this." She looked down at her hand. "The crystal has stopped."

Dessusdelit leaned over and peered at it, nodded.

"I need a drink," I said. "Miz Dessusdelit?"

"No, no, thank you. I think I need to go home and lie down. . . ."

She looked one last time at the dark knight on the white horse. When she was gone, LuEllen looked at me and grinned.

"That was strong," she said.

"Yeah. I hope I don't get in trouble with the tarot gods for fuckin' with the cards." She frowned, and I grinned at her. "No sweat. Let's get out on the river."

THE ANIMAL CONTROL compound was three-quarters of a mile south of the marina, at the far end of the town's small industrial district. Going downriver, we passed the tall white cylinders of a grain elevator with a barge dock, a series of warehouses surrounded by chain-link fences, a lumberyard, and then a stretch of empty riverbank, overgrown with brush. The animal control complex was the last sign of life before the river turned and slid out of sight. From the water we could just see the tops of the buildings. A couple of dogs were yapping, but there was no other sound except the boat motor and the water cutting around the bow.

"Goddamn it," I said. "I thought we could see in there."

"Why don't we go on down, tie off, and climb that little hill?" LuEllen asked, pointing across the water. A short, steep hill poked up just beyond the corrugated metal roofs. "We could take the glasses up with us, and we'd be looking right down on it."

"All right. Let's see if we can find a place to tie off," I said. We drifted down until we were a quarter mile below the complex, where the river began to turn away from the town. The near bank had been reinforced with concrete mats and made a decent landing. We tossed some foam bumpers over the side to protect the boat's hull, climbed the revetment, and tied off on a handy tree. A faint, twisting game trail rambled along the top of the levee, winding back toward town. We followed it toward the base of the hill, LuEllen in the lead.

Twenty yards down the levee she did a half hop and jump, blurted, "Jesus H. Christ," and took three hasty steps back toward me. "Big fuckin' snake," she said.

"Probably a garter snake," I said. "Sunning itself."

"Bullshit. I know garter snakes."

We eased up the path, and LuEllen picked up a

stick and swept the grass on either side of the
trail. A few seconds later we saw the snake again,
sliding through the grass. It had a wide reddish
brown head and brown bands across a thick
body. The snake turned, froze for the blink of an
eye, then uncurled into a tussock of dead grass.

"Copperhead," I said.

"Ugly." She shuddered.

"Poisonous. First cousin to a rattlesnake. We
better take this slow," I said. "If there are copperheads, there could be rattlers around, too."

With the snake sighting, it took another ten
minutes to climb to the top of the hill. LuEllen, a
city girl, was thoroughly spooked.

"If they know you're coming, they'll get out of
the way," I said, trying to reassure her.

"They're going to know we're coming," she
said, using the stick to whip the weeds in front of
us.

The crest of the hill was free of heavy vegetation, and though it wasn't particularly high, it
rose above everything but the grain elevators. The
view of the river was terrific, and a fire ring with
blackened stones suggested that the hilltop was a
popular camping spot. A dozen old beer cans
were strewn in a small depression just below the
summit, along with plastic bags and a rotting half
roll of toilet paper. We climbed past the garbage
pit to the grassy patch at the top and stopped to
catch our breath.

LuEllen had turned to say something, her mouth half open, when three shots banged out below us.

"Jesus," LuEllen said, dropping to her knees.

The shots continued, a series of three, then a couple more, a measured pause, then another three. By that time I was kneeling on the ground beside her.

"Target practice," I said. "Down by the dog-catcher's."

Crouched, we eased across the crest of the hill down next to a butternut tree on the far slope. Duane Hill and another man were standing forty yards away and seventy feet below us inside a rectangle made by a chicken-wire fence. Two lumpy burlap bags lay next to Hill's feet. The second man, a short, balding redhead who ran to fat, was loading the magazine into a heavy black automatic. A .45, I thought. I put the glasses on him. I wasn't positive, because I'd seen only bad newspaper photos of him, but I thought it was Arnie St. Thomas, the city councilman who ran the loan-sharking business.

"What are they doing?" LuEllen asked, puzzled. "And what's that noise?"

The noise was an ooka-ooka-ooka pumping sound coming from the animal control building. I had no idea what it was.

"I don't know and I don't know," I said. "Target practice, I guess. I hope they're not shooting up here."

The sound of laughter drifted up to us. The bald man suddenly dropped into a Weaver stance and fired four shots in sets of two: tap-tap, tap-tap. After the second set he straightened and called, "Whoa-oh."

LuEllen said, "There's something down there."

"What?"

"There's something in the cage. They're shooting at something," she said.

I scanned the wire enclosure but saw nothing. "I don't see anything. . . ."

Hill picked up the bag next to his feet and carried it down toward the end of the enclosure closest to the bottom of the hill, unwrapped a string, and shook it. Three cats fell out. Two were small, little more than kittens. The third was a big old tiger-striped tomcat. The tom had a dazed, frightened look about it and slunk toward a corner of the pen.

"Goddamn them," LuEllen said in a fury. She moved a little away from the tree, but I pulled her back.

"Guns," I said.

Hill walked back toward the other man. When he was six feet away, he whirled, Wyatt Earp style. A gun came out from under the back of his shirt, a chrome-plated revolver, and he fired almost without hesitating. The first shot missed, but the second shot blew up one of the kittens. The second kitten froze, but the old tom streaked toward the opposite corner of the fencing and hit it about four feet off the ground.

"Come on, come on," I muttered. The cat crawled up the chicken wire, and Hill had swiveled to take it when the bald man let go with the .45. At the first shot Hill went down, yelling, but the bald man fired three more shots. The cat was climbing, almost over the top, but the third shot took it in the shoulder and knocked it over the wire into the grass just outside the fence.

"You cocksucker," Hill yelled back at the bald man, but the bald man was laughing.

"You like to shit your pants, Duane," he called.

"You fuckin' peckerwood," Hill shouted back, and he was laughing too. Then quick as a snake, he pivoted, stretching and going flat at the same time, landed on his stomach, his arms outstretched, and he blew up the second kitten with a single shot.

There was another bag by the bald man's feet. He bent over to pick it up.

"Let's get out of here," said LuEllen, ashen-faced with anger.

"Look at the locks," I said. I handed her the glasses, and she put them to her eyes. There was only one real building in the complex, though there had appeared to be more from the river. The other roofs we'd seen from the water turned out to be simple shelter tops, mounted on poles over a series of stacked holding cages.

The main building was constructed of concrete block, painted white, with a green steel door. Small dark windows with metal casements punctured the two sides we could see.

"Standard shit," she said. "We can take it. We can probably use the power rake if we had to; there's nobody to hear it."

"All right."

"We could do it from the boat. Wear some boots or something so we wouldn't have to worry about snakes, walk back along the levee. Make sure there's nobody up here."

She was still looking through the glasses when a young black woman stepped out of the building door into the hot sunshine. She called to Hill, telephone, and Hill started back toward the building.

"Bring a couple more bags," the bald man called after him. He shook the bag in his hand, and three more kittens tumbled out.

On the way back to the boat LuEllen turned suddenly and said, "I'm glad I saw that."

"Why?"

" 'Cause now I'm not going to feel bad about taking those motherfuckers out. Prison's too good for those assholes."

BACK AT THE MARINA, we hooked up, and I called Bobby.

Any traffic?

Code word: Archball. May not help.

Why?

No auto-answer. Manual entry only.

Shit. How about the exchange monitor?

Set. Any call to engineer will ring here instead.

Probably tomorrow or next day.

We ready.

To get into a computer from the outside, the computer has to be on-line with the phone system. The Longstreet crowd, though, had a primitive setup: Instead of simply calling and getting right into the computer, somebody at animal control had to answer the phone, then switch the caller over to the computer. They probably didn't intend it as a security measure, but that's what they got. There's no better security for a computer than keeping it unplugged and plugging it in only for people you know. . . .

"WE'VE GOT TO GO IN?" LuEllen asked, looking over my shoulder.

"If we want the computer, we've got to go in."

"Let's do it," she said. "Let's run down to that Wal-Mart, buy some boots, and go for a midnight cruise."

"That's a lot of enthusiasm," I said.

She nodded, and I knew what she was thinking about. My cat is an old beat-up tom who roams the alleys and rooftops of Lowertown in St. Paul. One of these days he'll be squashed by a car or killed by one of the river dogs. I'll feel rotten about it, and so will LuEllen. She always worked solo and moves around too much to have a pet. But she and the cat get along famously, LuEllen lying on the couch, the cat on her stomach, both of them sound asleep in good fellowship. And I couldn't get the picture out of my mind, that old tom making a run for it, Hill and his asshole friend shooting him down. . . .

The sun was still hanging up in the hot, hazy sky when we drove out to the Wal-Mart on the edge of town, bought the green gum boots, and tossed them into the trunk. We ate at the Holiday Inn, stopped in the bar, and eventually ducked back to John's room. He was alone.

"I set you up," I said. "Told Dessusdelit that her future involves a black knight on a white horse, bringing welcome change."

"The Beemer's white, and I sure as shit am black," he said. He stepped over to the credenza, picked up a film cartridge, and flipped it to LuEllen. "Hope these are good."

"I'll look at them tonight." She glanced at her watch and turned to me. "We better get going. It'll be dark in half an hour."

"So tomorrow—"

"I'll talk to Brown about the land option," John said. "I hope Bobby's ready."

"I just talked to him. He's all ready. Is Marvel ready to move?"

"Harold's got the capitol crowd fixed. He told them that some heavy-duty crime is going down, that big money is being stolen, that something could happen this weekend. If he comes up with enough specifics, the attorney general will send in the state bureau of investigation."

"On a Saturday? For sure?"

"Any day of the week, any time of day, on six hours' notice."

"Can we trust them?"

"I think so. Crime is just crime, and most of the time they probably couldn't give a shit. But this is politics. This is a deal."

WE PULLED OUT of the dock just as the sun was disappearing over the highest of the old Victorian mansions up on the hill. The marina manager was leaving as we unhooked, and stopped by.

"Midnight cruise?"

"Little ro-mance maybe," LuEllen told him, rolling her eyes at me.

"Well, good luck with that." The manager

laughed, and he watched as we backed away, into the current.

We took our time going downriver, floating, easy. LuEllen stayed below, in the head, processing the film. I let the boat slip below the animal control complex, riding downriver for a dozen miles or more.

I could live out there on the Mississippi, I think, if I weren't eaten by the worm of Art. I could live there for the names alone. Longstreet was the only big town between Helena, Arkansas, and Greenville, Mississippi. Just in that stretch of 120 miles, from Helena to Greenville, you roll through Montezuma Bend, Horseshoe Cutoff, Kangaroo Point, Jug Harris Towhead, Scrubgrass Bend, Ashbrook Neck, and a few other places where you'd like to hop off the boat and look around.

The last of day's light was dying in the sky when I brought the boat around, took it back upriver, and eventually warped it against the revetment wall below the animal control complex. I killed the engine and the lights, dropped onto the main deck, and hopped ashore with the bow and stern lines. LuEllen came up, carrying the boots, as I finished tying off.

"Better take some repellent," she said, tossing me a spray can. "The mosquitoes'll be fierce."

"How'd the pictures come out?" I asked as I

sprayed my hands and rubbed my face and the back of my neck.

"Not sure," she said, frowning a bit. "Three frames look good. On the fourth, her thumb might be in the way. I can't tell on the wet neg, I didn't want to take the chance of scratching it. But holding it up to the light . . . we could have a problem."

"Goddamn it," I said.

LuEllen shrugged. "If we've got three digits and she's only blocking the fourth, it just means it'll take a little longer to get in. We might have to try a dozen combinations, but we'll get it."

"When can you print?"

"Tonight, when we get back. I can't do it on the river because of the engine vibrations."

THE NIGHT WAS still warm, but we wore dark long-sleeved shirts and jeans and the gum boots instead of shoes. I carried my portable in its black nylon case, and LuEllen had a daypack over her shoulder. We walked without talking, LuEllen using her miniature flashlight sparingly as we moved through the darkness. At the bottom of the hill she stopped, leaned her face close to my ear, and said, "Wait three minutes." I thought she was going up the hill, but instead, we simply stood in the dark.

When your eyes adjust from light to dark, the night vision seems to fade in, like a black-and-white slide coming into focus. What was pitch-dark when you first come out of bright lights is suddenly nothing more than twilight. It works the same for your hearing, although most people aren't aware of it. When you stand stock-still in a dark place, the noises that once resided in the background suddenly come to the fore. You notice the roar of far-off trucks climbing a grade, the motors and air conditioners, the insects in the trees, the sound of the wind. Human voices are an absolutely distinct sound; even from a long distance, when you can't make out the individual vowels and consonants, the rhythm or the rise and fall of the pitch tell you that you're hearing another human.

We heard all the background sounds, picked them up one at a time. No voices.

We waited the full three minutes, and then LuEllen was moving again. I trailed behind. The track along the levee broke out of the brush thirty or forty yards from the animal control buildings. The main building, the white one, was thirty yards away, across an open stretch of weedy lawn. A gravel driveway came in from the other side but stopped short of the building.

We waited for another five minutes in the weeds just out of the cleared area. There was one exterior light, up on a pole outside the main building. No lights were showing in the building.

"Glad the kennel's on the far side," LuEllen

said. She took her picks and a power rake out of her pack. "Let's try not to wake up the mutts."

We were absolutely exposed as we crossed the yard. If anyone was up the hill or anybody came up in a car, we were in the open. There was no point in being furtive but we were furtive anyway. LuEllen went straight to the door, tried the knob, found it locked. There was a window around the side, and she tried it. It was locked. She came back to the door and looked at the lock.

"I'll try the picks," she whispered. "Maybe we can avoid the power rake. Hold the light."

She opened it, but it took twenty sweaty minutes. The power rake would have done it in two, but it sounds like a spoon dropped in a garbage disposal. When the door was open, we took a quick look around the side of the building, then crossed the yard and waited in the weeds again, listening and waiting. If there were any kind of unseen alarm, somebody should be coming up the road.

The sense of hearing isn't the only thing that sharpens in the dark. As far as we were from the building, there was a light but persistent stench of animal urine and fear. And something else . . .

"Raw meat," LuEllen muttered. "From the shooting pen . . ."

Nothing moved on the road. We went back and inside. The lock on Hill's office door was nothing. LuEllen slipped it, and we were in. The computer was another old IBM. I brought the machine up and began dumping the hard disk to my portable. LuEllen went through the desk and found a box of floppies. When the disk-to-disk transfer was complete, I loaded the floppies one at a time, found two sets of files, and saved them to my machine.

That done, I slipped in a utility program I'd written myself. A hard disk is like an electronic filing cabinet, with lots of storage space for files. Unless the operator is running complicated accounting programs with enormous amounts of data or huge applications programs, there's usually plenty of empty space.

I checked and found the Longstreet gang had used less than a tenth of the available disk space. Good. My program—a gem, if I do say so myself—simply made a second copy of everything on the disk and then hid it in the free space. The copy would never show up on directories or in any other routine transaction unless the right code phrase was entered at the prompt. I made the code phrase *redneck*. And fuck 'em if they can't take a joke.

If these were the books, and the Longstreet gang got nervous and tried to erase them, there was an excellent chance that there'd still be a set left on the machine, hidden under the code. A set available to the state cops . . .

After LuEllen had unlocked the desk, she

checked a filing cabinet, found nothing interesting, and then went through the rest of the building. As I finished, she came in and said, "Come look at this."

I packed my machine and followed her into the back. There was a small loading dock at the rear of the building, with a pulldown door, like a small garage door. Built into the wall opposite the door were two cubicles, four-by-four-by-four feet, with heavy Plexiglas doors. There was a grille in the wall of each, and the doors had thick rubber seals.

"Gas chambers?" she asked. "For the animals?"

I looked at the seals and then at a pump apparatus off to the side. "No. It's a vacuum system. They put the dogs in the chamber and suck the air out. That's the way they do it most places now."

"Christ, it sounds awful."

I shrugged. "I don't know. It's supposed to be humane."

We left it at that. LuEllen made a last check of the building, to make sure we hadn't left anything behind, relocked the door from the inside, and pulled it shut after us.

Ten minutes later we were on the river. We didn't talk much as we pushed back upstream. LuEllen lay in the sunbathing well, looking up at the stars, and the tension drained away with the current.

BY TWO O'CLOCK I knew I had the books. I didn't know what they meant.

"They've used codes for all the categories," I told LuEllen. "The numbers are there, but I don't know what the categories are."

"Marvel may be able to figure it out," she said.

"I hope."

While I worked on the books, LuEllen set up the enlarger in the head. She made four prints, fixed them, washed them, and let them dry. By the time I was sure about the books, she was looking at the enlargements under a high-intensity light.

"We got three out of the four," she said.

She had enlarged the images of the safe dial to the size of an old-fashioned alarm-clock face. The numbers were clear enough in the first three. In the fourth, Wells's index finger covered the critical digit.

"So it's seventy-four, forty-four, twelve, and something between . . . say, fifty-five and seventy."

"Hang on." I got my drawing box, dug around, and came up with a compass and a set of dividers. Using the compass, I drew the missing portion of the dial over Wells's intruding finger. With the dividers, I measured the intervals between the visible numbers and marked them off around the rim of the dial.

"If this is the centerline," I said, indicating the line with a ruler and a sharp pencil, "then the digit is . . . sixty-six. Give or take a digit."

LuEllen looked at me and grinned. "You *do* have your uses. Other than sexual, I mean."

11

It was all coming together. Smoothly. Too smoothly, LuEllen said. She was born and raised in Minnesota and was automatically suspicious of pleasantness. No matter how nice the summer is, winter always comes . . .

With the printouts of the Longstreet books in hand, I called John and Marvel. We agreed to drive to Greenville, where we could meet in a motel without dodging the Longstreet locals.

LuEllen stayed with the boat. There'd be new people in Greenville, and she was paranoid about her face becoming known. At two o'clock Marvel let me into her room at the Sea-B Motel. John was there with Harold and a man I hadn't met before.

"This is Brooking Davis," Marvel said, nodding at the stranger. Davis was a slender, bird-boned man with a square chin, a dark mustache, and the liquid eyes of an Arab. "He's a lawyer and does appraisal work for the county assessor's office. Brooking will be our first appointment on the council. If Harold and I don't know where the bodies are buried, Brooking will."

"Well, we found you some grave sites," I said, handing over the printouts. "It looks simple enough, but I don't know how it breaks down."

Davis had two boxes full of city budgets, memos, and reports. He unloaded them on a credenza, and Marvel and Harold pulled chairs up to the bed. In two minutes the three of them were in deep discussion, comparing numbers on printouts with expenditures and collections in the city reports.

"How'd it go with Brown?" I asked John.

John smiled. "He was a little surprised when I turned out to be black, looking like I did—and driving that BMW—but we're all set," he said. He stepped over to a black nylon briefcase, unzipped it, and pulled out a sheaf of papers. "I gave him a cashier's check for a thousand dollars for a thirteen-week option on six hundred acres, at nine hundred and twenty dollars an acre. He was asking a thousand, but I dickered a little. I still paid too much, though. I wanted to seem anxious but like I was trying to hide it. And I wanted him talking around town about how he stuck it to the city boy."

"Does he seem like the sort to do that?" I asked. "I hope."

"Actually, no," John said with a grin. "He

seemed like a pretty decent guy. But the real estate dealer was an asshole. She'll talk. She asked me what I wanted the land for. I told them my heritage was in cotton farming and I was thinking of going back to it. She had to stick her hankie in her mouth to keep from laughing. I was wearing the wing tips. They figure I'm a crack dealer from Memphis. . . ."

"OK," I said. "So the word'll be around."

From the bed, Marvel was saying, "If *Outhouse* is the bar payments, what's *Suburb*?"

"Sounds like they're getting it," John said.

IT TOOK three hours to nail down the printouts. Davis, who'd seemed frail when I first met him, was as intense as Marvel or Harold, and they often deferred to him. But not always. There was one heated argument over a series of entries on recreational fees. The entries might have exposed the Reverend Dodge, and Marvel didn't want to take the risk. Davis, who apparently hated Dodge, did. Marvel won.

John whispered: "That woman can talk the bark off a tree."

"How's your . . . uh, relationship?"

John glanced covertly at Marvel, then looked back at me. "I'm trying as hard as I can, man. Sometimes I think she's about to haul my butt back to the bedroom, but then . . . I mean, Jesus, this is takin' longer than it has with any woman I ever met."

"Is she real, or is she teasing?"

"She's real, I think."

"Then that's probably a good sign," I said. "All the time . . ."

"You think so?"

We both looked at Marvel and realized that everybody in the room was looking at us. We'd been whispering in a way that immediately attracts attention.

"Uh, we didn't want to bother you, talking," John said.

"Uh-huh," said Marvel.

"HERE'S THE SITUATION," Marvel said, a half hour after her argument with Davis. She rolled off the bed and whacked a rolled-up copy of the printout against her thigh. "This is good stuff. It lays out the kickbacks and the payoffs, how much and where it went, but everything is done by code numbers. We *know* who the code numbers represent, but we couldn't prove it immediately."

"If the IRS gets it, they could check bank deposits."

"Sure," said Davis, "but that would take some time. If things drag out, we might not be able to get all of them out of the office simultaneously."

"Not even if they steal a hundred thousand bucks?" John asked.

THE EMPRESS FILE

"That'd do it, but that's an extra risk, and we don't know if that whole crazy con game with the bridge is going to work," Marvel said. "We were talking back in Memphis about blackmailing them out of office."

"Not the first three," I said. "Only the governor's redneck appointments."

"Why not try it now?" Marvel asked. "The bridge idea has always seemed kind of . . . shaky. If we can get around using it, we'd expose John to less risk, you and LuEllen to less risk, and we might get to the same place."

I thought about it for a moment. If we could blackmail them out of office, there *would* be less exposure. And LuEllen was worried already. . . . I looked at John. "What do you think?"

"Sounds OK to me," he said. He turned to Marvel. "How would we do it?"

"Harold will call Dessusdelit, tell her he's got to see her, that it's important," Marvel said. "She knows him, she knows he wouldn't bullshit. He'll go over to her house and lay the books on her. Tell her that all he wants is her resignation. Hers and St. Thomas's and Rebeck's. They quit, and he loses the books."

"Can you pull it off?" I asked Harold.

"I don't know," he said pensively. He shoved his hands in his pockets and looked at Marvel, and I realized he would do about anything she wanted him to. "It's worth a try, I guess.

205

Dessusdelit's a politician, and she used to sell real estate. She's been cutting deals all her life. Maybe she'll figure she can cool out the books and come back later. She won't know the rest of it—the part about us taking over the town."

I glanced at John again, then turned to Marvel.

"OK with me," I said. "But it's your call."

"Let's try it," she said with satisfaction. "If it doesn't work, John can still try the bridge scam, you and LuEllen can still hit City Hall, and we can still go to the governor. But if it does work, we avoid all that trouble."

"That's a lot to do before Friday," I said. "If we're going to work the bridge scam, it has to be on Friday, so we've got to move."

"We'll be back home before supper," Marvel said. "Harold can call Dessusdelit tonight. Maybe even go over tonight. And just in case, I'll start calling around and put the word out about John. Smart Memphis dope dealer just bought some land, and there's something happening with the bridge. It'll get back to the mayor and her crowd tonight, same time as Harold."

"Good. And if Harold can't convince Dessusdelit and the others to quit, we'll need some help next week, after the state cops come in. We'll need a half dozen people with white-southerner accents, to call the paper and the TV station, demanding that the council resign."

"That's fixed," Harold said simply. He was

wearing his brown suit again and sweating lightly despite the air-conditioning.

"What about the interim rednecks?" I asked.

"We've got two names, Marvin Lesse and Bill Armistead. Both are pretty wimpy, and we've got them by the balls on some illegal cement sales. We'll get them appointed, and when it's time to push them off . . . well, they'll go," Marvel said.

"We hope," added Davis.

We all looked at each other for a minute; then Marvel said, "It's scary," and John said, "Let's do it."

THE PROGRAM was complex.

Marvel would finish translating the books, stripping out the portions that applied specifically to Dessusdelit, St. Thomas, and Rebeck. Harold would show only those portions to Dessusdelit.

If Harold couldn't deal, we'd work the bridge scam.

The scam was a variation of the old pigeon drop routine. I figured if the pigeon drop worked a million times on Miami Beach, it ought to work once in Longstreet.

But instead of dropping an envelope of money on the sidewalk, we were dropping a bridge.

The bridge that Longstreet no longer had but desperately needed.

Marvel would plant the rumor that the state Department of Transportation was recommending construction of a toll bridge. But the bridge wouldn't come into the downtown area for engineering and cost reasons. Instead, it would cross the river just north of town, coming down on the Brown property.

The property John now held an option on. A property that would quickly sprout gas stations, fast-food joints, convenience stores, and maybe a small shopping center.

That kind of information is routinely held secret by state departments of transportation so that land prices aren't inflated before condemnation proceedings begin. The state DOT's engineering office would be the only place that could confirm Marvel's rumor.

Bobby was monitoring the Longstreet phone exchanges, checking lines out of the city offices, and at the homes of the most prominent members of the machine, scanning for the DOT's number in the state capital. When the number was dialed, a phone would ring at Bobby's place. An "engineer" would answer. No information could be released, he would say; studies were still under way. . . . But where did you get that information? That information is restricted.

In other words, *Yes, that's right, we're putting in the bridge. . . .*

It was a marvelous opportunity for a well-run machine, one we were sure it wouldn't overlook. Whoever controlled the land at the base of the bridge would make a lot of money. And that was . . . Brown. No? Some black dude from Memphis?

When John was contacted by a member of the machine, he would hint that he was working for a bigger Man in Memphis and couldn't act on his own. He'd be the reluctant bride, but he'd get back to them, quickly. When he got back, he'd say the Man would welcome participation, especially since it could grease the council votes needed on zoning matters around the bridge. But votes wouldn't be enough; the Man would also need money from the machine.

There'd be some back and forth, but Friday afternoon, after talking to the Man in Memphis, he'd tell the machine that he needed to see some cash. Right then. Before he went back. They didn't have to *give* it to him; that would make them too suspicious. They only had to *show* it to him. Show him that they could get it. A hundred thousand. He was leaving for Memphis in an hour. . . .

There was only one place they'd be able to get that much cash that quickly. The float. The float and the city's cash account at the bank. We'd work it so they had to take the money out of the bank but wouldn't be able to return it the same day.

St. Thomas, who ran the loan-sharking business, kept his stash at the City Hall, in the city clerk's safe. We figured they'd put the hundred thousand in the same place, for safekeeping until the banks reopened Monday.

If we could get the cash out, Marvel would be at the capitol. When we called, she'd go straight in to see the governor's hatchet man. He'd turn out the cops and accountants, and by Saturday night the council would be trying to explain what had happened to a hundred thousand dollars in cash—and why it'd been taken out of the bank in the first place.

Marvel and her friends would have delivered the doctored printout detailing Longstreet corruption and would also be singing a quiet chorus in the background. A hundred thousand? Probably dope, she'd say. Cocaine and crack. Run through the fire department. And with Marvel providing the details, there'd be enough meat on that bone to interest the state.

"I WORRY about you, Harold," I said as we were leaving. "It all sounds good in theory, but these guys . . . you don't run a machine like Longstreet's without being tough. They might not roll over so easy."

"I grew up in Longstreet," Harold said with an unhappy grin. "I know how it works. I can take care of myself. And Marvel thinks—"

"Yeah. Well. Good luck."

☐ ☐ ☐

BACK IN LONGSTREET, LuEllen and I climbed up on top of the *Fanny*'s cabin with gin and tonics, to watch the sun go down, and I told her about the change of plans.

"I don't like it," she said. "I'm getting spooked. In the bad old days, if I got spooked, I called off whatever I was doing. Walked away. I figured there might be a reason for being spooked, something unconscious. . . . If Harold can blackmail Dessusdelit and St. Thomas and Rebeck off the council, more power to him. We won't have to hit City Hall."

A small boat's bow light appeared downriver and cut an arc through the darkness as it came into the marina. A commercial catfisherman in a fat green jon boat. His wife was waiting up the levee with their station wagon and a stack of drywall buckets for the catch.

"I don't know," I said, finishing the drink. I crunched the ice cube between my teeth and sucked on the pieces. "It doesn't feel right."

We sat for a couple more minutes in silence; then LuEllen scraped her chair back and stood up. "Mosquitoes coming out," she said.

As I looked out at the river, in the hot, humid night, with the water burbling under the hull and the sound of car radio rock 'n' roll floating down the levee wall, it was hard to remember that winter always comes.

12

JOHN CALLED AN hour later.

"Harold talked to Dessusdelit. She says she'll see him at her house tomorrow morning."

"Did he tell her—"

"No. He just said it was important, that it involved corruption and high city officials. She agreed right away—nervous, I guess. He's supposed to be there at ten o'clock."

"Terrific," I said. John sounded unnaturally cheerful, and I heard Marvel's voice in the background. "Is that Marvel?"

"Yeah, I'm at her place."

"Let me talk to her."

"Just a minute," he said. I heard him call her; then there was a delay; then he came back on and said, "You gotta wait a minute; she can't talk to you unless she got her pants on."

I heard Marvel squeal and John laughing; then Marvel came on, somewhat breathless, and said, "You don't pay any attention to this liar."

"Hey, he's a good guy," I said.

She laughed and said, in an aside to John, "Quit that," and then to me, "He's been hanging over me since that first night. You know what finally did it? I think it was those fuckin' wing tips of his. He looked so cute in them."

"Jesus, that *is* perverted."

"That's me."

"I don't mean to bring you down, but something occurred to me. This woman out at animal control . . ."

"Sherrie?"

"Yeah. A black guy's going to show up at Dessusdelit's place tomorrow with a copy of the secret books. The question may arise, Where did he get them?"

"Oh, shit," she said. There was another pause. "I can handle it, I think."

"OK."

"I can tell her . . . to get sick, or something. If I tell her it's important, she'll do it."

"With no questions?"

"Nothing I'll answer. She's not too bright. . . . I can handle it."

"OK. I just thought I'd mention it."

"Good thought," she said.

"And listen . . . take care of John."

"Better'n he could possibly believe," she said.

□ □ □

LuELLEN AND I went to bed, LuEllen speculating about John and Marvel. Would they get married? Would it be a church wedding? Would Marvel wear a formal white wedding gown, and would that be right at her age? Would we be invited, and if we were, could we come?

She went on for a while, while I listened distractedly. Finally I got out of bed, picked up the phone, and called Bobby on a voice line. I outlined what we were doing and asked if he could monitor Dessusdelit's phones in the morning.

"We're putting a lot of pressure on her," I said. "If something goes wrong, or if she decides to run for it or figures out some kind of double cross . . ."

"I'll monitor it," he said. "If anything happens, I'll get back to you."

"Why do you want him to do that?" LuEllen asked when I hung up.

"I don't know," I said. "It seems like a good idea."

I WAS SOUND ASLEEP when the phone rang the next morning. I groaned, sat up, looked at the clock. Ten-thirty. I got to the phone on the fifth ring.

"This Kidd?" Bobby, his voice urgent, harsh, not waiting even for my "hello?"

"Yeah, Bobby? What's going on?"

"Get over to Dessusdelit's house," he snapped. "Something bad's happening."

"What?" I asked. LuEllen sat up, watching, roused by the tone of my voice.

"I was monitoring her line. About two, three minutes ago, the dogcatcher—"

"Duane Hill—"

"Yeah. He made a call. He was at her house. He called this St. Thomas guy, told him to get his ass over there, they had an emergency and he had to drive a car. That sounds like trouble to me. Hill wasn't even supposed to be there, was he?"

"No . . ."

"Anyway, St. Thomas said he'd be right there."

"All right, we're on the way. Call John, try his motel and Marvel's place . . . tell him . . ."

"OK."

EVEN WHEN you're in a hurry, it takes a long time to get going. We dressed, rushing, but it still took six or seven minutes to get to the car. Add that to the two or three between the time Hill hung up and Bobby got to us. . . . And I got us lost, trying to improvise a shortcut. We got tangled in a series of cul-de-sacs on the wrong side of the municipal golf course, and we had to go back out to my first wrong turn.

"What're we going to do when we get there?"

LuEllen said. "We just can't come busting up to the door."

"We could do that," I said. "Tell her we were in the neighborhood and just thought we'd stop by. . . ."

"She's too smart," LuEllen argued. "She'd make a connection. We're still strangers, too friendly too fast. Then Harold comes out of the blue. . . ."

"Maybe Marvel will think of something. When Bobby explains, all she'll have to do is call Dessusdelit, and say, 'Listen, we know you got him.' "

"Hope she does," LuEllen said. "Hope she does . . ."

SHE DIDN'T. And we were late. A white Ford turned out of the lane from the country club as we were approaching.

"That's the car Harold drove to Greenville," I said. We'd stood next to it for a few minutes, talking, before I left.

"Well, shit, maybe he's out," she said.

I accelerated, went on past the country club road, and closed on the Ford. There was a man inside, in the driver's seat. I couldn't see him that clearly, and closed further.

"No, no," LuEllen said. "Back off, back off. Take that turn."

"What, what?" I braked and swerved down a turnoff.

"That was St. Thomas, the guy who was killing the cats."

"Sure?" But I had no real doubt.

"Yeah, didn't you see the red hair?"

I hadn't, but I believed her and turned the car around, stopping at the highway, uncertain which way to go. "So where's Harold? In the trunk?"

"I don't know," she said. "What?"

I put the car on the highway, headed back toward the country club. I'd answered my own question. "If Harold drove that car to Dessusdelit's, he'd park either in her driveway or in front of the place," I explained. "If they whacked him, they wouldn't be carrying his body across the lawn to put it in the trunk."

"So . . ."

"So look for Hill's panel truck. It's white, and it says 'Animal Control' on the side. A Chevy—"

"There it is," LuEllen said immediately, pointing back over my shoulder. The van was winding through the country club streets, still a block or so away, but moving toward the stone pillars that marked the entrance road. I slowed and took the first turn on the opposite side of the road.

"Now what?" LuEllen asked. The van hesitated

before turning onto the highway, then accelerated away, after the white Ford.

"I don't know. Follow. See what happens . . . If we had a gun . . ."

"If pigs had wings . . ." Hill's van went past an obvious turnoff to animal control.

"Where's he going? Why's he going through town?"

"I don't know."

We found out five minutes later, after a nerve-wrenching job of tailing the white van through light traffic. On the northern highway business strip, just at the edge of town, the van slowed and turned into the Wal-Mart parking lot. We watched from the shoulder of the road as the van stopped at the front entrance. St. Thomas was waiting inside. He walked out and climbed in the driver's side of the van, which then started back out. By that time I'd made a U-turn and was parked behind the gas pumps in the Shell station.

"They ditched Harold's car in the Wal-Mart lot," LuEllen said.

"Let's call the cops."

"And tell them what?"

"That a guy was kidnapped—"

"We'll be on a tape—"

"Jesus, LuEllen."

The van went past on the highway, headed

back into town. I waited a few seconds and
pulled out after them.

"He's going out to animal control," LuEllen
said.

"Yeah. Can't get too close out there. There's
nothing else around."

I put several cars between us and the panel
truck and, when there was no longer any question
where it was headed, pulled over to a drive-up
phone outside a convenience store. I dialed Marvel's place, then John's, and got no answer at either.

"Let's go," said LuEllen.

We continued on to the animal control complex
and spotted the van parked outside.

"Where are they?"

"I don't know, but we can't go in," I said, continuing past the turnoff. We were on a gravel
road that had some traffic, but not much. Even
going by the place was a risk. "If they've killed
him . . . or are planning to . . . there wouldn't be
any reason not to do us."

"Maybe they're just talking to him," LuEllen
said. She didn't believe it.

"Maybe Hitler was only kidding."

"All right. Let's ditch the car."

Four hundred yards farther on, a track left
the main road to the right, away from the river,
and a sign said LEVI CREEK PUBLIC HUNTING. It
didn't look as if it had been used since duck sea-

son. I drove far enough down that a passerby couldn't see the car from the road, killed the engine, and we scrambled out. As I closed the door I noticed LuEllen's camera bag in the back seat.

"Bring the camera," I said.

"Got it," LuEllen answered. We jogged through the heat waves coming off the road, through some nascent wildflowers, toward the base of the hill we'd climbed on our last trip out. From this side a definite track wound up to the top. LuEllen, who is both in better shape and a better athlete than I am, led the way. When I came over the crest, she was crouched on the far side, peering down at the animal control building.

"Nobody around," she said.

I crawled up beside her and looked down. The van was twenty feet from the front door, which was closed.

"What *is* that noise?" I asked. Ooka-ooka-ooka. We'd heard it the first time we'd been there. It sounded like a broken pump.

"I don't know," she said. She opened the camera bag, took off the short lens she kept on the Nikon, and put on the biggest one she had, a 210mm zoom. Nothing moved. And the building stopped going ooka-ooka. Then started again. We lay on the bare patch, watching.

"If they beat him up, and if he's in obviously

bad shape, we want photos of him coming out with Hill. Maybe we could yell or scream or something, they wouldn't know who we are, but they'd have to let him go."

"Jesus, that worries me. Our security could be fucked."

"Yeah, but—" It suddenly dawned on me what the sound was. Ooka-ooka. I half stood and stared down the hill. "Motherfucker."

"What?"

"That's the pump for the fuckin' vacuum chamber. I bet that's what it is."

LuEllen didn't say anything but just stared, and the pump stopped. "You think?" she asked in the silence.

"Maybe they're trying to find out who else knows."

"Jesus, no. I don't believe it. . . ."

"We fucked up," I said. "We've gotta get to the car and call the cops. . . . Or maybe we can call them, Hill and St. Thomas. I'll try to disguise my voice, tell them we know they've got Harold."

I was headed for the path down the hill when LuEllen whispered, "Wait . . . wait. Here we go." She waved me back.

The door to the animal control building opened, and St. Thomas stepped out into the sun and looked around. There was nothing to see but the van in the driveway. He was agitated, jerking around when a dog suddenly started barking from the cages. He walked around the building, checking, then went back inside. A moment later he and Hill came out, carrying what looked like a body wrapped in a sheet. Hill used only his left hand; his right was around the arm of a black woman, who seemed to be weeping.

"Ah shit," LuEllen said, shooting off a string of exposures.

They carried the body to the levee, walking fast, looking around, then along the land side of the levee, down from the crest where you couldn't see them from the river. They went along until they got to the revetment where we'd tied up the boat. Erosion had cut a little notch out of the levee just above the concrete slabs. They dropped the body, both of them breathing hard, and St. Thomas stepped up to the top of the bank and scanned the river. They were in weeds and brush up to their shoulders, and there was nothing on the water. When he was sure it was clear, they unwrapped the body, dragged it over the levee, and heaved it in the river. It sank almost immediately.

With every step they took, LuEllen snapped another photograph.

With the body gone, the two men climbed back down the levee to where the black woman waited. She was half crouched, talking fast. We couldn't hear what they were saying, but Hill laughed and shook his head. St. Thomas said something to her, then stood and offered his hand, and they climbed back up the levee to the path on top, and he gestured into the river.

"Telling her not to worry, the body's gone," LuEllen guessed, looking up at me.

"No, keep shooting," I snapped.

She looked back through the viewfinder and triggered off a shot and then, without looking up, asked, "Why?"

"Because they're going to kill her," I said. I started to stand, thinking to shout, but Hill, already moving, stepped up behind the woman with his hand extended. It was holding the black automatic that St. Thomas had used on the cats. The woman never saw it coming. Hill fired a single shot into the back of her head, and she tumbled down the embankment like a broken doll.

"Motherfucker," LuEllen groaned. She took shots of them going down the levee, pitching the woman's body into the water, then coming back up. Hill was animated, laughing, and slapped St. Thomas on the shoulder. St. Thomas said something, and Hill took the pistol out of his belt, looked at it, and turned and pitched it into the river.

"Shoot it," I blurted. LuEllen was still looking through the viewfinder and fired a last shot just as the pistol hit the water. I tried to mark the spot in my memory and then said, "Let's get the fuck out of here. If they even get a smell of us or decide to check this place out . . ."

We ran back down the hill, down the road, and off onto the track.

"They'd know the car," LuEllen said, looking back toward the hill as we got in it.

"They were a hundred yards away, and they're both heavy guys, and they had no reason to run. Even if they're going up the hill, they wouldn't be more than halfway yet," I said. I turned the car around, rolled it back to the road, and went out the opposite way.

WE ARGUED about the killings.

"We can't tell anybody," LuEllen said urgently. "I don't want to quit, but I don't want to get involved in any kind of murder investigation. That'd blow me, that'd blow you."

"We can't just sit on it," I argued. "They fuckin' murdered them."

"So we handle it ourselves," she said. "We did once before."

I thought about the two bodies and what would be the now-rusty guns piled in the unmarked grave in West Virginia. Yeah, by God, we had handled it before, and it made me sick to think about. Not that we could have done anything different.

"I gotta think," I said. "We can't just let it go."

"OK, but please, please, we don't tell Marvel or John what happened. We don't tell anybody. This is for us, man." She was looking up at me and it occurred to me how small she was. "An investigation would drag us out in the open."

"For us." I threw an arm around her head and tightened up in a wrestler's headlock. She wrapped her inside arm around my waist. Not your basic *Gone With the Wind* clinch, but it felt right.

"Bobby will talk to them, tell them he called us."

"So we tell them that we went out to Dessusdelit's house, saw no sign of Harold's car, so we just kept going," LuEllen suggested. "We looked around for a while, checked animal control, but there just wasn't anything to see."

"Jesus." I ran my hand through my hair. There was an impulse to go out on the bow, take off the lines, and head south. That was impossible now.

LuEllen looked at me closely. "Kidd, sometimes you have these . . . impulses . . . to do the right thing. You've got to keep them under control. There's not a goddamned thing we can do for Harold or that woman. Nothing that would be worth going to prison for."

"I'd better call Marvel."

"What for?"

I shrugged. "To start working both ends against the middle."

MARVEL WAS frantic.

"I don't know," I kept saying. I suggested that she and her friends start hunting for Harold's car.

"You don't think he's hurt?"

"You know these people better than I do," I said, a sour taste in my mouth.

"All right. We'll get people out looking. Maybe I ought to go over to Dessusdelit's house, confront her—"

"No, no. Don't do that. If they have done something with Harold, you could be in trouble. Especially the way they've got the cops fixed. The best thing is, find him. Find his car. Figure out what happened. But don't do anything to derail the plan. If worse comes to worst, and something happened to him, it's more important than ever that we take the town."

It occurred to me that none of us was using the words *killed, murdered,* and *dead.* It was *if something happened . . . if he's hurt. . . .*

The day dragged by. Marvel launched her search, while LuEllen processed her film and began printing.

"You want something to weep about, look at

these," she said when she came out of the bathroom/darkroom. She was printing on RC paper to cut the wash time, and the prints were still soft and damp. She laid them out on the table like grotesque place mats.

The killings were graphically portrayed, as real as anything I'd seen from Vietnam, Beirut, or Salvador. She laid them out in sequence, from the time Hill and St. Thomas came out the door carrying Harold's body to the instant when the murder gun hit the river. If LuEllen had been a newspaper photographer, she'd have had a Pulitzer locked up.

"Christ, it could be out of the thirties; even the people look the same. Hill's got that haircut, those short-sleeve shirts. . . ."

You couldn't quite see the pores in Hill's face when he pulled the trigger on Sherrie, but close enough. If the photos ever got into court, they'd send the two men to the electric chair.

LuEllen slumped in a chair. "I'm feeling pretty bad for a cowgirl."

LuEllen had processed both the negatives and the prints wearing vinyl gloves, and I carefully avoided touching them, even when they were dry. Photo material is notorious for picking up and preserving fingerprints. When I was done looking at them, we sealed the prints inside a plastic garbage bag and taped them to the underside of a drawer.

Marvel called every hour or so. Finally she decided she had to see us. We'd meet at the Holiday Inn, at John's room, in an hour.

She and John were waiting when we arrived.

"Not a fuckin' thing," she said, pacing the room. "Can't even find his car. What do you think?"

"He wouldn't go off by himself?"

"No, of course not," Marvel said angrily.

"Then . . . I think . . . he may be dead."

She stopped, looked at John, and a tear ran down her face. "I think so, too," she said. "They couldn't just grab him and let him go later. . . ."

"No." I turned and looked at LuEllen, and her face was like a rock.

"Oh, God." Marvel sighed. She was standing close to John, and he slipped an arm around her waist and squeezed her.

Jesus, I thought, these people trust us.

WITH NOTHING MORE TO SAY, we left Marvel to continue her search and made a pro forma stop in the bar. Bell, the city councilman, was sitting at a table with a pretty, freckled blonde. He raised a hand to us, and LuEllen waved, but we turned away, found a corner table, and ordered.

"What's next, boss?" LuEllen asked with a light overlay of sarcasm.

"Just keep cranking," I said. "But now we've

got to put a little extra on Hill and St. Thomas. Dumping the machine isn't good enough anymore."

"I don't know," she said, now serious. "When I mess with you, things seem to turn violent. Before that time in West Virginia, I don't know if I'd ever seen a killed person."

"It's not us, not me—"

"You keep saying that."

"I've got to believe it," I said.

We talked for twenty minutes, through two drinks. Two is about as many as I can take before my lips start going numb. We paid, and LuEllen waved again at Bell. Bell nodded back, tipped up his glass, finishing a drink, and dug in his pocket for cash.

We were halfway across the parking lot when two car doors slammed with the kind of aggressive impact that makes you look around. Duane Hill was there, drunk, with St. Thomas on the other side. They each had a longneck beer.

"Hey, artist fuckhead," Hill yelled, wandering toward us.

"Keep walking," LuEllen said.

But I had the two drinks in me and, instead of walking, slowed down and stopped. Hill swaggered across the parking lot from his van, St. Thomas a step or two behind him. Two guys in broad-rimmed hats and cowboy boots had been sitting on the hood of a pickup down the lot.

Now they hopped down and sidled over to watch.

"Where's that old bitch Trent? You trade her in on some younger cunt?" Hill asked.

"Fuck you, asshole," LuEllen said in a tone of pure ice. For a second Hill stopped, nonplussed. He was a brawler, tuned to danger, and he heard it in LuEllen's voice. He didn't know quite how to take it.

"Gonna let the pussy do your talking?" he said after a minute, trying to recover. He was about fifteen feet away. He half turned to the two onlookers, to catch their reaction to this witticism.

I gave him my best southern smile and got my right foot planted, slightly splayed to the right. The most dangerous man in a fight is the one who likes it the most. Watching him, I decided he'd be a grappler; he'd come storming in and try to throw me, rather than punch.

"I do hang around with nice-looking women," I said. "Mrs. Trent said you mostly hang around with some guy named Arnie."

The words hung in the air for a moment; then I leaned a little to the left, peering around him at St. Thomas, and shook my head. "Can't say I like your taste, Duane. He ain't got that much of an ass on him."

One of the cowboys let out a happy "Whoa," while Hill bellowed something unintelligible, dropped his beer, and charged, his head down, his hands out, and his legs churning. I was ready, my right foot grounded, and I whip-kicked him with my left foot, catching him on the side of the face. He went bellydown on the parking lot, landing on the blacktop like a racing driver. The fury climbed on top of me, the image of the killings, and I punted him once in the ribs, and again, as he rolled away, then pivoted toward St. Thomas. St. Thomas was an older guy, out of his fighting days. He wasn't moving, but Hill was trying to get up.

"What's going on here?" We all turned, and Bell was striding across the parking lot.

"Your town thug decided to beat me up," I said as Hill got slowly back to his feet. His nose and upper lip were bleeding heavily, the blood glistening on his teeth and dripping down his chin. He wanted to come for me again, but his ribs were holding him back. Every time he moved, the pain flared in his eyes; I'd give odds that I'd cracked a couple of his ribs.

"What about that, Duane?" Bell demanded.

One of the cowboys, with the insouciant lack of fear that seems to mark the breed, cleared his throat. "Duane sure started it," he said cheerfully. "Called the young lady there a real bad name."

Bell looked us over again and then nodded. "Y'all go home and sober up," he said. "Fightin' in a parking lot doesn't do credit to anyone. And

Duane, I'll see you at City Hall tomorrow, ten o'clock sharp. Now git."

Hill, snarling, turned away, still favoring his ribs. Bell watched him go, then nodded at LuEllen, gave me a measured look, and headed toward his car, where the blonde waited with folded arms.

"Goddamn, this country is goin' to hell in a handbasket," one of the cowboys said, taking a hit from his beer bottle. He looked me up and down, taking in my artist's getup and beard. "Somebody's gone and taught the fuckin' hippies how to fight."

13

THE NEXT MORNING Marvel asked if we could meet her at the farm home of a friend, out in the country, well away from the river and the prying eyes of Longstreet.

"It's safe and quicker than Greenville, and nobody will see your car," she said. "Half an hour?"

"I'll be there."

LuEllen again decided to stay with the boat, away from new faces.

"You gonna be here when I get back?" I asked.

"Of course," she said gravely. "I'm not leaving until we find some way to grease Hill and St. Thomas."

MARVEL'S FRIEND'S NAME was Matron Carter, a plain, cheerful woman with short hair and good moves. She was shooting basketballs at a netless hoop hung on the side of a swaybacked, free-standing garage when I pulled into her yard. Marvel's car was around back, next to a vacant chicken coop. A rusty forties-style power mower appeared to be permanently parked in knee-high grass under lilac bushes at the edge of the yard, and a pear tree and a half dozen aging apple trees marched in military file down the edge of an overgrown field.

"They're waiting for you inside," the woman said, dribbling the ball as she talked. She faked one way, turned the other, and popped a fifteen-foot jump shot.

"Nice shot," I said.

"Do it for a living," she answered, running down the ball. Marvel told me later that she was a gym teacher at Longstreet High School and coached the girls' basketball teams.

The house was tired but comfortable. I went through the back door, through a kitchen, and into a small living room, where Marvel and John were sprawled on a broken-down couch.

"Harold's dead," Marvel said. She stopped me in my tracks.

"You found him?"

"We found his car. At Wal-Mart," she said wearily. "And he's gone. I can feel it. The motherfuckers took him someplace and killed him."

Tears started running down her face, and John

said quietly, "They go back to when they were babies. They were raised together."

"Jesus Christ," I said, running my fingers through my hair. I was gripped by the temptation to tell them the truth but instead blurted, "We need the FBI in here."

"I don't," John said sharply. "I've had some problems with those boys. And we've still got to take this town. That's the main thing."

"Maybe Harold is OK. Maybe he had to take off for some reason," I said fatuously. I wandered over to a window and looked out. Matron Carter was pumping a wrought-iron water pump and drinking from the spout as the water surged out of the ground. In the dappled sunlight in the yard she looked beautiful, not plain. "Maybe they scared him and he took off for Greenville or Helena."

"And left his car at Wal-Mart?" John asked.

Marvel, turning in John's arms, shook her head. "No. He's dead. I can feel him . . . gone."

There wasn't much more to say. Marvel insisted that we keep the takeover rolling.

"Matron will be the second appointee to the council if we bring this off," Marvel said. She'd be the third.

"Can she do that? If she lives out here, outside the city . . ."

"This is her folks' place. They're gone, dead,

and nobody lives here anymore. Matron lives in town."

"OK. You can name who you want, that's your call. I'm more worried about John and your contacts at the capitol—"

"Don't worry about that. I talked to an old friend of Harold's, one of the black caucus guys. I told him Harold was missing and that it was connected to our deal. This guy is smart; he knows something's going on, and he's helping. I'll take the fucking books to the governor's man and bring back so many cops it'll look like a convention. And one way or another, on my mama's grave, we'll find Harold."

"Then we've got to set up John's part," I said. "We've got to get the bridge scam going. Get the rumors started."

"I'll start now, from here, on the phone," Marvel promised. "Two hours from now everybody in town'll know there's a rich drug dealer down here snapping up land for the bridge. . . ."

"The more I think about it, the more this sounds like bullshit," John said. "The goddamn pin-striped suit and the car and the hair—why'n the hell would they believe some strange nigger from Memphis?"

"Same reason there are a million con men working the world and making money," I said. "Greed. You're going to offer them something for almost nothing; they'll have to show you some money, but that's it. They don't have to give it to you, just show it. They don't have to put up a cent until the bridge is coming in. By that time, the profit'll be guaranteed."

"A wonderful thing, greed," Marvel said. "Where would we be without it?"

John rubbed her head. "Fuckin' Commie," he said.

WHEN I GOT BACK to the boat, LuEllen was slumped in a deck chair with two bottles of beer and a glass, looking glum. A crumpled newspaper lay at her feet.

"Get a beer," she called as I came aboard.

I got one, climbed up on top, and sank into the chair beside her.

"Pretty bad?" she asked.

"Pretty bad," I said.

"Is John gonna do his act?"

"Yeah."

She squinted up at the city beyond the levee, the brick buildings, the peaks of Victorian mansions beyond. "The place looks like a museum," she said. "It's hard to believe this is all happening. . . . Look what I found."

She handed me the newspaper, folded to an editorial. The headline said LONGSTREET, AN ISLAND OF PEACE.

"Makes you giggle, huh?" she asked sourly, tipping her bottle up.

□ □ □

THE LONGSTREET RUMOR mill was as efficient as Marvel had said it was. She made her calls and sat back, while John drove around town, made several trips out to the supposed bridge property, and talked to an engineer about soil and perc tests. Bobby phoned again on a voice line.

"I just got a call on our phone cutout about the bridge," he said. "Archibald Ballem."

"The attorney."

"Right."

"Did he buy it?" I asked.

"Yeah, I think so. I got pissed and refused to answer questions. I wanted to know where he got his information and told him the whole thing was secret. I warned him that spreading the information might damage the prospects for construction. He tried to cool me off. I don't think he'll be calling back."

"Keep monitoring the number anyway," I said.

I CALLED JOHN with the news. "They'll be coming," I said. "Be ready."

John got a second call two hours later. Archibald Ballem, a local attorney, wanted to talk to him and to bring along a couple of business associates. I thought it would be Dessusdelit and maybe St. Thomas. It was St. Thomas all right, but Ballem opted for muscle instead of brains; Hill was with them.

"They all sat real close to me," John said later. "You could feel the threat. They were pushing, and they talked about it in advance."

The meeting, John said, started with the politely inadvertent racism that southerners fall into when they want something from a black: talk about basketball, break dancing, and hip-hop. St. Thomas liked it all, to hear him tell it.

After the chitchat Ballem put the question, What about the bridge? John asked, "What bridge?"

Ballem said, "We're all businessmen here and civic leaders. Mr. St. Thomas is one of our prominent city councilmen, and I'm the city attorney, and Mr. Hill is a city department head. . . ."

That got them down to it. Permits would be no problem. Zoning could be arranged. All for the future financial progress of the city of Longstreet. "Would there be any space for more investors, Mr., ah, Johnson?"

There might be . . . but I'll have to talk to my friend in Memphis. . . .

"They bought it all right," John said. He was with Marvel and Brooking Davis, and I could hear them talking in the background. "They were so hungry they were drooling on my fuckin' wing tips."

"OK. So do a little back and forth. If they don't call you, you call them to check on things. Talk about a Delaware company. They know about Delaware companies."

"I already started hinting about money. Let them know that they won't get in cheap, that the project's too big. . . ."

"Anything about Harold?" I asked.

"No, and there's something else . . . let me put Marvel on."

She took the phone and said, "Something else, I can't stand it. There's a rumor that Harold went off to Memphis with Sherrie. I don't believe it for a second."

"Is she missing? Sherrie?" I was afraid the fraud was audible in my voice. If it was, she didn't hear it.

"Can't find her," Marvel said. "I was supposed to warn her against going to work, but I was with John, and shit . . . I forgot. Fuck me, I forgot." There was a tone of finality in her voice, with an undertone of bitter anger.

"Jesus, *forgot*?" And now Sherrie was dead. I wanted to shout at her but I couldn't. "There's no chance that they did go off?" I was floundering, trying to react the right way, when I didn't feel any of it. I had already reacted to the murders the moment that I saw them and this, now, was just playacting, deceiving a woman I liked.

"No!" She almost shouted it. "What do you think they are?"

"Marvel, I don't know what to tell you. I didn't see this coming."

"Neither did I." She sighed. "We should have known. We're playing with fire."

"Keep hoping," I suggested. "Maybe . . . I don't know . . . Look: Let me talk to John again."

John came back on the phone. "Yeah?"

"Listen, if something was done to Harold and the woman . . . This Hill guy, the guy who came to see you with Ballem, is the town muscle. He's nuts, I think—a psycho. You can take care of yourself, but there's Marvel now, and her friends. People in town must know she was tight with Harold. . . ."

"I've got some people coming down from Memphis," John said. "Don't worry about us, and don't worry about what Duane Hill might do. If he gives us any shit, Duane'll need a new head."

JOHN TALKED to Ballem again the next morning, and this time Dessusdelit sat in.

"Like a crow," John said. "She sat there with her head bobbing up and down, like she was pecking on me."

John had parked the white BMW on the street outside the lawyer's office, where everybody might have a chance to look it over. In his time as an underground activist in Memphis, he'd picked up the language of municipal development; the three of them, John said, had an intense discussion of tax increment financing. When he left, Ballem was seeking references to TI financing in the state statutes.

They were excited, he said, but something else, too.

"This Dessusdelit woman, man, she looks fucked up. I mean, she looked a little crazy. Are you sure she's all right?"

"She always seemed wrapped a little *too* tight, if anything," I said.

"Not now," John said. "She looked frazzled."

John went to Memphis, more for show than anything, and returned to the Holiday Inn Friday morning, as Marvel was leaving for the capital. LuEllen sat in the Coffee Klatch Café across from the City Hall, watching the City Hall and prowling the adjacent stores. I was on the boat alone when Dessusdelit showed up. John was right: She seemed to be coming undone and asked if I was in the mind to do a reading.

"Guess I could," I said. "LuEllen's not here, she's up in town shopping—"

"I simply would like to see what the cards say." She was on the dock, and I was on top of the cabin, looking down. She was gray-faced, haggard. In the cabin I got out the deck, shuffled the cards, and pushed them across at her. She shuffled a dozen times, pushed them back.

"Cut?"

She hesitated, nibbling her lip, and finally cut.

The cards rolled out, and as happens in most tarot readings, there was no clear, dramatic direction. What the cards said was more subtle than that. The Five of Pentacles—sometimes interpreted as a poverty card—popped up, and her sharp intake of breath indicated that she knew what it was.

"Remember that everything is relative, and the cards have a hard time dealing with relativity," I told her. "I could roll the Five of Pentacles for a Rockefeller, and it might mean that he'd be cut back to his last billion."

"It's so much different from the last time," she said in a small voice, seeming almost lost.

The last card to come up was one of the major arcana, the High Priestess. I was startled but kept my face straight and started picking the spread apart.

"There's a secret," I concluded, tapping the High Priestess. "I don't know whether you have a secret or somebody has a secret they're hiding from you. But if the secret comes out, there'll be terrible problems. You can see how that influence in the High Priestess cuts right back to the Five of Pentacles, the loss card, the poverty card."

She was becoming increasingly agitated, clutching a wadded Kleenex in her fist, her knuckles white as marble.

"Is it going to come out?"

I shrugged. "I can't see that."

"Can we do another spread?"

I shook my head. "If you do too many, the influences tend to get mixed up. If you'd like a really good reading . . ."

"Yes?"

"Focus on a question. You don't even have to tell me what it is. But focus, spend the day and the night thinking about it, and come back tomorrow morning. Then we'll take out the cards, and we'll see if we can do something more definitive."

Her head jerked in assent. "Tomorrow," she said, getting up.

"Sure. But focus. We need that psychic energy."

"And you think we'll get something definitive."

"Uh, wait a minute." I scratched my chin. "Look, you've been awful nice to us, and I'm sure LuEllen wouldn't mind. . . ."

I got the crystal ball in its velvet sleeve and handed it to her. "Spend some time tonight, staring into it. Use it to focus; remember what the cards did to the crystal the last time? That can work in reverse. Focus tonight, and tomorrow we'll read."

"If you think LuEllen wouldn't mind . . ."

"Not at all," I said as I held the door for her, "and I'm sure it'll give us a much clearer look with the cards." As sure as a stacked deck could make it.

LuEllen was coming down the levee wall as Dessusdelit left, and they stopped and talked for a second before Dessusdelit went on.

"You loaned her the ball?" LuEllen asked as she stepped off the dock onto the boat.

"She's coming back tomorrow for a reading," I said. "I wanted an explanation for what the cards are going to do."

"She's shook up," LuEllen said. We both looked after the mayor. "Maybe she's got a conscience."

"I think she's mostly scared. The last time she was here, she had all this opportunity showing up. We just did a spread and got some very peculiar cards. Not nearly so happy."

"How'd you manage that?" LuEllen asked.

"I didn't. They just came up," I said uneasily. The cards sometimes make you nervous even if you don't believe in them. I changed the subject. "What'd you figure out?"

"We're in luck," LuEllen said. "That hardware store next to the City Hall has aluminum extension ladders."

"Say what?"

247

□ □ □

JOHN CALLED. When he returned from Memphis, he'd phoned Ballem and said he'd talked to the Man. The Man didn't mind some discreet, well-placed partners, but they wouldn't get in for free, even with the clout they could provide from City Hall.

The Man wanted a two-hundred-thousand-dollar investment, cash money: no checks, no stamps. And John had to see a piece of the money now. Half. A hundred thousand.

"I told them that my friend was used to dealing in cash, that it was a personal peculiarity," John drawled, still in character. "And I told them that he'd spent so many years dealing with bullshit artists he now insisted that one of his people actually see some cash up front, before any deals were made."

"They bought it?"

"Yeah. They think it's weird, but they figure I'm a dealer, which kind of explains some of it, in their eyes. We're meeting at the City Hall, quarter after nine. Ballem will be at the door to let me in."

"Why so late?"

"So it'll be dark. I asked, and they said they'd just as soon not have a lot of noticeable people getting together with me. And there was a hint there, you know, that I'd better stay in line. That there'd be a half dozen of them, and they wouldn't let in anybody but me."

"All right. Take a good look at whatever they're carrying the money in. Try to figure out if they'll leave it in the safe."

"Yeah, yeah. I'll do all that. Marvel called from the capital; she's all set. She's talked to the governor's man, and he'll see her anytime up to midnight. She'll go as soon as we call her."

"You be careful, man."

"Yeah. You, too."

AT NINE O'CLOCK LuEllen went back to the sleeping cabin and clattered around. After a minute she made a low, groaning sound and I stepped back. She was leaning against the cabin way, her eyes closed, her head cocked back.

"Not a fuckin' word," she said.

She did two more hits in the next half hour, while we waited. She was flying when John called.

"They had it, and it's in the safe, just like we figured. The safe was already open a crack. The city clerk was there, Wells, with Ballem and Dessusdelit and Hill."

"St. Thomas wasn't there?"

"No. Just those four. I went up the block to the Mobil station to use the telephone, and all four of them came out together, so they're gone. The money's in a bank bag, and they weren't carrying it when they came out."

"We'll take it from here then," I said.

"Good luck."

LuEllen is a great burglar for a lot of reasons, but the most important reason is her will to act. LuEllen can do outrageous things because she has the will to do them.

"I wouldn't take you, except I don't know what I'll have to go through inside. I might need some muscle to handle a ladder or get up on the roof," she told me as she selected the tools she'd take along.

"I'd worry," I said.

"I know." She pecked me on the cheek, checked her tools one last time, and we went.

The City Hall was effectively two and a half stories tall. The basement had windows at ground level, and the first floor was up a short flight of steps. The main doors were standard steel and glass jobs. LuEllen could open them any number of ways, but she'd be doing it in full view of the street, and illegal entry isn't always the quietest activity. That was out.

The back of the City Hall was also the entrance to the police department. There were eight cops on duty on Friday night, three pairs in squad cars, and manning the desk and a holding cell. We wouldn't be going in from that side.

The City Hall was on a corner, with only one side flanked by another building. That building was the hardware store, and it was a half story shorter than the City Hall. The two were separated by a ten-foot-wide strip of grass. A tree stood on the front lawn, its canopy blocking a front view of the roofline between the buildings.

The hardware store had a deep doorway at street level. The lock would be easy, LuEllen said. It was loose enough that we might be able to pry back the jamb and slip in without breaking it. Neither the hardware store nor the building across the street had second-floor apartments.

"I 'scoped them out," she said as we headed downtown. "The second floor across the street is a storage loft for a plumber, so nobody'll be watching from there. The second floor on the hardware store is a stockroom and an office. I don't know exactly where the roof access is, but there has to be one."

It was a hot night. We dumped the car on a side street two blocks from the City Hall and walked down the dark street, our arms touching, looking for other walkers. Nobody.

"Coming up," she said as we got close. She passed me a pair of flesh-colored latex gloves, the disposable kind intended to prevent dishpan hands. I pulled them on, and she dipped into her shoulder bag and took out a pipe, keeping it

against the leg away from the street. There was a
steel pry bar inside it. The pipe could be used as
an extension, for more leverage.

"You're sure this'll work?" A great time to ask,
I thought as the words came out.

"It should," she said. She slowed to look in the
window of an office equipment store and then
into the hardware store. The store was dark.
With a last glance around, we stepped into the
doorway like lovers looking for a moment of privacy. She slipped the bar between the lock plate
and the jamb, pulled the pipe out for leverage,
and pressed. "Push the door."

I pushed the door with the heel of my hand,
and the door hit the lock.

"Again," she said. She pressed her weight
against the pipe, and I pushed again, hard. The
doorjamb scraped and popped open. We were in.
"Hello?" LuEllen called. "Is anybody here?"

Not a sound, which was good. If anyone had
answered, I'd have had a heart attack. LuEllen
shut the door, grabbed the front of my shirt,
and led me down the aisles of the dark store, all
the way to the back.

"Stairs," she muttered. She stepped into the
stairwell, flicked on a pocket light, and led the
way up. On the first floor there had been a little
light, coming through the windows from the
street. Except for the flash, the second floor was
dark as a coal sack. At the top of the stairs we

turned left, toward the back, and stopped at a green door that looked as though it were painted in place.

"Gotta be it," she said. She tried the knob, found it unlocked, and pulled the door open. A short, steep flight of stairs led to a roof hatch. There were stacks of advertising booklets and old newspapers on the steps, covered with dust, and we stepped carefully around them as we went up. The hatch was secured by two simple hooks. She flipped them off, pushed the hatch up an inch or so, scanned the rooftop, then shoved it all the way off and we climbed through.

"Keep low," she said. We crept across the tarpaper and gravel roof to the parapet. The City Hall was ten feet away, and the top was eight to ten feet above us. The windows facing us were dark. LuEllen crawled along the parapet, looking at the buildings opposite, checking lines of sight.

"What do you think?" I whispered when she came back.

"We can do it, but if there's anybody on one of these other buildings, cooling off, we could be fucked," she whispered back. "No help for that, though. Let's get the ladder."

We went back down to the first floor and found an aluminum extension ladder. I carried it to the base of the stairs while LuEllen found a package of nylon anchor rope. Then I took one end of the ladder, and she took the other, and we went back up.

"What's the rope for?" I asked.

"We're pretty exposed. If somebody comes after us, there's the outside chance that we could tie the rope around one of the chimneys and go over the offside of the building and run."

"Yeah. Right."

"Hey. I've never done time—"

"OK."

On the roof we sat quietly, listening for voices and looking for lights on adjacent buildings. All we heard were the different hums of the streetlights and a thousand air conditioners. All we saw was a car roll past, its windows up. We wouldn't be visible from the street; the tree covered us on the front side. We would be visible from a cop car rolling down the alley.

After ten minutes we'd heard nothing, and LuEllen touched my arm. "Let's go." We unfolded the ladder, propped it against the top of the City Hall. LuEllen sat on the hardware store roof, her heels against the bottom rung of the ladder; she'd hold it in place while I crossed. After a last look down the alley, checking against police cars, I crossed. It was about as difficult as climbing a ladder to wash a window, as long as I didn't look down. . . .

I hopped onto the roof of the City Hall, treading lightly, and braced the ladder while LuEllen crossed. She moved like a cat, covering the gap in two or three seconds. I pulled the ladder across and laid it flat on the roof. We waited another minute, listening. Nothing. LuEllen crossed to the chimney, wrapped the rope around it, tied it, and left it lying in a heap. If we needed it, it would be ready.

Unlike the hardware store, the City Hall had a full-size door at the top, its housing sticking out of the roof like a wedge. LuEllen tried the knob, found it locked, and dug in her bag.

"Problem?"

"Naw, it's one of those old warded pieces of shit." She used what looked like two lengths of clothes hanger wire and opened it in fifteen seconds. The stairs were built in a steep spiral, narrow and dark.

"Wait until I call," she muttered. Wooden steps creak; they always creak, it's another of the basic laws of nature. She went down them slowly, her feet spread to the far edges of each step. There wasn't a sound. At the bottom she listened again, opened the door, peeked out, and called me down. I went down as quietly as I could; in my ears it sounded as if I'd stumbled through the cymbal section of the New York Philharmonic.

"We're in some kind of closet," she said. She had pushed the door open about three or four

inches; a filing cabinet blocked it from opening
farther. Worse, the filing cabinet was jammed
against another wall. I reached through, grabbed
the top of the cabinet, and tried to pull it farther
into the closet. It wouldn't budge.

"Now what?" I asked.

"Take the door off," she said. She found the
pry bar in her sack and pulled the pins from the
two hinges. We had to do some dancing, but
eventually we got the door off and enough out of
the way that I could boost her up on top of the
file cabinet. The door to the closet was also
locked.

"Pain in the ass," she whispered as she worked
on it. "If we want to close them all again . . ."
She was working blind on the closet lock, reaching down from the top of the file. After a couple
of curse words the bolt slipped, and she eased the
door open.

"Whoa," she said.

"What?"

She turned back and shone the light on her
own face. She was grinning.

"We're *inside* the clerk's office," she whispered.

"You want me to come?"

"No point."

She climbed down off the cabinet into the
clerk's office. I pushed myself up on top of
the cabinet, craning my neck until I could see.
She went straight to the safe, sat for a moment,

listening and watching the glass doors to the outer building, then stood, flicked on the light, and started working the combination dial. She hit on the third try, and the heavy door swung open. She spent a moment pulling drawers, dropped a white canvas sack behind her, pushed the door shut, twirled the dial, and came back to the closet. It took as long to lock the closet door as it had to open it. It took only a minute to put the stairway door back on and another minute to lock the door at the top.

"Got it," she breathed at me. "Jesus, stealing is better than fucking, you know?"

"Thanks," I said dryly.

"You know what I mean. . . ." Her voice sounded full, awash with adrenaline or some kind of special burglar hormone. We listened for another minute, heard nothing but LuEllen's breathing. Then she retrieved the rope; we recrossed the ladder and took it back into the store, hooking the hatch behind us.

"This is the worst," she said when we were at the front of the store. "This is where we really could get caught again."

"I haven't seen any cocaine," I said. The thought had just popped into my head, from nowhere.

"I thought I'd try it this way, doesn't feel too bad."

"So . . ."

"I still want it."

"That's the way it is, I guess." I slipped two fingers under her belt buckle and pulled her up against me. "You're more interesting without the coke."

She stood up on her tiptoes and kissed me on the lips, and it went on for a bit.

"This *is* goofy," she said, pulling away. "This is how you get caught. You forget for a minute. . . ."

We'd be going back out into the street blind. A car rolled by. We were ready to go when the lights from a second one showed. It passed, and we went. Outside, she used the pry bar to slip the lock in place, dropped the bar in her shoulder sack, and we were on the sidewalk.

I put my arms around her, and she pressed her head against my shoulder. Lovers, again, walking in the moonlight. We stopped once on the street before we turned down toward the car, to kiss and, incidentally, to drop the latex gloves in a brand-new Longstreet storm sewer.

JOHN WAS waiting for the call.

"You going?" he asked.

"Just got back," I said. I looked at LuEllen, who was stacking packets of twenty-dollar bills on the kitchen table. "It was smooth as silk."

"Jesus Christ, I'm starting to think Bobby was

right about you guys," John said. "I'll call Marvel. I'll send her in."

"I'll call her," I said. "There've been some changes. I think I've figured out how it'll go, all the way to the end."

14

WE HAD TAKEN out one hundred thousand dollars in cash. After counting it, we put it back in the bag and stuck the bag in the *Fanny*'s engine compartment, where it would be safe from accidental discovery. The boat was now a floating time bomb; on board we had LuEllen's burglary tools, the books from the Longstreet machine, a hundred thousand dollars in stolen city cash, and the murder photos.

DESSUSDELIT ARRIVED PROMPTLY at ten o'clock, and we cold-decked her. I almost, but not quite, felt sorry for her. She was as nervous as a hen, settling into the querant's chair with a series of twitches and unconscious starts. She'd been up all night, rolling the crystal ball in her hands. The ball had been dead, she said as she handed it back to LuEllen, except for a few moments around three in the morning. For a few seconds then she thought she saw her mother again.

"She seemed to be welcoming me," Dessusdelit said bleakly.

"Maybe that means you're going to visit her," LuEllen suggested ingenuously.

"She's dead," Dessusdelit snapped. "I thought I told you."

"Oh . . . I'm sorry," LuEllen said, covering her mouth in embarrassment.

We shuffled the cards, and Dessusdelit cut them. LuEllen reached out and touched her arm and said, "You can keep the ball for a while if that will help you reestablish a channel. . . ."

When Dessusdelit turned her head to reply, I switched the decks and started laying down the Celtic Cross. Out came the Tower or, as some tarots have it, the Tower of Destruction, symbolic of the wrath of God. The card shows a medieval tower struck by a lightning bolt, with two people tumbling out of it.

"Things seem to be stirred up," I said as Dessusdelit turned back. I tried to put the best face on it but let enough sickly kindness ooze into my voice that she had to know what I was doing.

Her mouth opened and closed a couple of times, and finally she blurted, "I've had some personal difficulties."

"That's what we're seeing then. But remember, the Tower doesn't always mean disaster," I continued with a patently false heartiness. "Remember when I told you that sometimes it's as simple as looking at the picture? One time I had an opening scheduled for a Chicago gallery. For me it was a big deal. I don't usually do the magical kind of tarot spreads, but I was worried about this opening; my career was in the balance. So I said, what the heck and did a spread—"

"And the Tower came up?" she asked eagerly. She was looking for reassurance, and since I had obviously survived the Tower . . .

"Exactly. Well, you can imagine how I felt. I even considered canceling the opening. But that was ridiculous. I couldn't do it. Food had been ordered, and wine. There were dozens of invitations out, including to the newspaper critics. Besides, I kept telling myself, it was just superstition—"

"What happened at the opening?" she asked, cutting me short.

"At the opening? Nothing. It went wonderfully." She allowed herself a small smile. "But *before* the opening . . . well, the question I had asked the cards was, 'How will my day go tomorrow?' Thinking, of course, about the opening. And I got the Tower. The next day I was eating breakfast, English muffins with orange marmalade. I was using a toaster to toast the muffins, and one got stuck and started to burn. When I thought about it later, I knew I'd been blindly stupid, but I wasn't thinking at the time. What I did was, I used a table knife to try to pry the muffin out. I got a terrific shock. Threw me across the room. My arm and hand spasmed for days."

Dessusdelit's smile slowly died.

"Everything was fine with the opening. The Tower was simply a picture that portrayed something that would happen to me. The card shows a lightning bolt, like the electricity in the toaster. I damn near electrocuted myself."

As I said that, the blood drained from her face. The state had the electric chair, and after Harold and Sherrie, it must have been on her mind.

"Could I look at your ball again?" she stuttered at LuEllen.

"Sure." LuEllen got it from its bag, and Dessusdelit rolled it through her hands. Nothing.

"No color," Dessusdelit said.

"Maybe things just aren't right," LuEllen said. "You've got to be able to focus. If you can't focus your mind, the ball won't have anything to react to."

"Goddamn," Dessusdelit muttered. I nearly dropped the cards, and LuEllen sat back, surprised. Dessusdelit's bony hands clenched on the table in front of her. Her mouth was running as though she were speaking in tongues. "We've got these goddamn niggers in town, goddamn nigger bitch, ruining it for ever'one, ruinin' ever'thing. Started happening when that shitheel dickhead cop shot that nigger kid trash fuckin' coon down on the tracks. . . ."

She rambled on insanely for a moment, then seemed to run down. She sat for another few seconds, staring blindly at her hands, then suddenly stood and walked out.

LuEllen followed her to the door, said, quietly, "Take care of yourself, Chenille," and watched her go up the levee wall. Over her shoulder she said, "The fuckin' mayor's cracked, Kidd. We cracked her open like a fuckin' egg. And it's amazing what leaked out, was it not?"

"First-degree murder ain't shoplifting," I said.

DESSUSDELIT LEFT around ten-thirty. At noon the state attorney general's auditors hit the town like the great flood of '27. They came in a convoy, six plain brown government cars and three state police cruisers. LuEllen and I were eating cheeseburgers at Humdinger's when they went by.

"The cavalry," LuEllen muttered over her chicken noodle soup.

"Too late for Harold," I said. "C'mon, let's go."

"Where to?"

"That hardware store we hit last night. I saw some really big magnets in there."

JOHN HAD TAKEN the BMW back to Memphis the night before and dropped it at the dealership where he'd rented it. After catching a couple of hours of sleep, he drove back to Longstreet in his

own car. He was hiding out at Marvel's, a non-
person, cleanly shaved, what little hair he had
cropped to a stubble, carefully wearing faded
jeans, old T-shirts, and ragged tennis shoes. He
looked nothing like the slick Mr. Johnson from
Memphis. If anybody made that connection, we
were sunk.

JUST AFTER NIGHTFALL LuEllen and I turned a corner downtown, John's Chevy stopped beside us,
and we climbed in back.

"Is Marvel back?"

"No, but she should be anytime now. She's
stopping at a friend's place—the cleaning lady at
the City Hall, Becka Clay. Becka was there this
afternoon when the state police came in."

"What happened with the governor? Marvel
took a long time."

"The usual bullshit. He wouldn't deal directly,
but he had to approve every little detail, so his
hatchet man was running back and forth like a
trolley car. By the way, when I talked to her on
the phone, she said you wanted Hill and Ballem
appointed to the city council, along with our
man?"

"Yeah."

"Why the change?"

"We figure if Harold is dead, Hill did it," I
said. "If Hill and Ballem are appointed along
with our guy, then we tip the state cops to the

computer out at animal control. They'll go in, grab the computer, find the books, and this time they'll include Ballem and Hill. Marvel can supply the state people with the code words I fixed in the machine. . . . And as soon as the state guys go in, Hill and Ballem both get anonymous calls. A woman, I think. Somebody who can do a white-southern-lady accent. She calls them up, says she knows Hill killed Harold and says she doesn't want to turn in a white man for killing a colored, but she doesn't want killers running the city either. So they have a choice: Quit or burn. They'll know that the cops have the books, so their council seats are probably gone anyway. When the woman calls . . . why would they fight it? They'll go."

John grinned. He liked it. "A little racist judo," he said. Then he frowned. " 'Course, if Hill didn't do it, he's gonna freak out."

"He did," I said shortly. John gave me an odd look, and I shrugged. "The tarot says so."

Marvel came in twenty minutes after we got to her house. She looked exhausted but determined.

"Harold?" she asked John. John shook his head, took her by the elbow, and led her to the couch.

"How'd it go?" I asked.

"The deal's done," she said. "The governor will appoint Hill, Ballem, and Brooking Davis just as soon as Dessusdelit, St. Thomas, and Rebeck quit."

"What if they don't quit?" John asked.

Marvel shrugged. "I don't see how they can avoid it. Becka fixed it so she was cleaning the second-floor toilets when the state people arrived. Wells and Dessusdelit were there. She said they went straight to the safe, opened it, and didn't find any money. She said Wells sat down right in the middle of the floor and started to bawl. Dessusdelit was talking about a lawyer."

"Did you talk to the newspaper?"

"Yeah. I called the managing editor, anonymously, and told him what happened—the missing money from the bank. I told him the TV was on to it, too. I told him I was with the state and wanted the word to get out before it could be covered up. He freaked out. He said he'd talk to the head auditor and confirm it. Then I called the TV and told them the same thing."

We sat and looked at each other for a moment. Then she said, "That should do it; I don't know what else we can do."

THE TELEVISION RESPONSE was disappointing. The local station's ten o'clock news mentioned that state officials were doing an audit of the city's books. "There are unconfirmed rumors circulating that some funds have been improperly transferred between accounts," the anchorman said with a fairly puzzled air. A reporter talked to St. Thomas outside his house, but St. Thomas, standing in a pool of TV light, claimed he'd been on the river, fishing, and knew nothing about it. Dessusdelit refused to comment.

At one o'clock John called.

"Drive up to the E-Z Way and get yourself a newspaper," he said. "Better hurry before they're gone."

There were four left when we got there. Elvis, the counterman, shook his head and allowed how the papers were selling like rubbers at an AIDS convention.

The paper led with the story, reporting virtually word for word what Marvel had told them. A hundred thousand dollars were missing from the bank. The state people wouldn't confirm it but didn't deny it, either, given several chances.

I called Bobby on a voice line.

"This has got to be between you and me and LuEllen," I said. "John's not to know, or Marvel. If you can't handle that, I'll go some other way."

He thought for a moment and then said, "Will it hurt them?"

"No," I said. "Their feelings would be hurt not to know, but they don't really need to know. In fact, if they did, they might do something that would hurt all of us. Especially Marvel—and John's in bed with her now."

"All right," he said after another minute. "You and me."

"You know Harold's gone missing?"

"Yeah."

"Hill killed him. And the Sherrie woman."

Bobby whistled. "For sure?"

"For sure. Put their bodies in the river. I need you to do two things. First of all, I need you to call Dessusdelit. You should tell her that you know Harold was at her house and you know what he was doing there. Tell her that you know that Hill took him away in the van and that Hill killed Harold and Sherrie. Tell her you know that she was in on it. Tell her she ought to quit the city council anyway, but if she doesn't, along with St. Thomas and Carl Rebeck, you're gonna turn her in. Mention the electric chair. Tell her you want her to quit Monday morning with the others."

"You want me to call her right now?"

"Right now. Shake her out of bed."

"All right. What's the other thing you need?"

"The Army Corps of Engineers runs computer models of the Mississippi on all kinds of things."

"Yeah?"

"I want you to get into their data base in St. Louis, or maybe it's down at Vicksburg, whatever, and run a model on a body dumped into the river just below Longstreet. See where it'd get in a week."

□ □ □

SUNDAY.

I had the feeling that mobs should be in the street with torches, storming the castle gates. But Dessusdelit didn't live in a castle; she lived in a rambler. And instead of mobs in the street, we got church bells from three different directions. I sat on the upper deck and sketched, while LuEllen would pace the cabin, come up and sunbathe for a while, then go below and pace some more. Halfway through the afternoon we both started drinking gin and tonics and got mostly in the bag, something we rarely do.

With our blood alcohol levels about as high as they get, we had a wonderful idea. We talked about it for a few minutes. Then we went below and called Rebeck's house. His wife answered.

"I gotta talk to Carl," I said urgently.

"Can I ask what this concerns?" The voice of a politician's wife.

"Well, uh, I just been talking to one of them state boys," I bumbled. "You better tell Carl to get his ass on this telephone, this is important."

Rebeck picked up an extension a minute later. "Yes?"

"Carl, I don't want to say who this is 'cause I could get in trouble myself. But you know me, and I know you, and I'm here to tell you, those state boys have got more than some money shuffled around. Somebody's got themself hurt. I don't know who, but they got homicide investigators comin' in. If I was you, I'd go have a talk with them state folks. Maybe you can get out while the gettin' is good. . . ."

"What—" he started, but I hung up.

"There," I said drunkenly, "that'll fix things."

"You need another gin and tonic," LuEllen said, and we fell around the inside of the cabin, laughing about Rebeck.

AT FOUR O'CLOCK Bobby dumped to the computer and tapped the alarm. By that time we were sobering up, and the call to Rebeck no longer seemed like such a good idea.

"What the fuck were we doing?" LuEllen moaned.

"Shit, it'll be OK," I said, grimacing. I hadn't gotten loaded in two years.

When I brought up Bobby's file, I found a series of calculations based on current, channel shape, and flow that suggested that the bodies would be anywhere from three to twenty-five miles downstream. He listed a series of probabilities for each location but warned that "the bodies could have gotten hung up on something two minutes after they went in the water and maybe went nowhere."

On the other thing, he said, "I did Dessusdelit."

"Fuck it," I said to LuEllen as I crawled back up the ladder. "Let's go out on the water."

The marina operator was reseating planks at the end of the dock, working with a power drill, a couple of crescent wrenches, and a stack of two-by-sixes. LuEllen waved to him, glass in hand, as we went out, and he waved back with his own beer bottle.

We headed south past the warehouses, elevators, and the tank field, past animal control. There was nobody in sight at the complex, and at the revetment, where Hill and St. Thomas had dumped the bodies in the water, I put LuEllen ashore. She jogged up the levee path, watching the weeds for snakes, and peeked at animal control. Nobody home.

She came back, and we examined the last of the murder photos, the shot of Hill throwing the pistol into the river. I had no idea how much the lazy current would deflect something as heavy as a pistol, so we anchored ten feet above where it had gone in the water and began working with the magnet. LuEllen didn't have a great deal of faith in the possibility of finding it. I thought it was mostly a matter of patience.

I was using a muskie rod to cast with, with the magnet tied on instead of a lure. The magnet was heavy, but if I got my shoulders into it, I could toss it twenty-five or thirty feet downstream and then crank it back upstream to the boat.

And I found the pistol, just about the time my arms started to tighten up. There was a clank transmitted through the rod, and I said, "Whoops," and gave the rod to LuEllen and went back and eased up on the anchor. When we had the line running pretty much straight up and down, I slowly retrieved it. It was a .45. A good old government model from Colt. I detached the gun from the magnet, cut the magnet from the line, and threw it overboard.

"Why'd you do that?" LuEllen asked.

"I hate magnets. Damn dangerous things, around computers and software."

We spent another hour poking along to the south, scanning the banks for any sign of a shirt. Bobby's note said the shirt was what we'd see, since the decomposition gases gathered in the abdominal and chest cavities.

Nothing. I cleaned the gun as we went along, lubricated it with some WD-40, and put it back together. Good as ever. Some people like guns, some people don't, but you can't deny their quality as machines.

We hid the pistol with the money bag, down in the engine compartment; as the sun went down, we turned the *Fanny*'s nose upstream and headed back. Five minutes after we arrived at the marina, Marvel called.

"They're going to quit," she exulted. "It's all over town. They had a meeting at Dessusdelit's house, and St. Thomas went home and told his wife. They're out of here."

□ □ □

ON MONDAY Dessusdelit called at nine-fifteen. I was still asleep, and LuEllen crawled over me to answer the phone, then handed it over.

"I'm ... I really need ... some help. Would it be ... could you come to the City Hall, my office? And bring your tarot?" She sounded ragged, desperate.

"Now?"

"Yes. Right away. You'll have to hurry. I've got a meeting at ten."

We took quick showers, then grabbed my tarot and LuEllen's crystal ball and drove up to the City Hall. Dessusdelit's office was in the city council suite. There was a secretary's desk in an outer office, a conference room, then a series of four closet-size offices for the councilmen, and a double-size closet for the mayor. A dozen people milled around the ground floor, outside the council meeting chambers, and a couple more slouched against the walls in the council's outer office.

The harried secretary said, "Mr. Kidd?" as soon as we walked in, and ushered us through to Dessusdelit's office. Dessusdelit was with one of those young-old people you find in corners around city halls, a guy maybe twenty-five, who'd seen fifty years' worth of corruption and showed it in the weary, overly wise crinkles around his eyes.

As tired as he looked, Dessusdelit looked
worse. She'd aged ten years in two days. She'd
tried to cover her distress with makeup, but now
she looked like a painted puppet.

"Could you excuse us for a minute, Robert?"
she asked the young-old guy. "I have to talk to
these folks privately for a few minutes."

"What's happening?" I asked. "I saw the
papers. . . ."

"There's been a serious problem," she answered. She glanced at her watch. "I have a question about your tarot. Must I ask you a question?
Explicitly? Or can I just hold the deck and *think*
a question?"

"You can do it either way," I said. "A lot of tarot readers don't believe the question should ever
be spoken. I think it clarifies a reading, but no,
you don't have to speak it."

"I'd like to try it that way if we could."

We couldn't cold-deck her, so I simply took the
deck out of its box, unwrapped it, shuffled a few
times, passed it to her, and had her go through
the routine. She might be asking any of a number
of questions: Should I quit the council? Where did
the hundred thousand go? Will the murders be
found out?

"You know, stress can twist a reading," I said
conversationally as she shuffled the cards.
"Maybe we should wait until you're a little more
relaxed. . . ."

She stopped shuffling long enough to glance at her watch and shook her head. "No. It has to be before the meeting."

So. It had to do with the meeting. That most likely meant that she was asking whether she should quit, although I couldn't be sure how she would formulate the question.

"Don't try to formulate a precise question. Just let your mind settle on a situation, and let's see what the cards have to say about it. They're really not best for yes or no answers."

I rolled the cards out. We got a spread that could have meant a lot of things. Her eyes darted around like a bird's looking for a worm, past the Three of Swords, a deadly card, to the Nine of Pentacles, a card suggesting attainment, and finally settled on the Hanged Man. I tapped the card with my index finger.

"This is the key," I said in my most portentous voice. "It stands for sacrifice, giving up something held dear, to clear the way for greater gains in life. This is what I call a forked reading because you can see that the possible futures"—I tapped the Three of Swords and the Nine of Pentacles— "are wildly split. You're at the crux of a situation. If you make the sacrifice, the road leads to the Nine. If you don't, it leads to the Three."

The Three shows three swords driven through a red heart, a card of sorrow and loss.

"I see," she said softly. She swiveled in her

chair and looked out the window. LuEllen rolled
the crystal ball out of its velvet sack and passed it
to her.

"Look inside, focus on yourself," LuEllen said.

Dessusdelit rolled the heavy ball in her hands,
moving it into the light from the window. "So
much inside," she said almost dreamily.   .

She sat like that for a moment, then turned and
said, "Thank you."

We were dismissed. "Is this meeting open?" I
asked as we went out.

"Yes. All meetings are open. But I'm afraid it
won't be a happy one."

By the time we left Dessusdelit's office, a few
minutes before ten o'clock, the council chambers
were packed. We were standing in the hallway,
looking over the heads of the crowd, when an argument blew up down the hallway. Carl Rebeck,
wearing a suit and sunglasses and escorted by a
state trooper, was standing nose to nose with
Duane Hill. I hadn't seen Hill come in, but he had
apparently been waiting for Rebeck.

"What the fuck are you doin', Carl?" Hill
blurted. The trooper moved between the two
men.

"I just wanna go vote and have it done with,"
Rebeck said, staying in the shadow of the cop.
The cop had one hand on Hill's chest, but Hill
kept peering around him.

"You gotta come talk to us, Carl. You don't

wanna be listening to a bunch of bullshit put out by these piss-ant state jerk-offs," Hill said, his voice rising almost to a shout.

The state trooper, who wore mirrored glasses and had a face like the sharp side of a hatchet, said something to Hill and shoved. Hill gave a step, and Rebeck slid past with the cop.

"Maybe it wasn't a bad idea, calling Rebeck," LuEllen muttered.

The argument in the hall had pulled some of the crowd out of the meeting room, and we managed to push inside. Marvel and two men were sitting toward the back, to the right. We went to the left and stood against the wall. The meeting started twenty minutes later. Lucius Bell showed up right on time and took a seat, looking around expectantly. The Reverend Mr. Dodge, wearing a dark suit with an ecclesiastical collar, showed up a couple of minutes later, carrying a sheaf of papers, and sat at the opposite end of the curved council table. Even from where we were standing, you could see his collar was soaked with sweat.

Dessusdelit, St. Thomas, and Rebeck came in a few moments later and settled behind the table. There was no talking. Dessusdelit pounded a gavel twice, called the meeting to order, told Mary Wells to turn on her tape recorder, and started.

Money was missing, she said, taken in the night from the City Hall safe. It had been withdrawn from the bank with the approval of herself, St. Thomas, and Rebeck as a test of the bank's and the city's accounting procedures. Now it was gone, and there was a state investigation. They were innocent of any wrongdoing and were sure that the state would find it so.

Further, she said, there were unfounded allegations that other funds had been diverted. Again, these were allegations from a small minority and had been given undue weight by state investigators. They also would be proved false.

"It now seems clear, however, that I, Mr. St. Thomas, and Mr. Rebeck will have a full schedule simply demonstrating to the state that these charges are incorrect. Therefore, we feel we have no option but to leave the council, at least for the time being. We all look forward to running again in the fall if, by the grace of our Lord, the state has realized the falseness of these allegations. . . ."

Dessusdelit seemed to be holding up well, after the near breakdown we'd seen on the boat. I glanced over at Marvel; she was sitting forward, half smiling, watching with rapt attention. Dessusdelit first stepped down as mayor, and Lucius Bell was unanimously elected to succeed her. Bell took the gavel. Then Dessusdelit, St. Thomas, and a tight-lipped Rebeck, each asking to be recognized in turn, read short messages of resignation. When they were done, there wasn't a sound in the chamber until Dessusdelit pushed her chair back, and the leg scraped on the wooden floor.

Suddenly everybody was talking. A half dozen people gathered around Marvel, chattering at once. Bell remained seated, looking at the gavel in his hand, talking to Dodge. Dessusdelit said a few words to St. Thomas, ignored Rebeck, and walked out toward her office.

"That's it," LuEllen whispered. We were trapped in a corner and were among the last to get out of the meeting room. Marvel was in the hallway, talking animatedly with another woman. As we passed, she suddenly, without thinking, reached out and squeezed my arm. I instinctively smiled but kept walking. When I turned away from her, I saw Hill standing on the steps going to the second floor, to Wells's office.

He'd seen Marvel reach out to me and squeeze. His eyes narrowed, and he fixed on me. While I kept walking, swiveling my head as though I were simply interested in watching the crowd, the little man in the box at the back of my brain was chanting, "Damn, damn, damn . . ."

15

"WE'VE GOT TROUBLE," I told LuEllen as we stepped out in the sunshine. A dozen people milled around on the sidewalk below us, as though they'd just come out of a church wedding.

"What?"

"Marvel squeezed my arm when we walked through the hall. Hill saw it. He knows . . . something. Or he'll figure it out."

"Shit," she said. She raked her fingers through her hair in a gesture I recognized as one of mine. "Why now? We're so close."

"She's not a pro. She wasn't thinking." I squinted up the street, into the sun. Longstreet looked hard and dusty, and more than that: priggish, self-righteous. I've been in a lot of river towns, some of them a shambles compared with Longstreet, all of them tough. But they were all more or less likable. Longstreet was not. It wasn't so much tough as mean. "We've got a couple of more things to do, and then we go."

□ □ □

WE WENT back out on the river, hunting downstream. The river off Longstreet had been thoroughly contained by the Corps of Engineers, the banks stabilized, the current directed by submerged wing dams. For long stretches it was as much a canal as a river, and that was our best hope for finding the bodies. There just wasn't a lot they could get hung up on.

We ran the hunt with a program-editing technique; computer programming teaches you things that often have nothing to do with computers. Searching for bodies was one of those things.

When you finish writing a computer program, there are always a few bugs—mistakes. Some are obvious and easily corrected. Some are not. Finding the hard ones can be a nightmare; imagine reading a phone book, looking for a number that should be 6966996 instead of 6996996, without knowing precisely what you are looking for.

THERE ARE two ways to go about debugging.

One is intuitive: You jump around the program, looking for spots where the trouble may be.

The other is logical: You start at the most likely place and methodically search every possibility until you find it.

The intuitive approach has its proponents. You may find the problem very quickly. On the other hand, you may never find it; the mistake may not be where you think it must be. The logical approach gets the job done, but it's glacially slow.

I tend to go with the intuitive because the logical is boring. But to hunt for the bodies, where we couldn't fuck up and where intuition was blunted by a lack of knowledge of the river, the logical route was a necessity. We searched downstream from the point where the bodies had gone into the water, giving detailed attention to Bobby's highest-percentage areas.

"There's too much river," LuEllen said. "And if we keep looking at it in the sun, we're going to get . . . snow-blind, whatever you'd call it."

"If we find them, though, that'll be the last thing we need."

We never did find Harold.

The Bolivar County Sheriff's Department found him, in the river above Rosedale. Or rather a catfisherman did. The body was floating off a wing dam. The catfisherman called the sheriff, and the deputies pulled the body out, just about the time the city council was meeting. We got the word from Bobby that night, when we came off the river.

I'd put in the hookups and gone back for a shower when the phone rang; Bobby had been auto-dialing every minute or so, waiting for our return. I answered it, got the carrier tone, and punched up the computer. A block of newspaper text slid onto the screen:

ROSEDALE, MISS. (AP)—The body of an unidentified man
was found in the Mississippi River near Victoria Bend above
the city of Rosedale late Saturday, according to a spokesman for the Bolivar County Sheriff's Department.

The body was partially decomposed and apparently had
been in the river for several days, the spokesman said. The
dead man was black and was wearing a yellow dress shirt
and gray dress slacks. No identification was found with the
body.

An autopsy is scheduled for this week in Greenville. The
sheriff's spokesman said there was no sign of foul play.

Appended to the story was a note from Bobby:

That's all. Could it be Harold?

It seemed likely. The body had been found in
one of Bobby's high-probability areas. And if
Harold's body had gotten there, maybe Sherrie's
had, too. I called Bobby back.

*Don't talk to Marvel or John about the body.
We'll tell them later, OK?*

There was a moment's hesitation as he thought
it over, then:

OK.

LuEllen and I were looking at the corps's navigation maps of the lower Mississippi when Marvel called.

"There's a meeting tonight," she said. She was quietly triumphant. "The governor has announced his appointments, and Bell called a meeting at eight o'clock to swear them into office. Ballem, Hill, and Brooking Davis."

"Was anybody upset by Davis?"

"No. He's an attorney, and the governor's people were running around telling everybody that it was political—a gesture to the black caucus in the legislature. They understand that kind of politics down here. It's considered smart and harmless. Especially with Ballem and Hill going on the council . . ."

"All right. It's time for you to talk to Reverend Dodge."

"We're ready."

"Take John with you. Just in case. You've got to get him by the balls—"

"We got him."

"Then just sit tight. We'll take care of Ballem and Hill."

WE SPENT the rest of the evening talking, sitting on the top deck, watching the river go by. We were almost done, we agreed. We should take the boat on down the river, to New Orleans. Hang out awhile. French Quarter. Take our time heading back up north.

"Maybe you could stay with me awhile," I suggested.

"That's kind of scary, Kidd," she said.

More river went by. "Listen, I kind of wanted to ask . . . is your name really LuEllen?"

She looked amused. "Yeah, it really is."

Marvel called at ten o'clock. It had worked, she said. Hill, Ballem, and Brooking Davis had been sworn in as the new city councilmen.

"And the Reverend Dodge's ass is mine," she said. "His ass, and his vote."

"Did he freak out?"

"Nope. He was cool as a cucumber," Marvel said. "I told him about this one girl, and then a second one, and he just reached out and patted me on the knee, and he said, 'Marvel, what exactly is it that you want?' I told him, and he said, 'Well, I guess you got me,' and asked if we wanted a beer."

"That's cold," I said.

"I actually kind of admired him, the way he kept his shit together," Marvel said.

At the meeting, she said, Ballem tried to get a "consensus of the council" that committed the new members to resign when the former members were found innocent of wrongdoing.

Only Hill voted with him.

Then two black members of the audience got up and demanded a new investigation of the shooting of Darrell Clark. After some heated discussion—and a recess, during which Marvel spoke to Brooking Davis—the proposal was rejected, three to two, with Bell and Dodge voting in favor. Both Bell and Dodge were surprised by Davis's decision to vote with Hill and Ballem, as were the black members of the crowd.

"Brooking is going to take some shit, but we figure we've got to lay back. We don't want anybody having second thoughts about who is on that council. We want him solid with the whites in town. I'd have told Dodge to vote against, too, but he'd already suggested a new investigation, so he couldn't."

After a few more angry exchanges about the state investigation, Bell was about to adjourn the meeting when Davis brought up the bridge. Instead of looking to the state legislatures for money, he said, the city should look into the possibility of a revenue bond issue and build its own bridge. A toll bridge, if necessary.

Bell said the idea had been proposed before, and the financing looked impossible. Davis insisted that it was worth exploring. Ballem was positively enthusiastic. There'd been some problems, but there'd been problems before, and the machine always kept rolling. Revenue bonds were just the thing to fuel it. The vote was unanimously in favor of Davis's idea.

"We figured that would get Davis in solid with Bell, just in case we need him later," Marvel said.

"Now, the real question is, When can we dump Ballem and Hill?"

"Right away," I said. "We'll start working on it tonight."

"How're you going to do it? The state cops could take a while with those books."

"Don't worry about it. You just be ready to move."

EVERYTHING WAS rushing together.

We got up early the next morning, drove to Greenville, and mailed sets of LuEllen's murder photos to Ballem and Hill. We'd give them a chance to stew over the photos, and then LuEllen would call them. Using her best phony southern-belle accent, she would say that she had been on the hill, making landscape photographs, and that she'd seen Harold's body and the shooting of Sherrie. She wouldn't want to send a white man to the electric chair for killing a Negro, she'd say, but she would, if they didn't quit and leave town.

"How're we going to convince Ballem? He wasn't even there."

"Hill's his errand boy. Everybody in town knows it. When he sees the pictures, he won't argue. Not right away. He might go looking for the photographer later, but the first thing he'll do is quit. Just to keep things quiet, so he can maneuver. When he does that, we're outa here," I said.

We were back in Longstreet before noon. The

marina operator told us that Hill had been there and had asked after us but hadn't left a message.

"I heard that you and him had a misunderstanding sometime back, outside the Holiday Inn," the marina man said.

"It cleared up," I said.

"Yeah. Well, you take care," he said, spitting in the river.

We cut the boat loose and headed downstream again, looking for Sherrie's body. As we passed the animal control complex, we could hear the ooka-ooka-ooka of the vacuum pump, working the death box.

Late in the afternoon, a couple of miles above Victoria Point, LuEllen took the binoculars down from her eyes and pointed out over the water.

"Over there. Yellow."

"Another float?"

"Doesn't look like a float. Looks like it's stuck on a tree."

Sherrie's body was hung up on a dead cottonwood sweeper near the Concordia Bar Light.

"Jesus," LuEllen said as we drifted up. The smell of decaying flesh was overwhelming. I had intended to tangle the body in a wad of heavy monofilament fishing line and tangle the line in some brush, to anchor it, but in the end, neither of us had the stomach for the job. Instead, we calculated the distance the body lay above the light and turned back upriver.

"We'll call it in as soon as we get back," I said. The run back upstream was depressing.

"How come we keep getting people killed, Kidd?" LuEllen asked.

"You keep asking, and I keep telling you: We don't," I said. "They get themselves killed. We're just unlucky enough to be around when it happens. Harold knew what he was doing."

"How about Sherrie?"

"I won't take the blame," I said. "Hill's a fuckin' psycho. Period. It's not us. It's them."

"I'll try to remember that," she said. And after a minute: "The money we took from City Hall—I think we're going to have to give it back."

"What?"

"When we were over at Marvel's house, she mentioned a couple of times what they could do with the money. Give some of it to the family of the kid that got shot—they've got a couple of more kids—or give some of it to Harold's family. She was talking like the money belonged to all of us."

"Huh." I'd planned to keep it.

"The point is, everybody knows our faces. And they know what we've done. Some of it, anyway. And so far you'd have a hell of a hard time proving that anybody else has done anything wrong. If we take expenses out—she'd expect that—and give them the rest and they spend it, then we've got something on them. I like Marvel, all right, but she's a politician."

"I see," I said. And I did, sour as the taste was.

A COUPLE OF MILES below the Longstreet landing a sleek glass bass boat was goofing along the shoreline. One man was on the back deck; the other, on the bow. When I first saw them, I assumed they were casting. I didn't immediately look closer because a tow had rounded the bend above us, pushing a string of barges. The first priority on the river is to avoid the tows; they can't stop in time to miss anything that they're close enough to see.

We took the tow down the right side. When we cleared it, the bass boat was arrowing out from the shore on the other side, to intercept us.

"That's fuckin' Hill," LuEllen said. She put the glasses on the bass boat. "And that's St. Thomas up front. Bet they were looking for the bodies."

There was no chance of running—the *Fanny* was a pig, and the bass boat was carrying a big 115-horse Mariner outboard—but I pushed the throttle full forward. If we could fend them off long enough to get to the marina, they'd be limited in what they could do.

Ten seconds later they were on top of us, throwing off a fat, curling wake, the outboard's normally deep roar climbing toward a scream. Hill stood at the bow while St. Thomas sat behind the wheel, maneuvering to come beside us. Hill was shouting something, but with the two motors and the sound of the water breaking under the hulls, I couldn't make it out. I waved him off and kept drifting right, away from the bass boat.

When Hill saw that I wouldn't voluntarily let him come aboard, he shouted something back to St. Thomas, then stepped up to the edge of the bow casting-deck and crouched, one hand on the low gunwale to steady himself, ready to leap aboard the *Fanny*. He had a lump on his hip under his white short-sleeved shirt and when his shirt flapped in the bow wind, I could see flashes of gun-metal blue.

The *Fanny* had a rail all the way around and her deck was a foot higher than the low-riding bass boat's. Coming aboard could be tricky.

St. Thomas, his brow wrinkled in concentration, brought the bass boat six feet from the *Fanny*, then edged closer. I stepped away. He bored in again. This time, I flipped the wheel toward him, and the distance between the two hulls went from six feet to nothing. The bass boat was faster and more maneuverable, but the *Fanny* was bigger. If the two hulls hit, the bass boat would fold like a beer can. Anything caught between the two hulls would be crushed. St. Thomas flinched.

Hill had been tensing to jump. When I cut in, St. Thomas almost jerked the boat out from under Hill's feet. He staggered, swayed, caught himself, and screamed something either at Hill or at me, his face red with rage.

They came back in. This time they came an inch at a time. St. Thomas was watching me now, instead of the boat. If I moved the wheel, he was right with me.

Hill put his hands up to grab the rail and LuEllen was there, facing him across the rail. She'd cracked the boat's emergency kit and was pointing an emergency flare gun at Hill's chest from no more than three feet away. Hill reached back and I thought for a second that he was reaching for his pistol. LuEllen must have thought so too, because the barrel of the flare pistol drifted up until it was leveled at Hill's eyes. They stared at each other for a beat, then two, LuEllen's face as hard as a chip of flint, before St. Thomas flinched again. He took the bass boat to the left, paced us for a moment, then accelerated away, hotfooting it back toward the marina.

"Guess Hill wanted to keep his face," LuEllen said laconically, as she climbed up on top. "Wouldn't know why."

HILL WAS WAITING on the dock when we came in. St. Thomas was up toward the top of the levee, hurriedly walking away. There were a half dozen people around, messing with boats, talking, coming and going. We nosed in, coasted, bumped, and LuEllen tied us off.

Hill walked down the dock and yelled up at me: "What the fuck you think you were doing?"

"What the hell were *you* doing?" I called back. "I thought you were going to sink us."

He was operating in the kind of blind rage that infects psychotics when they're countered. His hand went to his hip, but he wasn't actually far enough gone to pull the pistol with witnesses around. "I'll get you, computer man," he screamed. "I'll be looking for you."

LuEllen was watching him climb the levee when I dropped down to the lower deck. "Computer man?" she said.

"Somebody's been doing research," I said. "If they found out I do computers and suspect I'm with Marvel, then they may have put together the whole thing: the state having their books, John coming in, everything."

"Time to leave," she said.

"Soon," I said. "We're close."

LATE THAT NIGHT we got the City Hall money out of the engine compartment, agreed that seventeen thousand dollars was about right for expenses, and took the rest of it to Marvel's friend's house in the country.

"We took expenses out," I told Marvel, handing her the package. "There's eighty-three thousand left. You can't give it back. That might jeopardize the case against Dessusdelit and St. Thomas, and there just wouldn't be any explanations."

"We've got some things we can do with it," she said. "Thank you . . . I mentioned to John that I thought the money should be for all of us, but he said it was yours. . . ."

John, who was lounging in an easy chair, shook his head. "It ain't right," he said. "You two are working an angle somewhere, but I can't figure what it is."

I shrugged. "You could just give us credit for a selfless act."

He looked at us for a moment, then said, "Nah."

BACK ON THE BOAT I called Bobby:

Will tell John/Marvel about Harold body. Will call cops anonymously and give them IDs. Will tell John/Marvel you found body reports in data searches. Please back up if John inquires.

He came back:

OK. But need long talk soon.

He was getting nervous, thinking about friends and loyalties. I answered:

Yes. Tomorrow, day after. Soon.

16

THE NEXT MORNING I phoned the Bolivar County Sheriff's Department. Posing as a reporter for a Memphis television station, I asked a couple of airweight questions about bodies pulled from the river. A woman had been found, a deputy said, but hadn't been identified. There'd be no further comment pending an autopsy.

I called another meeting at the country place.

"It's about your friends, the ones you've been looking for," I said cautiously, talking to Marvel on the telephone.

I went to the meeting alone, LuEllen shying away again. John and Marvel showed up at the rendezvous, tense, expectant.

"What? What?" Marvel asked as I came through the door.

"It's about Harold and Sherrie. I think they've been found," I said. "They're dead."

"Oh, no," she whispered, sinking onto a couch. John stood beside her, a hand on her shoulder. He had an odd look on his face: I wasn't fooling him, not entirely.

"Bobby called. He's been doing a data search . . . and he found that the Bolivar County Sheriff's Department has pulled a couple of bodies out of the river near Rosedale. A man and a woman. Both black. The man was dressed like you said Harold was. The woman, I don't know . . . they said a yellow blouse. . . ."

"It's them," Marvel said. She was dry-eyed, but on the thin edge of an explosion. "She was wearing yellow; her mama told us that."

"We've got to let the cops know; we've got to bring it back to Longstreet," I said.

"What do you want us to do?" John asked.

"I want you to get Marvel . . . or somebody . . . down there and identify the bodies. Tell the deputies you heard it on the radio. Find out how they were killed. Tell the deputies what you suspect—that Harold had gone to visit Dessusdelit—but tell them you don't know why. Tell them that Harold had some information about this political scandal that's going on. That'll put a lot of pressure on Dessusdelit."

"All right. I can do that," Marvel said. Her fingers were dug an inch deep into the tough fabric of the couch arm.

"I'll go with her," John said. "What are you doing?"

"We're getting ready to leave. We're about

done, but I'll tell you what. You better get back here quick if Brooking Davis and Reverend Dodge are going to elect you to the council. Hill and Ballem will most likely quit this afternoon."

"What'd you do to them?" she asked.

"Squeezed them," I said.

"With Harold and Sherrie?" she asked.

"Look," I said, "I didn't want anybody to get hurt, but some people got hurt anyway. We're using Harold as a little extra encouragement for Hill to leave, above and beyond the computer material. That's all."

She was no longer sure of me, and her face showed it.

"If you manipulated Harold . . ."

"You know what happened to Harold," I said harshly, "because you sent him. We aren't playing fuckin' Ping-Pong here. We're ruining some people's lives, and they are hard people. They'll fight back."

"If I'd known . . ."

"Nobody can know," I said. I looked at John. "You keep her close. Hill, Ballem, and the others, St. Thomas, are in a pressure cooker. Hill's a psycho. I can't predict what he'll do."

I stopped at a supermarket on the edge of town and stocked up with sandwich meat, bread, soup, pasta, cereal, and milk for the run upriver. When

I got back to the boat, LuEllen was waiting. So was Dessusdelit.

"Mr. Kidd," she said as I stepped aboard.

"Miz Dessusdelit. What can I do for you?"

"You know about our troubles?"

"Yes, after our talk ... and I was at the meeting. . . ."

"Our animal control officer, Duane Hill—"

"I know him."

"He believes you have something to do with it, that I've been a fool with these tarot readings, with the crystal ball."

She sounded like a magnolia, her voice slow and dreamy, something out of a Tennessee Williams play, like Blanche. . . . And she was pleading.

"That's bullshit, if you'll pardon the expression. You know about my history with Hill?"

"I believe there was some kind of confrontation on the river."

"It goes farther back than that. He attacked me, for no reason at all, outside the Holiday Inn. He was drunk. Actually he called LuEllen a rather unacceptable four-letter word, which I won't repeat, and I was forced to respond. There was a fight, and he lost. Then Mr. Bell intervened and sent him on his way. Ever since then he has been watching me, and yesterday he tried to run us down with a speedboat and board our yacht. I believe he was carrying a gun. Personally, Miz Dessusdelit, I think he's crazy."

"He says you're in league with a local Communist, a Negro woman—"

"Miz Dessusdelit, I don't know what to say, other than the man needs treatment. I don't know anybody in this town, other than you and a few people I've encountered casually. And frankly Hill frightens me. He's crazy. He's so crazy that LuEllen and I are leaving. Because of him."

She thought it over and then said, "I don't know what to do."

"I wish I could help you, but we've got to go."

She thought for a moment more, then sighed and said, "Once more with the cards?"

We weren't set up to cold-deck her. I don't even know what cards we would have planted. As far as I was concerned, she was in a box, and there was no way out. But LuEllen, standing behind me, poked me in the spine, and I nodded at Dessusdelit.

"All right."

In the cabin I got the deck from the Polish box, unwrapped it from its silk binding, and handed it to her.

"I still don't know how far to trust you, Mr.

Kidd," she said, still with the dreamy expression.

"Then don't trust me," I said harshly. "You know that tarot spreads are artificial constructs. So let's skip the spread. Pull out four cards and lay them down: past, present, future, and final outcome. You can do your own interpretation if you like. If you have questions, I'll try to answer them."

A spark showed in her eyes as she stared across the table at me. "Yes," she said. She shuffled the deck seven times, then spread it across the table. Her hand hovered for a moment and pulled a card.

"Past," she said, and flipped it over.

The Devil. A man with a goat's head and horns and bat wings, with a man and a woman chained to his throne. Usually interpreted as bondage to base emotions—greed, for example, or the urge to personal power.

"Present," she said, and flipped the second card.

The Nine of Swords. A woman sitting up in bed, weeping, nine swords racked on the wall behind her. She's suffering great losses of all kinds, as are people who are important to her. All of it's accompanied by great anguish. Dessusdelit nodded.

"Future," she said, and flipped the third card.

The Ten of Swords. The body of a man on the

ground, with ten swords protruding from his back and neck. Final ruin.

"Final outcome," she said. Her hand paused at one card, but she stopped without turning it, moved to another, paused again, and flipped it over.

The Tower of Destruction. The lightning bolt striking the tower.

"My old friend," she said weakly. "I've seen it a lot lately."

I reached forward and turned over the card she'd almost chosen. The Sun. A card of success.

"You almost chose this card. Why didn't you?"

"I . . . don't know," she said.

"You made a choice in the recent past that perhaps led to these problems you're experiencing. That's reflected in this choice, isn't it?"

She was silent for a moment, staring unseeingly at the cards, then nodded.

"I made the choice," she said.

It was as close as anyone would ever get to a confession. Hill and St. Thomas had killed Harold and Sherrie. But Dessusdelit had made the call. The mayor got shakily to her feet and started toward the door. LuEllen, solicitous, asked, "What are you going to do?"

"I don't know," Dessusdelit said.

"Could I give you some . . . advice? Something to think about?"

Dessusdelit stopped with her hand on the doorknob, looked carefully at LuEllen, then nodded.

"I was once involved in a situation . . . well, it wasn't the best situation, and there were some police involved. I don't want to say more. But I will tell you something about the American legal system: It's quite difficult to convict anyone of anything, and when time passes, it becomes almost impossible. You know what I did, when I had my . . . trouble? I went away. And nobody really looked for me. It was too much trouble, I guess. I went back four or five years later, talked to some people who were involved with me, and it was like . . . nobody even remembered that the police once were looking for me. Nobody cared."

"You're saying I should go away?"

"I don't know what your problems are exactly," LuEllen said. "I'm just saying that . . . there are options. There are some really wonderful places in the world and here in the United States. Longstreet isn't everything."

Dessusdelit nodded a last time, stood silently for a few more heartbeats, then said, "Thank you," and walked out.

When she was on the levee, LuEllen turned to

me and said, "She told Hill to kill Harold and the woman, Sherrie."

"Yes. I think that's what she was telling us," I said. "What was all that bullshit about running from the cops?"

"Give me the car keys," LuEllen interrupted. "C'mon, quick."

I handed her the keys. "Where're you going?"

"After Dessusdelit," she said hastily. "You call Bobby. Ask him to monitor Dessusdelit's phones. We want to know if she's going anywhere tonight or if anybody's coming over."

LuELLEN WAS GONE for four hours. I filled the boat's diesel tanks and got some gas for the auxiliary generator, then climbed up on the top deck with a sketchbook. John called in the early afternoon.

"Two things," he croaked, as though he were losing his voice. "We identified Harold and Sherrie. Marvel and I stayed away, though. Sherrie's brother did it. He freaked out and told the cops that Sherrie was screwing Hill and about how all this weird shit was going down in Longstreet. . . . I suspect the deputies will be calling on Hill—or the Longstreet cops will."

"You didn't tell her brother?"

"We didn't tell him anything except that we'd heard it on the radio. I told him that he had to make the identifications because Marvel couldn't stand to do it, and I didn't know either one of them. He went along."

"Was it bad?"

"Man, Marvel is fucked up. I'm going to have to take some time with her."

"Jesus, John, I'm sorry . . ."

"And there's the other thing," he said. "The council's called another special meeting, but it's not until tomorrow night."

"Hmph. I would have thought . . . I guess that's OK, but I would have thought they'd do it quicker."

"Maybe stalling for time. Maybe trying to figure out who knows what. You take care."

"Yeah," I said. "You, too."

When LuEllen returned, she was wearing the intent look she develops when she's working, when she's turning a job in her mind.

"Where were you?" I asked.

"Greenville," she said. "I shadowed Dessusdelit back to her place and waited for a few minutes, to see what she'd do. She came back out, got in her car, and drove down to Greenville."

"To do what?"

"Visit a bank," LuEllen said. "She had a briefcase with her when she came out of her house. She was carrying it by the handle and threw it in the backseat of the car. When she came out of the bank, she was carrying it with both hands."

"She took something out of the bank," I said.

"Yeah. Out of the safe-deposit box in a town where she's not known."

"She had some money stashed."

"She had something stashed, and now she's got it in her house. She's thinking about running."

"And you ..."

"I'm going to hit her again. She killed Harold and Sherrie, and she's got to pay."

"You weren't that close to Harold, and you never even knew Sherrie."

"They're fuckin' Nazis," LuEllen snarled. Then, in a milder voice, she said, "Besides, there's some bucks in it. Truth be told, she's the kind of fat cat I'd hit just for the money, and the first time around we never really touched her."

BOBBY REPORTED a flurry of calls between Dessusdelit, Hill, St. Thomas, and Ballem, all cryptic but increasingly testy. Ballem had gone to the chief of police about the burglary of his house but hadn't formally reported it, Bobby said. And he'd gotten the murder photos in the mail, delivered while Dessusdelit was in Greenville.

"He didn't tell her what the pictures were, but he wants to see her tonight. They're meeting at his house after dark. He's only about three blocks from her, so she's going to walk over. Hill's going to be there, but they haven't said anything about

St. Thomas. I think they're cutting St. Thomas out."

"Or planning to set him up for the murders," I said.

HILL WAS INSISTING that the "goddamn artist" had something to do with the machine's problems, but the others weren't listening, Bobby said. "Dessusdelit told him she knew all about the problems between you and Hill. She said that if they wanted to get out of this trouble, they had to stop fantasizing and understand that they caused the problems themselves, by making a mistake, and now they have to straighten it out themselves."

"Sounds like she's recovering herself," I said to LuEllen when I passed on Bobby's information.

"It also sounds like she's going to be out of her house tonight," LuEllen said.

We argued about whether to hit Dessusdelit, and LuEllen won.

"Look," she said, "the heart of the machine is Ballem, St. Thomas, Hill, and Dessusdelit. We know we can take Hill and St. Thomas, because the cops have the bodies, and we have the photos. We already ripped Ballem for those stamps, and now we're siccing the IRS on him; plus he'll be tarred with the killings whether or not he's convicted of them. But Dessusdelit—Dessusdelit slides free, unless the IRS gets her for evasion or the state gets her on a corruption charge. That's not enough. But if we take her stash, we take her heart out. Everybody says that she lives for money. Even the cards said so, didn't they?"

"The cards are bullshit," I said.

"Yeah, right."

LuEllen took Dessusdelit by herself. The house was an easy target the first time, and it was easy the second. It was, however, a little tough to watch, so we watched Ballem's instead.

Dressed in navy blue sweats and running shoes, we parked in the country club lot—there was a dance going on, and the lot was full—and jogged along the edge of the golf course to a small copse of trees off the third tee. From there we were looking right down at Ballem's front door. Hill arrived first, a little before nine, and then Dessusdelit walked in. We jogged back to the car, called Dessusdelit's place from a pay phone, and, when we got no answer, nipped off the receiver.

As we drove down to Dessusdelit's, LuEllen unscrewed the car's dome light, so it wouldn't come on when the door opened. I took the car into the cul-de-sac, as though lost, and slowly rolled through the turning circle. When we passed Dessusdelit's driveway, I stopped just for a second, said, "Go," and LuEllen rolled out the back door. She pushed it shut before she

311

crawled away, and I continued out onto the road.

LuEllen said ten minutes max. I drove back to Ballem's house and parked on the street near the entrance to the country club. Hill's car was still in Ballem's driveway, and I once saw a shadow on a curtain, moving across the living room.

Eight minutes. I started back. At nine minutes, forty-five seconds, I was a block from the entrance to the cul-de-sac. I stopped at a corner, reached back, and opened the right rear door. The only turn I had to make was a right turn, so it shouldn't swing open. . . .

At ten minutes and ten seconds I rolled through the cul-de-sac a last time. I paused again at the end of Dessusdelit's driveway. LuEllen popped into the backseat, staying low, and held the door shut with her hand.

"Get it?" I asked.

"Yeah, but I don't know what I've got," she said. "It's the briefcase, but I didn't find it until about a minute before your pickup. She had it hidden behind some built-in drawers under the linen closet."

When we were well away from Dessusdelit's, she screwed the dome light back in and climbed into the front seat. We were sitting at a downtown stoplight when she dug into the briefcase and came up with a handful of small white envelopes, the same kind I'd taken out of the wall cache.

"More stones?" I asked.

"A fuckin' river," she said, dumping a glittering tracery of light into the palm of her hand. "Diamonds. Emeralds. Some rubies. Jesus Christ, Kidd, there's so many you could make a snowball out of them."

"So she's paid."

"Oh, yeah. She's paid."

17

John walked down to the boat the next morning, just as we were getting up.

LuEllen had gone out to the main cabin, wearing only a pair of underpants and a T-shirt. I was sitting on the bed with my feet flat on the floor, suddenly bone-tired, when she called, apprehensively, "John's coming."

"What?" I stood up, pulled on my artist's shorts and a T-shirt, and padded barefoot into the cabin. John was at the bottom of the levee wall, just stepping out on the pier. I went out to meet him, shading my eyes in the bright morning sunlight. He was wearing jeans and a T-shirt with Beethoven's face on the front. He waved cheerily to the marina manager, then came right up to the boat.

"Hey, Kidd, how's the work going?" he called in a voice loud enough for the manager to hear. He scrambled aboard, and we shook hands.

"I'm John Smith, Memphis artist," he said

quietly. He was sweating harder than seemed necessary, even with the heat. "We need to talk. I didn't think you could risk coming to Marvel's, and we don't have time to go out in the country."

"Come on inside," I said.

"Bizarre shit," John said as soon as the door was shut. "Did you hear about Dessusdelit?"

"What about her?"

"She's dead. The cops think it was suicide. Last night."

LuEllen stared at me, deadpan.

"Jesus Christ," I said. "Do you know anything else?"

"They found her in bed, wearing a pink nightgown. She took a bunch of pills and whiskey, I guess. There was a note, but I don't know what it said. The cops are talking to Ballem, I know that."

"What about the meeting tonight?"

"That's still on, as far as I know, but I thought you needed to hear about Dessusdelit, and I was afraid to call on the phone. Quite a few people know she was seeing you, getting her cards read. . . ."

"You think the cops are coming here?"

"I don't know. I don't know what the note said."

"Jesus."

□ □ □

"Time to go," LuEllen said when John left.

"We can't now," I said. "If the cops want to talk to us, we've got to be here. If we take off and they come looking for us . . ."

"What a fuckin' mess. We did another one," LuEllen said.

"How're you gonna know?" I said. "Assholes aren't supposed to kill themselves."

"We've got to clean the boat out," she said. "If they go through it, they'll find my tools."

We decided to go out on the river.

"That was an artist guy from Memphis, haven't seen him in years," I told the manager as we cast off. "He's always going up and down the river collecting stuff for his sculpture."

"Oh, yeah? He does river stuff?"

"Yeah, out of water-worn glass and old bottles and driftwood and shit," I said.

"I'd like to see some of that," he said, and he sounded as if he did. When we were out of the marina, I turned upstream. LuEllen wanted to keep on going to St. Paul.

"Hill's fucked," she argued. "We send some pictures to the cops and forget it. Toss the gun overboard."

"The photos might not be enough if the cops don't know where they come from. A good defense attorney might be able to keep them out of evidence. And we can't tell them where we got them, unless we want people looking at *our* backgrounds. . . . But if they find the gun out at animal control . . . that'd seal it up tight."

"I'm getting scared, Kidd. We're walking the edge, with Hill and the cops and everybody."

"I know. One more night, and we're out of here."

A mile or so above town we cut through a side channel behind a sandbar. The channel was too clogged to go all the way through, but it got us out of sight of the main river. LuEllen tossed her burglary tools over the side, one by one, along with the case. All could be replaced, and she had not an ounce of sentimentalism for them. She held the lockpicks out; we'd need them at animal control.

Her camera equipment I could claim as my own, if the cops searched us and asked about it. I'd say I used it to shoot landscapes. We still had the extra prints of the murder photos, the gun, and the jewels. LuEllen hid the jewels by cutting tiny holes halfway through the carpet in the corner of the bedroom. She pressed the stones into the holes until they were out of sight, but before they came through the underside of the carpet. Even if somebody lifted the carpet, the jewels would be invisible and secure.

That left two sets of photos and the negatives. Working with gloves, LuEllen packaged the prints and wrote short notes, in block letters, to the county sheriff and to the commander of the state police district headquarters. The negatives she put in another envelope. We'd mail that to a reliable friend in St. Paul, an old lady who lived in the apartment below mine and who took care of my cat while I was gone.

Finally, the gun.

"There's nothing we can do with the gun except keep it hidden," I said. "We need to hide it only until tonight."

"What if there's a reception committee waiting back at the dock?"

"Then we're fucked anyway, because we've still got the photos. . . . Look, the main problems are the jewels and the lockpicks. The jewels they won't find, and we can throw the picks overboard if we see somebody waiting. We can't dump the gun or the photos, but we can explain them if we have to. We say we were taking landscape shots from the top of that hill, saw the killings, and were afraid to do anything because we believed Hill was psychotic. Because we didn't know the town, and we were scared, and because Hill was friends with all the cops—"

"Sounds like bullshit," she said.

"It's all I got," I said.

THERE WAS NOBODY waiting for us. Even the marina manager had gone off somewhere. We stuck plenty of stamps on our packages and put them in separate mailboxes.

As we were walking back to the *Fanny*, LuEllen asked, "Is there anybody in this whole thing that we haven't lied to at one time or another?"

I had to think about it for a minute. "Bobby," I said finally. "I don't believe we've lied to Bobby."

AFTER SOME ARGUMENT we decided I should go to the city council meeting that night, while LuEllen went to the animal control complex with the gun.

"What if somebody wonders what you're doing there?" LuEllen asked.

"I just tell them I'm hanging out, that Dessusdelit was a friend. Shit, at this point I don't care. Hill and Ballem will be there, if only to quit. But I've got to see them. If something went wrong . . ."

"OK."

"I'll call you from City Hall. If Hill and Ballem are there, you can drift the boat down, tie off on that wall. If it's clear, you go in, dump the gun—put it up in the ceiling maybe—and get out. Coming in from the river, at night, you should be OK, if you're careful about scouting it out. . . ."

"I'd rather go without you anyway," she said. "Safer that way."

"Yeah. And as soon as I see what's going on at City Hall, I'll cruise animal control, just in case. If there's a problem, turn on a light. If everything's OK, get out. I'll see you back here."

"And we leave tomorrow morning."

"As soon as I get the car back."

The meeting was scheduled for seven-thirty. I left the boat fifteen minutes early, expecting a mob at the City Hall. When I pulled into the lot across the street, there was already a crowd on the sidewalk. Neither Hill nor Ballem seemed to be around, but I waited, watching, until people began drifting inside.

The city council chamber was a small semicircular auditorium with seats for perhaps fifty people. Folding chairs had been brought in, and thirty lucky spectators were occupying them. Another dozen people were standing against the wall. The air-conditioning couldn't keep up. The temperature inside must have been in the nineties, and the sweating townspeople used stacks of agendas from the last meeting to fan themselves. Nobody was giving up a seat.

Marvel and Matron Carter, the basketball coach who'd be the fifth council member, were sitting together near the front. John was absent; still a little nervous about showing his face, he was waiting at Marvel's.

The word about Dessusdelit had gotten around, and it was the major topic of conversation as we waited for the council to show. The wait went on for ten minutes, fifteen. Then Bell came in through a side door, looking harassed, and said to a long groan that the meeting would be delayed until eight o'clock.

I stepped outside, relieved to be in the relatively cool hallway, and walked down to a pay phone and called LuEllen.

"Wait," I said. "I haven't seen either Ballem or Hill, and they've delayed the meeting. I don't know what's going on."

"I'll wait," she said.

At ten after eight Bell reappeared, apologized again, said the meeting had been delayed another twenty minutes, and suggested that the townspeople adjourn to the sidewalk.

"You all are starting to parboil," he said. Then he looked out into the crowd, searching the faces, and stopped when he got to mine.

"The artist fellow back there? Mr. Kidd? Could you come down here and talk to me for a minute? And Miz Atkins? Could you come down here, too?"

A buzz went through the crowd, and I thought about walking out the back, down to the boat, and leaving for St. Paul. I could dump the car in the used-car lot where I'd rented it, with a couple of hundred bucks under the seat. . . . But there was no way out, with everybody watching. Marvel had walked down as soon as Bell called her name, and I picked my way down the center aisle, trying to look puzzled.

"Come down this way," Bell said to me. He let

Marvel go first, and I tagged along behind, until we were in the hall, and then he led the way to the council offices. Ballem was there, looking frightened. Hill was with him, wild with rage but holding it in. St. Thomas was standing down the hall with Rebeck. The chief of police was there, with four or five men I didn't recognize.

"Motherfucker," Hill said, standing up when Marvel and I came in. "What're you and this bitch up to?"

"You watch your mouth, Duane," Bell said. His voice was like a knife, and I suddenly understood why Bell had done so well in the big-time farming business. He was not a man to fool with.

"I don't know what's happening," I said to everybody in general. "What in the hell am I doing here?"

We were in the narrow hallway outside the tiny council offices, the only place there was enough space for us all.

"Duane, here, says you and Miz Atkins are involved in some kind of conspiracy to drag the city down," Bell said. "He said all the weird happenings here the last few days are because of you."

"Duane's a fruitcake," I said. Hill started up, and I braced my feet, but Bell put his hand on Hill's shoulder and shoved him back down. "The first time I ever saw him was on the day I came to town. He came up and hassled me on old Mrs. Trent's yard, where I was painting. Mrs. Trent

323

came out and ran him off—says she knew him from the days he used to shoplift out of her stores—"

"I never," Hill said.

"There's a police record in juvenile court," I said. "That's what Miz Trent says anyway. Then the next time I saw him, I was down at the Holiday Inn, and he came after my ass; I still don't know why. You were there, Mr. Bell. He called my woman friend a . . . four-letter word you don't normally use on respectable women, or any kind of woman, for that matter, if you got even an ounce of breeding—"

"This is bullshit," Hill said, twisting up to look at Bell. "Ask him about Atkins!"

Marvel looked at me and shook her head. "I saw the man only one other time, when Miz Dessusdelit and the others quit. I thought he was a friend—I only saw him from behind. I thought he was Lou Shaffer from the school—and I squeezed his arm, but when he turned around . . . I was embarrassed."

Bell looked from one of us to the other, not quite believing.

Then I said, "Fuck it—excuse me, ma'am. But I'm getting out of here. You're all crazy people. I'm taking the car back to Miz Wells's brother, and I'm getting in my boat, and I'm getting out of here."

Bell sighed. "I don't know," he said. He looked

at Ballem and Hill. "Come on, you two. If you're going to do it, let's do it."

Marvel and I left first, not looking at each other, and turned in opposite directions once we were in the hall. I walked straight down to the phone and said, "They're all here: Ballem, Hill, St. Thomas, and Rebeck."

"Go?"

"Go."

I UNDERSTOOD from Bell's comment as Marvel and I left the council offices that Hill and Ballem were ready to quit. I almost left after talking to LuEllen but decided at the last minute to stick around for the finale. When I went back to the city council room, people were packed in the hallway.

"What happened?" I asked.

"I don't know. Duane's saying something about his quitting," said a yellow-toothed courthouse regular standing in the doorway. Hill stopped talking, and Bell said something I couldn't understand, and Ballem started talking. Two minutes later it was done, and the two men walked out through the side door, leaving Bell at the council table, along with Brooking Davis and Reverend Dodge.

Davis was talking to Bell, and the yellow-toothed man turned and said in a panicky voice, "That Davis is asking about electing new members. Son of a bitch, there's two coloreds against Lucius."

There was some further exchange at the council table, and the gavel rapped, and Bell, Davis, and Dodge got up and walked out. "Lucius called a recess," Yellow-tooth said. "By golly, this could be bad."

Whatever was happening, I couldn't change it. Time to go. I was out the door, crossing the street to the parking lot, when I heard somebody coming after me. Hill, I thought, and I pivoted. It was Marvel.

"Gotta talk," she said in a harsh whisper.

"Jesus Christ, Marvel, if anybody sees us, the whole thing comes unglued. . . ."

"I can't help it," she whispered. I pointed to the other side of the car as I unlocked the door and said, "Lay down on the backseat."

When she was in, I started the car and rolled out of the lot, turned away from the courthouse, and started around the block.

"What?" I asked.

"A problem we didn't see." Her voice was disembodied, floating over the backseat. "Bell caught on, of course, as soon as Davis suggested nominations for new members."

"What can he do about it? He's outvoted, two to one."

"He can do two things that we didn't think of.

He can refuse to go back to the meeting. Without a quorum there's no vote," she said.

"Shit." I gnawed at a thumbnail. "He can't stay out forever, though."

"And he can quit. That would do it. The governor would have to appoint replacements again, and there'd be three more white boys. And Bell's talking about doing just that."

"Goddamn it. Who's he talking to? Everybody? Or just Davis."

"Just me and Davis. I think he's still trying to figure out what we're doing. And he really doesn't want to quit; that'd be the end for his precious bridge."

I took a couple of more blocks, worrying it. There was only one out. "You gotta deal with him," I said. "You. Or Davis. Somebody. You've gotta find a way to cut a deal with Bell."

"How?" she asked. "He doesn't even want to live here. He wants to live across the river, in a whole 'nother state. He's here only because he thinks it'll help him get that fuckin' bridge."

"Then get the bridge for him," I said.

"I can't. Everybody's tried. And they've tried about everything they could think of."

"Well, I'll tell you what, Marvel," I said. "If he walks out of that City Hall without going back to the meeting, the white pressure'll get heavier and heavier, and he won't be able to move. If he goes back tonight and you get elected to the council,

he can always claim that it didn't occur to him to
boycott the meeting. If the meeting gets put off
until tomorrow, there's no way that'd work. By
tomorrow everybody will have thought of it."

"You got nothing for me?" she asked. "Nothing?"

"Man, I'm a technician. I can get you to a
point, but after that . . . you're the politician.
What you need is a deal, to cut a deal." I looked
at my watch. "And I've got to take you back now.
You've got about two minutes to get to Bell. Two
minutes to figure out how you're gonna get a
bridge for him."

"Ah, Jesus," she groaned. "We're so close. So
close. What am I going to do?"

18

I DROPPED MARVEL in a pool of darkness a half block from the City Hall, hoping that nobody would see us or recognize us. She hurried away, not looking back. The outcome of our attack on the city was now in her hands. I had no ideas for her.

And I had LuEllen to worry about. She should have been out of animal control, but I had to check. I was supposed to keep track of Hill and St. Thomas, and in the encounter with Marvel, I'd lost them.

The road to animal control, after it got past the tank field, was dark as pitch. My headlights on the lonely gravel road would attract the attention of anyone at the place, but driving without them was impossible. I finally left them on, kept my speed up, and blew past the turnoff into the complex. There were lights on in the building, and Hill's van squatted under the pole light in the yard.

"Goddamn it," I muttered. I smacked the steering wheel with the palm of my hand. LuEllen should have seen their headlights coming. But if she'd been inside, looking for a spot to hide Hill's pistol, it was just barely possible that she'd been trapped. I went on down the road, parked, got a flashlight out of the glove compartment, and jogged back.

The night had cooled, and the smell of mud, road gravel, weeds, and something else rode on a river breeze. Goose bumps popped up on my arms as I ran, and I finally identified the "something else" as the stink of decomposing flesh, probably from Hill's killing pen.

At the entrance to the animal control complex I slowed, cut a corner through the weeds, prayed that all copperheads were asleep, and stepped over a fence. The complex was in a flat, open area cut in the riverside brush. I skirted the open area, cut behind the pen where we'd seen Hill and St. Thomas killing the cats—the smell of rotting flesh grew stronger, and I started breathing through my mouth—and climbed the levee. Nothing; I was too far away to see whether or not the boat was tied to the wall. I started down the levee, picking my way along the nearly invisible game trail. The boat loomed up like a ghost in the night, just a light spot in the humidity, a trick of the eyes. In another fifty yards it had solidified. No lights, nothing moving around it.

"LuEllen? LuEllen?"

Nothing. Cursing under my breath, I turned back up the levee. I could hear somebody inside. A voice, a banging of drawers. There was a window on the far side of the building. If I could get to it, I should be able to see into the main work area.

I started around the clearing, staying in the brush as long as I could, then darted into the cage area at the rear of the main building. Most of the animal pens were simple wooden or wire cages stacked six high inside a chain-link fence, but there was also an open pen for puppies. A couple of half-grown spotted mongrels stood up in the pen as I went by, watching curiously, and I prayed for silence. One continued to watch me, its nose pressed through the fence, while the other one turned in its tracks and settled down again. Neither barked.

Standing in the darkness of the pens, I waited a second, listening, then poked my head out. A shaft of light came out of the window onto the grass. Then a man spoke, but I couldn't make out what was being said. I stepped out from the pen area, staying close to the building, moved up to the window, and carefully looked in, moving slowly. . . .

Hill was there, his back to me, stuffing paper into a plastic garbage sack. The file cabinets around him were standing open. He was cleaning

the place out. That was OK, as long as they didn't
physically trash the computer. The voice I'd heard
came from the radio, a local sports talk show
about the high school baseball team. I let out a
breath and started to step back.

"Don't fuckin' move." The voice came from
ten feet away and nearly stopped my heart. I
turned my head, and St. Thomas was there. He
was wearing loose, soiled khaki slacks and a light
short-sleeved shirt, which was half open over his
fat belly. With one hand, he fumbled with his fly.
With the other, he pointed a shiny chrome pistol
at my head. I froze.

"Duane, get your butt out here," St. Thomas
hollered. Then to me he said, "Picked a good time
to take a leak, didn't I?" Then louder again:
"Duane, goddamn it . . ."

Hill came around the corner of the building
and stopped, his mouth half open.

"God-damn," he said. He broke it into two
words, dragging out the *God*. He didn't exactly
smile, but he was delighted. "I knew you was the
nigger in the woodpile."

"I talked to the mayor before I came—"

As I started the sentence, Hill walked up to me
and, before I had a chance to raise my hands,
swatted me openhanded on the face. The blow almost knocked me down, semiblinded me, and the
taste of blood surged into my mouth.

I put my hands up to defend myself, and St.

Thomas screamed, "Put your hands down, motherfucker, motherfucker. . . ." He shook the pistol at me, and I was sure it was the last thing I'd see. I put my hands down, backing away, watching the gun, and Hill hit me with a left hook and then a right cross, hit me first in the eye and then in the nose. My nose broke with a crunch, and I went down, banging backward into the side of the shed, then dropping forward on my hands and knees.

"Busted my fuckin' ribs," Hill shouted. He grabbed the hair at the sides of my head, jerked me upright, and threw me back against the building. "You was the nigger in the woodpile, wasn't you? You was the one what set this all up, this whole thing, nobody'd believe me, nobody'd listen. . . ."

He punched me in the forehead. My head banged back against the building, and I went straight down, to a sitting position, and he kicked me below the armpit. I rolled with the kick and crouched, ready to roll again, and Hill started screaming, "On your feet, motherfucker, on your feet."

St. Thomas danced around beside me, giggling, waving the gun. "On your feet, on your feet . . ."

"What're you looking for out here? What're you looking for? Were you in that car? What were you doing, cocksucking faggot?"

I got up again, sputtering, blood running out of

my broken nose into my mouth. I had my hands half up again, and said, "Listen, goddamn it, I talked to the mayor—"

"Fuck Bell. You hear me, cunt? Fuck him—"

Hill screamed. He screamed all the time, never dropped his voice, never laughed, always screamed. "Hands down, cocksucker. Arnie, you shoot the motherfucker in the nuts if he puts his hands up. . . ."

"I will," St. Thomas squealed. "I'll shoot you in the nuts, faggot motherfucker. . . ." He pointed the pistol at my crotch. Hill squared up again, and St. Thomas was squealing, and I dropped my hands, trying to edge away, but St. Thomas danced around in front again, blocking me, and Hill hit me in the nose again, and I went halfway down, trying to fall, and he hit me twice more, hard, in the right eye again and on the nose. The world went black and red, and I was down, nearly blind, feeling the grass under my hands, the blood running down my throat. . . .

"Get up, motherfucker," Hill screamed, his face two feet from mine. "Get him around inside, Arnie, let's get him around inside."

I couldn't get up. I tried but couldn't. "Get up, motherfucker," Hill screamed, and kicked me in the thigh. I tried and stumbled. He kicked me again.

"Kick him in the ass," St. Thomas yelled.

"Kick him in the ass, Duane. Kick him in the balls."

Hill kicked me again, and I crawled some more, and he screamed, "Crawl, motherfucker." I crawled another six feet toward the door, and he kicked me in the side, and this time I didn't see it coming, couldn't roll, and a couple of ribs went. You can feel ribs when they break because the muscles between them go into spasm. The pain can bend you in half.

I went down on my face and thought: Keep breathing. Keep breathing, keep your arms around your head, LuEllen's out here somewhere; maybe she's gone for help. . . . And I had an image of the *Fanny* slowly slipping off the revetment and downstream, LuEllen cutting the boat loose, satisfied that she hadn't been seen.

When I went down on my belly, Hill flew into a fury, kicking me in the legs, the hips, and along the side. Most of the kicks to the side hit my arm. Somewhere along the nightmare crawl to the door, the arm broke below the elbow. I didn't realize it until he kicked it a second time in the same place, and the pain ripped out as a groan out of my chest.

"That's right," Hill brayed. "Let's hear it, motherfucker, what you done to us, you oughtta hurt. . . ."

St. Thomas was as excited as Hill, out of his mind, waving the pistol, and as Hill was kicking me, he fired a shot into the ground next to my head. Dirt blew up into my face, embedding itself in my cheek, but by then I didn't care. . . .

SIX FEET from the open door Hill, impatient, grabbed me by the hair on the back of my head and dragged me into the building. My broken arm bumped over the concrete doorsill, and I may have fainted.

Water splashed off my face. Hill was pouring it out of a paper cup. It was cold, out of a bottle cooler, and trickled off my forehead, down across my nose and chin onto my neck. I opened the one eye that still seemed to work, and found myself lying on my back on the concrete floor, my legs spread, my head propped up against the wall.

"Can you see, motherfucker? I want you to see," Hill brayed. I could see and tried to say something. St. Thomas was there, still grinning, still waving the gun, though he didn't need it. "Look at this. You see this? This is the vacuum chamber, motherfucker."

Directly across from me was the Plexiglas door of the killing cage. Hill pounded it with his hand.

"The vacuum chamber. We put big fuckin' dogs in there, boy. We put Doberman pinschers in there. We put German shepherds and rottweilers in there. Big, dangerous dogs, we can't take no chances. Once you put a dog in there and close these latches, no way he's gonna get out. If he got out, he'd tear your fuckin' liver out, boy, so we built these latches strong. You know what we're gonna do, boy?"

He waited for an answer, but I was in no shape to make one. He seemed vaguely disappointed.

"We're gonna put you in there," he screamed, smacking the plastic door again. "Then we're gonna get a couple of lawn chairs and some beer, and we're gonna push the button on you, and then we're gonna sit here and watch you try to scratch your way out. Just like TV. Like a big-screen TV. I'm gonna do a little more work on you, cocksucker, because I want you to hurt before you go, but I ain't gonna kick you in the head, and you know why?"

He turned to St. Thomas. "You know why I ain't gonna kick him in the head, Arnie?"

"No. Why?" Arnie was grinning, the straight man in a comedy act.

" 'Cause I want him to know what's happening to him. You hear that, motherfucker? I want you to know." He grabbed one of my feet and jerked me away from the wall. The back of my head bounced off the floor, and Hill booted me in the side. It was the good side, the side where I hadn't been hurt yet, but more ribs went. I tried to move, tried to roll, tried to cover with my hands, but he was in a rage, screaming, spitting, kicking, howling. . . .

I had the good eye open, watching myself being

kicked to death. St. Thomas was there behind him, encouraging him, laughing, with the little silver pistol, a cheerleader.

Then LuEllen was there with him. She came out of nowhere, like a rabbit out of a hat. She had Hill's old weapon, the .45, the one we'd fished out of the river, and she put it next to St. Thomas's ear. At the very last second he sensed her presence and started to go stiff, but she pulled the trigger and blew his brains all over the wall of the animal control building.

Hill spun, staggered, caught himself on the wall, got around, his mouth hanging open in shock, and looked straight down the barrel of the .45.

"Don't," he croaked. I don't think I could hear him, but I could see him say the word: *Don't.*

I saw LuEllen's mouth moving but couldn't hear what she was saying. The world was going pink on me, and I realized that while I could see the shot go through Arnie's skull, I hadn't actually heard it, or the noise hadn't registered. I thought I might be dying.

A few seconds later I was moving. Trying to focus. Trying. We were outside, the cool air on my face, and then I was in the back of the station wagon, lying flat on my back. I could see LuEllen, all black and white, like a black-and-white film, holding the pistol with both hands, marching Hill away. . . .

Sometime later, I don't know how long, the car was moving. Bouncing. LuEllen's voice came in, finally, and from far away, with static, like a Juárez radio station when you're driving at night across Montana. . . .

"Hold on, Kidd," she said. "Hold on, Kidd . . ."

Some long time after that, it seemed, another woman leaned over me and said, "His pressure's OK, but we're gonna want a peritoneal lavage, blunt trauma, looks like the ribs, mostly, let's get some film on his skull . . . keep that neck straight. . . ."

I can barely remember three other things before the black plastic mask came down over my face, three things that I wonder about. Were they dreams, or were they real?

I can remember the catheter going in. That's not something you forget, no matter how skillful the nurse; it doesn't particularly hurt, but it's a memorable feeling.

And I remember somebody talking to LuEllen, almost chanting: "Has he been drinking, using street drugs, allergic to aspirin . . . ?"

And I remember driving out of the yard at animal control, the yard light spinning by the window like a sudden moon, and the sound through the window, the sound coming back, that familiar ooka-ooka-ooka. . . .

19

THE AFTERNOON WAS getting on.

I'd left New Orleans the day before, heading north. The winter and spring had been dry, and both days were hot and hazy. From the highway you could see long trails of gravel dust kicked up behind the plantation pickups as they rolled along the good earth to the west.

The first day I went only as far as Vicksburg, with the excuse that I'd never inspected the battlegrounds as thoroughly as they deserved. And I like Vicksburg; back in '80 I rode down the river on a pontoon boat and camped on a Louisiana island in the Vicksburg harbor. I was sitting there, eating freeze-dried beef Stroganoff, when a dozen wild turkeys rambled by, beautiful birds that looked to me as large and foreign as ostriches.

AFTER THE LAST NIGHT in Longstreet I woke up with LuEllen beside the hospital bed. Consciousness came slowly. I didn't hurt anywhere, but I'd been pumped full of drugs. When I did come up, we were alone.

"Can you hear me?" she asked.

I could hear her, but she seemed to be several miles away. And I wasn't much interested anyway.

"Water," I mumbled.

"Fuck water," she said, her voice as harsh as the light that was breaking through my eyelids. "Listen to me. We drove up last night, just to get some ribs. We left the car by the waterfront and wandered down some alleys, looking for a rib joint in a basement. We got lost, and we got mugged. You tried to fight three guys. White guys. Long hair. One of them broke his glasses. . . . You got that? I ran."

"Water."

"Fuck water, Kidd. Listen to what I'm telling you. . . ."

THE MEMPHIS COPS came by but, after hearing my story, decided there wasn't much to go on. They were apologetic, but I told them I figured I'd screwed up, it wasn't their fault. They said no, no, people ought to be able to walk in the streets, but I could see they agreed with my assessment. The dumb Yankee fucked up. . . .

I stayed in the hospital for two weeks. When I got out, LuEllen drove me south to New Orleans. It was a painful trip. When we arrived, I was generally confined to my apartment for the best part of a month. An invalid, I was, afraid to laugh or sneeze or cough or sit up too quickly, afraid of the tearing pain in my chest and sides.

Hill had done a good job on me: eight broken or cracked ribs and a punctured lung, bruised kidneys, broken arm, massive bruising down my arms and legs, broken nose, cracked cheekbone, a concussion. I'd never gone back to Longstreet. John had come to see me at the hospital, and Marvel.

"We've got the town," Marvel said. "It's ours. They'll never get it back."

There wasn't much more to say.

Bobby called when I got a laptop set up, and we went back and forth for quite a while. Mostly about loyalties.

It worked.

Barely.

Good enough. Thanx.

Most of a year had passed since then. I was more or less back to normal, returning to St. Paul in time for the Minnesota fishing opener. LuEllen, last I heard, was in Singapore.

LuELLEN HAD picked up St. Thomas's new gun, left the old one beside him, turned out the lights, and locked the animal control building. Then she drove me straight out of Longstreet to Memphis.

"Just praying you'd stay alive," she said. "I kept asking, 'You OK, Kidd?' and you kept saying, 'Jes fine,' and I figured you were dying."

At the hospital she told them the rib story.

" 'Crank,' one of the docs said. 'He must have run into a pack of speed freaks.' That's what they told me," LuEllen said.

When they took me away to the operating room, she drove back to Longstreet as fast as she could, then ran through the night to animal control. Everything was as she had left it. She climbed the levee, walked down to the boat, set it loose, and took it up to the marina. Then it was back in the car, and Memphis again.

"I waited until you woke up and gave you the story. Then I took the car back, paid, got on the boat, and brought it up to Memphis. I got here at five o'clock in the afternoon," she said. "No sweat."

No sweat. By the time she arrived in Memphis with the boat, she'd been up for a brutal thirty hours.

I LEFT VICKSBURG in the early afternoon. North of Greenville, I was on remote control, flying through the flat bean and cotton fields with the window down, through the stink of anhydrous ammonia and rotted cow manure, up the river, the sun burning my left arm and the sound of gravel banging up under the fenders.

The ice cream social was scheduled to start at six o'clock. It would be something of a political event, Bobby said, when he called on the wire to relay the invitation, part of Marvel's campaign to get Longstreet's blacks and whites talking to each other.

I rolled into town a few minutes early and took a turn past the marina. From the levee you could see the new bridge going up. The pilings were already in, and part of the superstructure. A couple of work barges were tethered below the pilings, with warning blinkers already operating on the river-side corners. If John had actually bought the land we'd used in our Brooklyn Bridge scam, he'd have lost his shirt. The bridge was going in at the opposite end of town.

When I got to Chickamauga Park, a swarm of kids covered the slides, the swings, the teeter-totters. Ladies in pastel dresses scooped ice cream out of cardboard buckets and cut cakes out of aluminum baking pans. Marvel was directing traffic at the kitchen end of things: more ice cream there, we're running out of cake, like that. She didn't notice me. I got in line at the ice cream tables, paid a dollar for an adult ticket, got a scoop of Dutch chocolate and a healthy chunk of carrot cake, and went and sat on the rim of a tractor tire being used as a sandbox.

Marvel was as beautiful as ever, and then John showed up, no longer the phlegmatic radical I'd met in Memphis. He was laughing, fooling with her. In love.

A few minutes later, while I was waiting to catch Marvel's eye, another body settled in next to me.

"Mr. Kidd," Bell said. He was wearing his seersucker jacket and had a paper plate full of ice cream and cake, just like mine, and a red plastic spoon. "I *thought* it was you. You've changed your dress."

"Just passing through," I said easily enough. I was wearing a blue work shirt and jeans and was clean-shaven again. The Gauguin image died on the operating table in Memphis. "Closed the place in New Orleans. I'm heading back to Minnesota for the fishing opener."

"Lot of excitement down here 'bout the time you left," Bell said, taking a cut of the ice cream.

"Yeah. I heard Miz Dessusdelit killed herself."

"She wasn't the only one. Had a murder-suicide out at the animal control. Grisly thing; the whole town was in an uproar," he said, shaking his head.

"Yeah?" I didn't want to ask because I'd already heard enough about it. "What happened?"

"Don't know exactly. But it looks like Arnie St. Thomas forced Duane Hill . . . you remember Duane, the guy you fought in the parking lot?—he forced old Duane into the vacuum box they used to kill dogs and pushed the button on him. Duane died scratching at the Plexiglas doors, trying to get out."

"Goddamn," I said.

"It was ugly," Bell said, licking the spoon. "He could just barely get a grip on the edge of the Plexiglas doors, and he broke off all his fingernails trying to pull them open. Blood all over the place in there. . . . There was a lawn chair set up in front of the doors. We think old Arnie sat there and watched him try to scratch his way out."

"Jesus."

"He had very little to do with it, I'm afraid," Bell said.

I'd never asked LuEllen about the death of Duane Hill, and I never would. If she wanted to tell me about it someday, I'd listen. . . .

Bell was still talking. "After Duane died, Arnie must have killed himself. Took us all day to figure out what happened. We thought at first that somebody else might have been involved. Then the police started getting photographs. Somebody took some pictures of Duane and Arnie killing these two black people, man and a woman, putting their bodies in the river. One of them was Hill's girlfriend. The other one, the man, was a guy around town here. We think he maybe was bumping the girl, and Hill found out."

"So he killed them? Hill did?"

"No doubt about it," Bell said. "We had the photographs, and when the state crime lab checked Arnie's gun, they found it was the same one that was used to kill the black woman. Test bullets matched the ones they took out of her body, and Arnie had powder traces on his hands and face, like you get from firing a gun. And a couple of boys who worked out there said, 'Yeah, it looked like a gun Arnie sometimes shot out there. . . .' "

"Hill was nuts," I said. "I kept telling people that. I don't know about St. Thomas."

"You were right about Duane, though I didn't see it at the time," Bell admitted. "All the river towns have a Duane Hill somewhere. I knew he was rough, but I didn't know he was insane. Not until they did the autopsy on the black fella."

"Hmmm?"

"They couldn't figure out what killed him at first. After Hill was killed in the vacuum box, the pathologist down at Greenville suddenly had an idea what it might have been. They did some tests, and sure enough, it seems like the black fella had been killed in a vacuum box. Just like a big old German shepherd."

"I love the South," I said, finishing the ice cream on my plate. "Your ways are so quaint."

"Well, I just thought you might like to know how it came out, you having left so soon after, and all."

"It is interesting, in a sort of distant way. I mean, not being from here, and all," I said. Time to change the subject. "Nice bridge you've got there," I said.

The bridge's superstructure was painted with a reddish anti-corrosion paint. You could see the top of it over the park trees, glowing in the setting sun.

"It's the mayor's doing, and it's gonna save my financial butt," Bell said. He looked across the grass at Marvel, standing behind the table with a scoop in her hand. "The empress of ice cream."

"I saw her picture on *Time* magazine when she got it," I said. "She's a pretty woman. The Red Marvel, they called her."

"*Time* magazine. We couldn't believe it. The only American town with a Communist mayor."

"She says she's not."

"Yes, yes, she says she's a social democrat. Nobody believes it. Not down here. 'Course, she's got reelection locked up, since she brought in the bridge, and the way the council went and gerrymandered the new election districts. But I don't care, as long as the bridge comes along."

"*Time* says the state legislators were stumbling over themselves, approving the funding."

"They had a remarkable change of attitude," Bell said dryly. Then he laughed. "Two weeks after we elect her mayor, with the town in an uproar, she drives into the capital, meets with the

governor and the old redneck who's the speaker
of the house, and they all get their picture taken
on the capitol steps, shaking hands on the deal.
That stopped a little traffic, I'll tell you."

"It'll be a pretty bridge," I said. "There are lots
of pretty bridges over the Mississippi. I'm happy
to see you keeping it up. . . . How about you? For
reelection?"

"No. I'm gone," he said, shaking his head. "I
never did like this peckerwood town anyway. I
moved back across the river, where I belong. Besides, it took the folks about fifteen minutes to
figure out what I should have done that night:
that I should have walked out and prevented a
quorum. They figure I made a deal with Marvel."

"Did you?"

He squinted down at me with a small grin.
"Yep."

I nearly choked on my last bite of cake, laughing, and Bell stood up and brushed off the seat of
his pants. Then he dug into a pocket and took out
a computer key. The key, if anyone had bothered
to check, would fit the front panel of my North-
gate IBM clone. I'd had it in my pocket the night
I went into animal control.

"You know what this is?" he asked.

"I don't believe so," I said, taking it from him.
"Looks like what, a key to a Coke machine?"

"Maybe," he said, taking it back. "The police
found it under St. Thomas, out at animal control,

when they picked him up off the floor, dead. It didn't match up with anything of his."

I tried to look puzzled. "Why would I know what it is?"

He shrugged. "It's just kind of a mystery. I've been walking around for a year, asking a lot of people. Nobody recognizes it."

"Me either," I said.

"And it's about time to bury the past," he said. He pitched the key toward a fifty-five-gallon oil drum being used as a trash can. He was no basketball player, and the key bounced off the side, into the sand.

"Never be in the NBA," he said, echoing my thought. "Say hello to Miz LuEllen for me? If you see her?"

"Sure."

He wandered away. I watched him cross the park, speak to Marvel and then to John, then drift over toward the City Hall. He stopped at the corner, looking down toward the river. From there he should be able to see the bridge just fine.

I got seconds on ice cream, served by Marvel herself.

"Tonight, about ten o'clock, at my place?" she said.

"Sure."

I finished the ice cream, watching kids on the slides and the swings, and then strolled down to the river to watch the light die on the bridge. I took a sketch pad with me and got a fair view of the thing, but I doubt I'll ever do a painting. The angles are all wrong.

JOHN WAS at Marvel's.

"June wedding, up in Memphis," Marvel said. "You're invited. And LuEllen. Bobby's set for best man. On a computer."

"You're looking pretty fuckin' smug," I said to John.

"What can I tell you?" he said. "I'm old, bald, and dumb, and she said she'll marry me."

"Let's not talk about old," I said. "You've got about three weeks on me. Let's talk about somebody else being old."

Marvel said she had been disappointed by the ice cream social. Ninety percent of the kids had been black, she said. They had to do better with the whites.

"We'll do better," John said. "It'll take a while. Maybe we should have another social in the summer."

"Maybe," she said. "I sure do like ice cream."

"How'd you figure the bridge out?" I asked her.

She shook her head and turned away.

"He's got a right," John said softly. "Wasn't no white boys beat him up in Memphis. You know that."

She looked at me, and I shrugged.

"Tell him," John said.

"I bought it," Marvel said. "With the money you took out of the City Hall."

"Bought it?"

"Ain't it wonderful?" John asked.

"I did what had to be done," Marvel said. "I called up my man at the capital, told him in one minute what was happening—how close we were to taking the town—and then I asked if seventy-five thousand dollars in untraceable cash would buy me the bridge. He said if I got it to the right three or four legislators, it'd buy me a bridge and two ferryboats if I wanted them. I said the bridge would be enough, but I had to have a commitment quick. He got a phone number from me, for Bell's office. Then I went and sat there, chewing my nails, and fifteen minutes later, with Bell getting pissed, the phone rings, and the speaker of the house tells Bell he might be able to work some kind of deal on a bridge. . . . Said I 'was a pretty convincing gal,' is what he said."

"And Bell went out and voted against your ticket, but you had the votes," I said.

"That's right."

I looked at John and remembered that he'd said something about Commies and hobby politics. "Doesn't sound like hobby politics to me," I said.

"Woman learns quick," he said.

"What about Darrell Clark and his family? Did you reopen the case?"

"No, no, we didn't," Marvel said, her eyes shifting away from mine. "We were having control problems. We didn't want there to be any more uproar than there already was. Not until we got the election districts redrawn."

"How about now?"

"Well, it's just kind of . . . awkward," she said.

"Not good politics," I said, "to reopen the case."

"That's right. And Darrell's gone . . . can't get him back. And there's no money left for the family. That all went. . . ." She gestured in the general direction of the state capital.

As I was leaving, I asked, "Was it worth it?"

"Yes," she said, looking straight into my eyes. "Harold would have died for this. He would have told you so himself. And he did. But we got what he wanted."

"If you're satisfied . . ."

"I am, but that doesn't mean I'm not sad. Harold's murder damn near killed me. And there are loose ends all over the place. Archie Ballem is oozing around like a slug. He's got trouble with the IRS, but he's still kicking, and he hates me. And we can't pry Mary Wells out of the city clerk's office. Not yet, anyway, because of civil service. Carl Rebeck got immunity to testify against the machine and now thinks he can run on a clean house ticket—and he's already going around calling me a Commie nigger. . . . But for now I'm satisfied. Satisfied and sad."

"All right," I said. "Maybe that's the best you can hope for."

ON THE WAY out of town I stopped at Chickamauga Park, scuffed around the trash can until I found the computer key, and pocketed it. Then I drove on to the E-Z Way and bought a couple of Diet Cokes. I'd need the caffeine for the run into Memphis.

It was still hot when I got to the store, and a billion bugs were diving around the pole lights. The fat guy sat behind the counter, mopping his face with a rag that once was a T-shirt; you could still see the yellow deodorant stains in the armpits.

"Hot," the counterman said, in a sort of neutral way. He was ready to agree with a different opinion if I had one. It was that kind of town.

"Yeah." I put a dollar and a quarter on the counter. He slid it into the palm of his hand and poked at the cash register. He was wearing a plastic pin that said ELVIS, and under that, in smaller letters, NIGHT ASSISTANT MANAGER.

He gave me a nickel back. As I was going out the door, I thought he said something to me and half turned. He was looking out the open window at the pole lights, with a dreamy look in his little pig eyes.

355

"Pretty fliers," he crooned. His mouth was half open, his heavy pink lips glistening in the overhead lights. "Pretty, pretty fliers."

LuEllen.

She hung around for a month or so in New Orleans, while I was recovering. One morning at breakfast she said, "Do you love me?"

I said, "Yes."

"I don't know if I can handle that," she said.

"I don't know what to tell you," I said.

"I'm going away for a while."

"Like Charade, or whatever her name was," I said.

"Chaminade," she said absently. "But not like her. 'Cause I'll be back."

"For sure?"

"Yeah." She has dark eyes like great northern lakes. "For sure."